SAFELY TO THE GRAVE

SAFELY TO THE GRAVE

Margaret Yorke

ARROW BOOKS

Arrow Books Limited
20 Vauxhall Bridge Road, London SW1V 2SA

An imprint of the Random Century Group

London Melbourne Sydney Auckland
Johannesburg and agencies throughout
the world

First published by Hutchinson 1986

Arrow edition 1987
Reprinted 1992

3 5 7 9 10 8 6 4 2

Printed and bound in Great Britain by
Cox & Wyman Ltd, Reading, Berkshire

ISBN 0 09 947350 X

1

Mick liked frightening people.

On Hallowe'en when he was eight he had played Trick or Treat with two bigger boys, and one old lady had shown real terror when she opened her door and saw the fearsome masks worn by the three sheeted figures. She had swayed and clutched the doorpost, a thin hand at her chest, and had uttered a faint shriek. Then, regaining self-control, she had scolded them but, ashamed of her own timidity, had found them each a sweet.

Mick never forgot the thrill he felt at her obvious fear. He and his friends had run off laughing, and had startled other people too that night, but it was the first old lady's frightened face which Mick remembered.

He was careful. At school he waited for his victims until they were alone and unprotected and at first he rarely used direct violence. He would waylay a smaller boy in an alley and pin him against a wall using only the threat of his own superior size, until the child dissolved into tremulous sobs and surrendered the contents of his pockets – money, a penknife, a battered bar of chocolate, whatever he possessed. What Mick craved was not so much material profit as the sense of power he experienced when he saw terror in another.

No one suspected. His deeds went unreported by his victims who dreaded reprisals, and he kept out of open trouble. At school he was a poor achiever, playing truant much of the time in his final year, and at home he contrived a near-invisible existence, the quiet one between his older sister and his younger brother.

As he grew up he learned other ways of scaring people.

* * *

Peter had found the car at half-term. It was an old green Morris Minor saloon, its once sturdy body now badly rusted; one door had hung open, the hinge broken. The leather seats were torn and wild creatures had nested under the rotten matting, but the windscreen was intact and one of the windows could still, by the use of his maximum strength, be wound down an inch or two.

Peter had managed to close the gaping door. He sat in the driver's seat holding the steering-wheel, turning it as far as it would go and pretending he was at Brand's Hatch. It began to rain, and he stayed there while a short autumnal shower pattered through what leaves remained on the brambles which, in the hollow where it lay, concealed the car from casual passers-by. Peter found the wiper switch, but of course it didn't work.

It must have been driven along the path through the copse and pitched over the ridge into the tangle of brambles below, Peter supposed. You couldn't have driven it up again. He wondered whose it had been and why it had been abandoned. Perhaps it had been the getaway car in a robbery, he thought, and decided to look in the boot in case any loot had been left behind.

But there was nothing, not even a spare tyre. The car must have been there for some time, for the thicket of brambles about it was quite dense. Peter cleaned a section of windscreen with his handkerchief and resumed the driver's seat, now a police driver chasing a villain, making siren noises as he peered ahead.

He had gone back the next day taking some packets of crisps and two tins of Coca-Cola which he'd put in the boot with a copy of *The Beano,* and a notebook and pencil with which to record anything special he observed on his rambles around the district. He might find an insect never noticed in these parts before and become famous. On Saturday, before Peter's father arrived to fetch him, he paid a final visit to the Morris after lunch. He went to the copse on his bike, pedalling along the dry paths between the trees from which most of the leaves had now fallen, and hiding the machine under some bushes near the car.

Peter had divided feelings about leaving Didbury. It would be nice to be back with Dad although he didn't really see all that much of him. On weekdays they both left home at much the same time, but Peter returned from school long before Dad arrived back from the office. And now there were Caroline and the baby Sarah. It wasn't like it used to be. Once, Mummy had fixed things – taken him on trips and to the cinema, or he'd gone to play with friends. He did that much less often now because Caroline didn't know the various parents, and as she'd been rather sick with Sarah, he hadn't liked to ask if he might invite them round.

He had stayed with his aunt in Didbury for over three weeks in the summer holidays, during which time Sarah was born. He and his father had spent almost every weekend at Lime Tree Cottage after Mum had left them and gone to New York, before Dad had married Caroline. During those months Mrs Walker had looked after them in London, coming daily from Catford where she lived with her husband and three cats. Her husband drove a bus, and Peter had been on it once. Peter had been sorry when she left after Caroline arrived, not that he minded Caroline – he quite liked her – but she was so busy, now, with Sarah, whom he quite liked too, but babies couldn't do much except eat and sleep. And yell.

In spite of the large lunch he had just eaten, Peter finished a packet of crisps in the car. He noted the date in his book. He'd be back after Christmas. He packed everything carefully away in the boot and began climbing the side of the hollow to reclaim his bicycle. Peering through the bushes, he saw a long tawny body slinking between the trees some distance away. It was Cleo, Laura Burdock's golden Labrador. Peter's first impulse was to call the dog, who was a friend of his, but he knew Laura could not be far away. She was a friend, too, a very particular one, but Peter didn't want to tell even her about the car; that was to be a secret. Besides, if a grown-up knew it was there, they might get it taken for scrap. Peter didn't know who owned the copse; it didn't belong to any of the farmers who worked the land nearby. Perhaps it was no one's.

He hid behind the screen of bushes until dog and owner had moved away. Then he scrambled up the incline and rescued his cycle. He meant to catch up with Laura; he'd been to say goodbye to her that morning but it would be nice to go back with her to the village. However, as he followed her, he was side-tracked by a small spider which he watched swing itself aloft, and a scuttling beetle which he caught and put into a match-box carried in his pocket for this purpose. He let it go before he got home; he couldn't take it to London; it might be eaten if he turned it out in their Putney garden, and it would starve if he left it here in his room. He couldn't expect his aunt to fetch food for it; most women didn't like beetles at all.

Peter was back in time to bid farewell to his various treasures: his conker collection, apart from six monsters he was taking home; two ammonites; a piece of string and some wire; and the skull of a sheep which he'd found with Nicholas on the farm. He knew Aunt Marion would leave them safely in the room that she kept completely for him. He'd see them again after Christmas.

'Aren't I going to stay with Mummy?' he'd asked, and when Marion said, no, not this time, he had been relieved.

He had been to New York once. The flying part, across the Atlantic, had been a great adventure, and it had been wonderful to see Mummy, but he hadn't liked living high up in a tall apartment block with no garden to play in, and he hadn't been allowed out on his own. Besides, Mummy was so busy all the time. She worked for an advertising firm, and for the duration of his visit had brought work home. He had been a nuisance, Peter was sure, and he didn't much like Geoffrey, Mummy's new husband. Geoffrey had called him 'old son', but Peter wasn't his son and he didn't like being treated as if he were four years old. Peter knew he would have to go again one day, but he was in no hurry for that.

Now that he was married, home for Mick Harvey was a council flat in the old part of Merston, where a warehouse and a laundry had been demolished and four three-storey blocks built some eighteen years ago. Theirs was a top-floor flat, which meant that Beverley had to carry the pushchair up and down every time she went out with the children, just as earlier she had lugged the carry-cot with its wheeled frame which she had used instead of a pram. Mr Duke, from the flat below, complained of noise over-head when Mick came home late, which was often, and the only place to hang washing was on the balcony. It seemed that they'd never get a house, though they had had their name down since long before Mandy was born. Now she was six months old and teething, and not only Mr Duke had complained when she cried in the night.

On Saturdays Mick took little Cliff to the park. He would put the child on a swing and push him high, ever higher, till the child's excited yells turned to screams of terror. Mick knew that Cliff almost enjoyed his fear; he would set him down at last, when the cries became piercing enough for people to stare.

Beverley was always tired these days. There were mounds of washing and ironing to be got through after the broken nights, and the hungry baby, still partly breast-fed, sapped her strength. She was only twenty, but she had already lost her bloom.

Mick found her easy to frighten. She was so puny and feeble that it was not very satisfying, but even so, every so often, he needed to experience the sudden surge of energy and heightened awareness that came with creating fear.

No one had connected him with that business four years ago when one of his scaring episodes had gone too far. He'd meant only to frighten the girl, pay her back for not wanting to go joy-riding with him in the car, but when he saw her terrified face he'd felt compelled to carry it further. He'd dumped her in a ditch and she hadn't been found for three days.

The car had been stolen. He had left it in a multi-storey car-park thirty miles away and stolen another to get back home. He'd learned how to do that sort of thing when he had a spell in Borstal; you met all sorts there and could pick up many useful tips. Mick had been sentenced after being caught thieving. It was very unfair; people should be more careful about locking up: open windows and doors were just asking for anyone passing to take a look round. He had hated being confined; when the cell door clanged behind him at night, it was his turn to know fear. One spell inside was enough and he had been careful not to get caught again.

Mick drove a delivery van for a furniture store in Fordbridge. He liked the freedom the job gave him and it took him about the district with an excuse for being late back at The Buildings if he needed one. He'd look at the people he met on his rounds and imagine how frightened they'd be if he suddenly turned on them and stopped being the helpful delivery man. But he never yielded to that temptation with a customer, for they had the power to get back at him.

Beverley never did; she was much too weak and timid. It was quite some time since he had terrified anyone else.

Before Peter's parents had parted there had been a country cottage in Sussex. Every Friday they had piled into Dad's car and driven down there. Dad would spend most of the weekend working in the garden, digging and planting vegetables, cutting the hedge or mowing, and, in winter, painting and renovating the interior. Peter would look for interesting creatures – once he saw a mole, and there was a badger's set in a local wood – and go for rides on his bike; on warm summer days they went to the sea and swam. Mummy often asked her friends to stay, and one of these friends was Geoffrey, who had taken her off to New York. He had heard Dad say something to Marion about hoping it would blow over but then the whole edifice had collapsed when Geoffrey went to America. Peter didn't know what an edifice was; he'd looked it up in the dictionary and discovered that it was a building. Dad's remark was a bit puzzling as their house in Putney hadn't fallen down, nor the cottage, though that had been sold.

Just before all this happened, Uncle George, who was Aunt Marion's husband, had died. He had been in the Army and had retired only a few months earlier.

After Mum left, Dad and Peter had spent most weekends with Aunt Marion. Dad had explained that they must do all they could to cheer her up. Things had just seemed to be settling down when Dad had met Caroline, and in less than a year they were married.

Dad had arrived by the time Peter reached Lime Tree Cottage.

'I'm not late,' Peter said at once, consulting his digital watch which did a number of things besides tell the time.

'No – it's all right, I'm early,' said David Cartwright. He had driven up expecting his son to come rushing out for a joyful reunion and had been disappointed when he found that Peter was having a last ride on his bike, which was kept at Didbury now.

'He's probably down at the farm,' said Marion.

'He and Nicholas are still friends, then?' asked David.

'Yes. He spends hours there,' Marion answered. 'I think Nick's glad of some masculine support, with those two pony-mad sisters.'

'It's so good for him, coming here like this,' David said. 'Being able to run wild, like we did as kids.'

'You certainly did,' said Marion, smiling. She was David's half-sister. Their mother had been widowed early in the war and had remarried. When David was born, Marion had been sent off to boarding-school. She still remembered the resentment she had felt at the attention the intruder attracted, although he had turned out to be an attractive child of whom she had grown fond. It was her memory of this early attack of insecurity – the loss of her father, the swift remarriage of her mother and her own sense of displacement – that had made her anxious to stretch out a succouring hand to her nephew, in case he felt the same.

'How are Caroline and the infant?' Marion asked.

'Caroline's blooming, and the babe is good. I left them both asleep,' said David. He laughed, a little sheepishly.

'I feel as if I'm playing truant,' he added. 'I'm off duty now, till Peter turns up.'

'Isn't it a bit exhausting, being a new papa?' Marion said.

'In some ways, yes,' said David. 'Broken nights – all that.'

'You're looking well,' Marion observed. David was a partner in a firm of solicitors in the City; towards the end of his marriage and for weeks afterwards he had been grey-faced and haggard – working much too hard, she had supposed until she knew the truth.

'I am,' David said. 'I'm rejuvenated. I've been very lucky.'

Time would tell if that would last, Marion thought, and was shocked at her own cynicism.

'Good,' she said, and then asked him, 'How do you like my new chair?'

Last week, she and Peter had gone to Fordbridge to swim at the indoor pool, and then they had bought a new wing armchair at Patchett's Fine Furniture. It was upholstered in mushroom pink velvet and was extremely comfortable.

'Very nice,' said David, who had been sitting in it without realizing it was new.

'Several springs had gone in the old one,' said Marion.

'What have you done with it?'

'It's in Peter's room,' said Marion. 'He's very pleased with it – he doesn't mind the bumps.'

'I should think he is,' said David. 'You call that his room, then?'

'Mm, of course. He stays here more than anyone else and I keep the real spare room for other visitors. Then he knows that anything he leaves here will be safe until he comes again.'

'You're sure it's not becoming a bind?'

'Not at all. Makes me feel useful,' said Marion. 'And I can take a proper part in parent talk when I socialize.'

David glanced at her. She was small and wiry, with curly red hair cut short, and she still had a dusting of freckles on her nose. How she'd hated those freckles! Her father had had red hair. She had not had a settled home for years; she and George had often lived in Army quarters and he had just finished a posting in Germany before he retired. They had bought Lime Tree Cottage twelve years ago, lived in it while he was at the Ministry of Defence, and let it when he was sent overseas. They had been unable to get their tenants out when George went on a tour of duty to Northern Ireland, and Marion had rented a flat in London. She had worked for a pharmaceutical firm where her fluent French and good German had been useful. Now she supplemented her Army pension with translation work which she could arrange so that she had time free for Peter and anything else she wanted to do. David thought she had made a good job of readjustment, as was to be expected of a soldier's widow, and having Peter to think about must have helped. This was hardly the moment to tell her that Caroline, a country girl, had decided that while life in London was tolerable for an infant, since there was space in the small garden for a pram, it would not do for raising the several children she planned to have. She wanted to move to the country, so David was going to become a commuter and Peter would be changing schools. Caroline had said that she would be able to do more for Peter then, and Marion's help would not be so necessary. David did not look forward to the travelling but supposed he would get used to it; as Caroline had pointed out, he could work on papers in the train.

'They delivered the chair the very next day,' Marion was saying. 'I was amazed that they were so prompt. The young man who brought it carried the old one up to Peter's room for us – he thought we wouldn't manage it ourselves.'

He'd offered to do it, the curly-headed young man in the leather jacket. Marion and Peter had been having tea in the sitting-room when he came and she had felt she must offer him a cup, as he'd been so kind. He'd eaten a bun which they had toasted at the open fire, something the delivery man said he had never seen done before. Peter had asked where he lived and was told in a flat in Merston.

He'd said he had a son aged two, and a baby girl. While they were upstairs, Peter had mentioned Sarah and had explained that he lived in London but that he had another home here, with his aunt.

'You're really lucky,' the young man had said, looking round the comfortable room, and Peter had agreed.

After he had gone, Marion was pleased at her democratic handling of the episode; when she was a colonel's wife she would have given a delivery man his tea in the kitchen, but she lived a different life in Didbury and a lot had happened since those days.

2

Whenever he arrived home from work, it seemed to Mick that the children were always screaming. He would pick up one or both of them and try to tease them out of their tempers. Cliff liked being thrown up in the air and caught, but sometimes Mick would make for the window as if to toss him out of it, and then there would be a hint of hysteria under the little boy's ecstatic yells. Once, Mick opened the window and loosened his grasp as he pitched the child towards the aperture, and this time the hysteria surfaced. Beverley, who was feeding the baby, began screaming too.

'Leave him be,' she yelled. 'Can't you see you're scaring him out of his wits?'

Mick knew it was true, but he couldn't stop. Again and again he swung the child towards the window, where the cold air from outside blew in towards them. Cliff had to learn to take it, anyway: kids must, if they were to survive in the world.

Beverley had put the baby, now crying too, on the floor and began pounding at Mick with her fists, trying to take Cliff from him. He turned to thrust her away from him, at the same time dropping Cliff on to the sofa which was littered with toys and magazines and Beverley's knitting. Luckily the needles were tucked into the work, points down, and Cliff was unharmed, but his high-pitched wails continued. As Beverley dropped on her knees to comfort him, Mick caught her by the arm and hit her hard across the face. She collapsed on to the small form of her son, cradling him against her, and the two clung to one another, sobbing. Mick stood, fists clenched, irresolute, looking down at Mandy who still bellowed, and for a moment Beverley thought he was going to threaten her too, but then he stormed from the room and she heard the outer door of the flat bang to behind him.

They were safe for the present. Beverley gathered both the children close to her, and all three sobbed together.

Mick ran down the concrete stairs and out into the street, where his battered white Maxi was parked by the kerb. He got into it and drove off down the road, the engine roaring to echo his defiance. He hadn't meant to provoke such a scene but the kid must learn to take a joke. Why, he was such a manly little fellow as a rule, and they had a big thing going between them; if Beverley hadn't interfered, Cliff would soon have been all smiles.

The pubs were not yet open, so he couldn't go into the Cricketers, his local. Mick drove on through the town, and from habit took the Fordbridge road, his daily route to work along which he had only just driven. He went past Patchett's shop, a black unlit blob between the bright lights of a supermarket and an electrical store. What made it tolerable to work for someone else was that the job took him out of doors, on his own. When he was in the delivery van, Mick was his own master. He didn't like anyone telling him what to do, and old Patchett knew it; Mick often changed his planned round just to assert himself. Patchett knew better than to make an issue of it, for he needed Mick, who was strong and could load and unload articles which would need two weaker men to handle; look at how he had hauled that big, sagging armchair upstairs for the red-headed old bint at Didbury the other day. She might have been a looker once, Mick thought, though she

17

was too small and scrawny for his taste. Beverley was like that – thin and bony. He'd had enough of her, with her skinny tits and sharp hips.

Mick dreamed of becoming a long-distance lorry driver. That would take him away from Beverley for weeks at a time; he'd meet all sorts of birds in Turkey and such places. But he needed a heavy goods vehicle licence first and there were problems about that. Still, he'd do it one day.

He stopped at the Bull where he had two pints, and then went on to the Five Horseshoes. For a while he played the machines but for most of the evening he drank alone in a corner of the bar, staring at the wall and thinking alternately of his own domestic trap with his feeble, wretched wife, and of voluptuous belly-dancers. He thought, too, of the power of a vast container lorry; thundering over wide rolling roads behind its wheel, he would be the captain of his own ship with the little cabin behind the seat where he would sleep. He'd escape from everyone. And the pay was good.

At closing time, Mick was in the Black Horse and very drunk. He blundered out into the yard, relieved himself against a row of dustbins and then got into his car where he sat for a bit waiting for his head to stop swimming. He'd have to go home now, there wasn't anywhere else. A tiny part of Mick had been ashamed of the scene he had left behind, but the drink had blotted out all conscious sense of contrition whilst aggravating his sense of grievance. What sort of life was it, with the kids always crying and Beverley complaining? He was only twenty-one, for Christ's sake, with his life before him. Was he to go on like this till he was forty and as good as dead? There'd be more kids, probably; Beverley wouldn't take the pill – said it upset her and gave her headaches. She'd got the coil now, but that didn't always stay in, did it? You'd think she'd get something better organized.

He started the car and joined the late-night traffic leaving town. A ballet company playing at the theatre had attracted a large audience, and there were a lot of cars about. Mick was feeling drowsy and slightly sick as he took

18

the Merston turning, and he was driving quite slowly, weaving about all over the road, when the headlights of another car came up behind him. Reflected in the mirror, they dazzled him as the driver sought a chance to overtake.

Angered by the dazzle, Mick became alert, cursing aloud as he pulled into the centre of the road so that the other car could not pass. Its lights were flashed once as a request to move over, but the next stretch of road was twisty and even if Mick had obeyed, it would not have been safe to overtake there so the driver dropped back. When sober and in a good mood Mick was a competent driver, and automatically now he pulled back to the left, though still steering a somewhat wavering course. This gave the following driver a chance and as soon as the road straightened out again the car, a blue Golf, went past.

Mick was instantly enraged. He changed down and stepped on the accelerator, roaring past the Golf with his old Maxi exerting every ounce of its power. He saw that there was a dark-haired woman driving, and he pulled sharply in front of her, cutting in, forcing her to check.

'Bloody cow! Thinks she owns the road!' Mick banged the wheel in irritation.

He let his speed slacken, all the time holding the crown of the road, forcing the Golf to stay behind and travel slowly. More than once he had to pull over to let traffic going the other way get by, and after one of these occasions the driver of the blue Golf saw her chance to overtake once more.

Mick dropped gears, roared after it and passed it on a bend, then cut in as before, forcing it to slow again. For a mile the two cars went in procession along the road. More lights came up behind and the Golf's driver dropped back to let two other cars pass. Mick, too, let them go by and then slowed right down until he was crawling along close to the side of the road. Now the Golf kept its distance, and again another car came up behind and overtook it. Mick had almost stopped by now; the driver of the Golf seized her opportunity, accelerated hard and, close behind the other car, went by. Mick's Maxi no longer had the compression to pick up enough speed to catch up at once, and by the time he had done so, they were almost at Merston. Mick sat behind the Golf, his headlights at full beam to annoy the driver. He could see that there was a passenger in the car, another woman judging by the shape; he could not make out any details as he stayed right on their tail. When they reached a mini-roundabout on the edge of Merston Mick shot past them, going round the mini-roundabout in the wrong direction, anti-clockwise, and at the same time brandishing a heavy spanner out of the window. If they passed him again, the threat was clear; he would hit out with this implement and at least would probably smash in their windscreen.

Laura Burdock slowed down and took a left turn.

'Well, we've got rid of him, thank goodness,' she said.

'We should still go to the police station,' said Marion Quilter. They had decided to do this as they approached the town; the Maxi would hardly follow them there. They had hoped to meet a police patrol car, but of course there was never one about when you needed it. Marion had memorized the Maxi's registration number. 'It's our duty,' she added.

Laura, shaken by their adventure, agreed, and they turned in to Merston's small police station to make their complaint. Mick, meanwhile, had lost them in his driving mirror. They'd given him the slip; what a pity; he might have forced them to hit a lamppost, which would take some explaining when they were caught wrapped round it and he'd gone. Once, he'd forced someone off the motorway like that; he hadn't waited to see the extent of the damage as the car slid down the embankment, and he'd got away with it.

He drove home, parked outside The Buildings, and was climbing the concrete stairs as Marion and Laura began their tale in the police station.

Beverley lay utterly still on the very edge of her side of the bed, her back turned to his space. He knew by her breathing that she was only feigning sleep. She wouldn't get away with that. It was only his right, wasn't it?

Mick pulled the bedclothes from her and exerted that right. Because he had had so much to drink his own effectiveness was diminished, and she had to be punished for that failure.

The trip to Fordbridge had been Marion's idea. When advance notices of the ballet's visit appeared in the local press, she had suggested to Laura that they might all go one night. Ballet was not in Tom's line, Laura said, but he was going to be in South America on business then, so she gladly agreed to go. They had both enjoyed the performance and were discussing it on the way home.

'I love that haunting music,' Marion said. 'Poor Giselle – she reminds me of Ophelia when she goes mad.'

'I hadn't thought of that,' said Laura.

'Same cause – spurned love,' said Marion.

'The head of the Wilis was a bit of a tartar,' said Laura.

'Yes – she looked a real old bossy-boots, didn't she?' Marion agreed. 'Perhaps she was afraid of slipping on that stage. I believe ballet companies don't like it because the surface is bad.'

'All those fairies with wings on their backs,' said Laura. 'What's that Gilbert and Sullivan thing with a chorus like that?'

'*Iolanthe*,' said Marion. 'Yes – the Wilis in middle age.'

They were laughing about this when they caught up with Mick Harvey on his wavering progress home.

The duty sergeant in Merston police station listened carefully to their story.

'You wish to bring charges?' he asked Marion, who had been the spokeswoman.

Laura looked uncertain, but Marion said that they must.

'The driver must have been drunk,' she said. 'He could have caused a serious accident.' As they overtook the white Maxi she had seen the blob of the driver's profile and thought it was a young man, but she could make out no features. 'If he gets away with this, he'll do it again to someone else who may not be as lucky as we were. And there are two of us – it won't all rest on the word of a single witness.'

The police computer provided the owner's name and address while statements were being taken from both women, and a call was put out for the car. The driver might be caught while still on the road so that he could be breathalysed on the spot, and the nearest patrol car was sent to the owner's address, which was in the town.

'I'm glad I wasn't alone,' Laura confessed, when they had left the police station and were driving the last few miles back to Didbury.

'He probably hoped we'd get out and confront him,' Marion said. 'When he slowed right down like that.'

'What – and be bashed up?' Laura asked. 'No thanks!'

'You did a good bit of quick thinking, finally getting past him when you did,' said Marion.

They had discussed turning and driving off in another direction, but had decided the trouble-maker might turn too, and pursue them; there had been no handy side road which they could take to evade him.

'It seemed the only thing to do,' said Laura.

'Come in for some coffee or tea,' Marion suggested, when Laura drew up outside Lime Tree Cottage, but Laura refused.

'I'll get on home,' she said. 'Cleo will be wondering what's become of me.'

Marion did not press her to change her mind. She had to translate a highly technical paper for a scientific journal the next day, and was tired.

'Thanks for the lift,' she said, and stood in the doorway watching as Laura drove off. Poor Laura: she had every-thing that money could buy but she had no child and was often alone. She did not read a great deal or listen to music; Marion thought the days must often seem long for her at Clyde House. She was wrapped up in Tom and in running the house smoothly, treating him, perhaps, as the child she had never had. Tom depended on her, found tranquillity with her, as he had once confessed to Marion, who occasionally did translations for him.

'She's made me feel safe,' he confessed. He meant that she had rescued him from the pitfalls of the sexual jungle, where Tom had felt threatened. He had had an unsettled childhood: his father was in the Indian Army and Tom and his mother had been sent back to England soon after independence. There, his mother had suddenly died. Tom had simply been told she had gone away, with no further explanation, and had only realized the truth when he was whisked to his grandmother's house and heard her cook talking about it to the daily woman. He was packed off to boarding-school, and after his grandmother's death spent his holidays with either an uncle in Leeds or, more often, at a holiday home for children whose parents were abroad. His father eventually came out of the Army and took up farming in a part of Africa which later became very unsettled, and he was killed in a riot.

Tom left school when he was sixteen. His uncle then told him that there was no money left; it had all been spent on his education and upkeep; and in the same interview he revealed that Tom's mother had committed suicide.

'She was always unbalanced,' his uncle said.

How unhappy she must have been, was Tom's thought: and how little she must have cared for him to leave him like that. Laura had eased all this early hurt, and in return he had provided her with security of a more material kind. He ran his own export business, which he had built up from a small agency dealing in a few potentially lucrative items until now he employed a staff of three working in rented premises near Slough, and had an impressive office with a thick pile carpet and a large mahogany desk, and a few tasteful prints selected by Laura on the white walls. He made frequent short trips overseas to deal with his agents in the field, and often he and Laura entertained clients at home.

Cleo, the golden Labrador, was pleased to see Laura when she had put the car away in the garage behind the house in what had once been stables. The dog went out for a final run in the garden, and while she snuffled about among the trees across the lawn Laura slowly paced round the gravel sweep in front of the house, her hands thrust into the pockets of her coat. The night air was damp and cool, with the scent of autumn leaves still just discernible. She wished Tom were at home to share it with her, but she wasn't alone; Tom had given Cleo to her to keep her company when he was away and she was now very fond of the dog, who had an affectionate, gentle disposition and was more likely to welcome any intruder with a wagging tail than fearsome barking.

After the night's adventure, Laura was too wide awake to fall asleep quickly; besides, she rarely did when Tom was away; she missed his large bulk beside her in their wide bed. She had enjoyed the ballet, which to her had seemed like a pantomime without the happy ending. The incident on the way home had been alarming; she supposed Marion was right to insist on reporting it, but left to herself Laura would have driven on home and tried to put it out of her mind. After a while her thoughts moved on to plans for Christmas. Tom would have a few days off then, at least, although last year he had spent much time on the telephone to Bahrain, where the festival was of no significance in the world of commerce. It would be nice if they could get away in the New Year, go skiing again, as once they had done before the business became so demanding. Without Tom it almost ceased to exist and he took very few holidays, but the house with its large garden and swimming pool was so perfect that she felt churlish for wanting to get away. Certainly they had everything necessary for recreation here at home.

Next week they were having a client to stay. Laura fell asleep while she was planning the dinner menu.

A constable thumped at Mick Harvey's door soon after he had rolled off Beverley and fallen into a sated slumber. It was she who heard the knocking and, rather than rouse Mick, went to answer it.

'Mrs Harvey?' asked PC Coates, as she peered round the door. 'It's Police Constable Coates from Merston police station. If I could just have a few words with your husband?'

Beverley could see the officer's uniform. She undid the door and let him in, to deny the neighbours the rest of the interview.

'He's asleep,' she said, and at that moment Mandy woke and began to wail. 'That's the bedroom.' Beverley pointed at it and went into the children's room.

But Mick had heard their voices. He appeared in the tiny hall, shaking his head in an effort to clear it, naked except for a towel tied round his waist.

'Michael Harvey?' asked Coates.

'Right. What's that to you?' Mick replied.

'Owner of a white Austin Maxi saloon, registration number – ' the constable read it from his notebook.

'Well?'

'You have been reported driving dangerously on the road between Fordbridge and Merston at approximately eleven-fifteen p.m. tonight,' stated Coates.

Mick stared at him, his head still muzzy.

'That's a lie,' he said. 'I've been home all evening.'

'Your car was seen on the road at that time, proceeding towards Merston in an erratic manner,' said Coates. He had seen the car in question parked in the street outside The Buildings, and had felt the bonnet before entering the block of flats. It was still just warm, and condensation was only beginning to form on the windows, whereas it was dense on other cars nearby. 'It is further alleged that when entering Merston at the Four Roads crossing, you traversed the mini-roundabout in an anti-clockwise direction.'

'I tell you, I haven't been out all night,' said Mick.

'Your car was seen by two witnesses,' said Coates.

Those two bloody cows! They'd gone to the nick!

'Well, someone else must have been driving it,' said Mick. 'I wasn't.'

Beverley, with Mandy in her arms, had appeared in the doorway of the children's room.

'Come here, Bev,' ordered Mick, and reluctantly she obeyed. As she moved towards him, Mick caught her arm, his own hard grip concealed by the baby bundled in her sleeping bag. He pinched her hard. 'You'll tell the officer I've been home all evening, won't you?' he said.

Beverley swallowed a sob and nodded.

'Nice and loud, so he can hear,' Mick instructed.

'That's right,' Beverley echoed, but feebly. She looked down at the ground, avoiding Coates's eye.

The constable glanced at her. He could see a bruise on her cheek. Once again he repeated the allegation that Mick's car had been seen being driven dangerously, and once again Mick denied being the driver. The man was lying, and Coates knew it, but unless he admitted being out in the car at the relevant time, or unless the woman could definitely identify him, he could not be charged. Coates noted again Beverley's drawn, pinched features and the bruise. He saw that he was not going to get an admission now, but he was not prepared to let the matter end here.

'You'll hear more about this,' he warned. 'I shall be continuing my inquiries into the incident.'

'You do just that,' Mick said. 'See where it gets you.'

3

By the next morning Mick had managed to bury all recollection of the night's events except for Beverley's role.

She prepared breakfast in silence. The bruise on her face was now well defined, but Mick felt no remorse; she'd asked for it and he'd do it again if she didn't show him respect. She was properly meek now, moving stiffly, pale and thin in her grubby pink dressing-gown; it seemed odd that he'd ever really fancied her. Mick turned his attention to Cliff, who was sitting at the table supposed to be feeding himself Rice Krispies. His sister now used the high chair where she sat wedged with cushions; this meant that, on an ordinary chair, Cliff's nose was level with the table top, and for every spoonful that went into his mouth, another was scattered over the floor.

'See how far you can throw them,' Mick urged, so the little boy loaded his spoon and, with a sideways sweep, discharged its contents over a wide area.

'That's meant to go into him, Mick, not round the room,' said Beverley.

'He can have some more,' said Mick.

'Food costs money,' said Beverley. 'Besides, he's got to learn to eat nicely. Just look at the mess.'

Mick ignored her.

'Open your mouth,' he instructed the child. 'See if Dad can score a goal.' Mick opened his own mouth wide to show the child what he meant.

Obediently, Cliff opened his mouth like a baby bird its beak, and Mick, after carefully cutting a cube of toast from his thickly spread slice, took aim. Soon ten or more segments of toast had missed their delighted target and landed on the floor. Cliff managed to catch one in his fat little hands and smeared butter and jam all over his face and his fingers before eating what was left. By now, however, Mick was bored with the game. He cut a further thick chunk of bread for himself, spread it, and still chewing it, went out of the room. A few moments later the outer door banged shut behind him.

When he had gone there was silence in the small kitchen. Beverley was always relieved when Mick left for work; she had long forgotten that there had been a brief time when she had clung to him, not wanting him to go. Now, she was too exhausted to feel much emotion until despair surfaced as Cliff began to cry. Soon Mandy joined in, and Beverley sat at the table with her head in her hands, crying too, wondering how she could cope with the future.

PC Coates was on day shift that day and came on duty at ten. The complaint against Mick Harvey had been noted in the Occurrence Book, and before he went out on the road one of the other duty constables mentioned it.

'Works in Fordbridge, that bloke, doesn't he?' he said. 'Drives a van for old Patchett.'

'Does he?'

'Yes. My mother-in-law lives round the corner from him and I've seen the van outside The Buildings a few times when he's probably supposed to be making deliveries. Wasn't he up for something not so long ago? I remember wondering if old man Patchett knew about it.'

'Is that right?' So maybe Harvey already had some points on his licence. 'The car's an old heap,' said Coates. 'I wonder if he's got his MOT?'

'Could be worth asking,' said his colleague. 'Since he's denying all knowledge about last night.'

'He'd been out all right,' said Coates. 'But he made his missus say he hadn't. She looked none too good to me – had a bruise on her face.'

'Got it falling over, didn't she?' said the other policeman sarcastically.

'I didn't refer to it,' said Coates. 'Didn't want to make things worse for her after I'd gone. Pity I couldn't have got there in time to catch him with the car. But I might find myself in that vicinity when he gets back from work,' he added. 'I might need to look at his papers.'

'Surprising how things work out, isn't it?' said the other constable.

Coates waited for Mick that evening. He parked near the mini-roundabout at the Four Roads Crossing where the alleged offence had occurred, and he saw the rusty white Maxi approach. It was travelling fast and it swept round the circle without waiting for another car already moving on to the roundabout and having precedence. Coates fell in behind and when he came up close enough to read the Maxi's registration number, made sure it was his quarry. He followed Mick through the town and back to The Buildings. The Maxi's speed dropped sharply when the driver realized that there was a police car behind him. Coates noticed that one of the Maxi's brake lights was not working. He drew in behind it outside the flats and was standing on the pavement blocking Mick's way when he approached the entrance.

'You failed to yield right of way to another car that was approaching the Four Roads mini-roundabout from your right just now,' Coates stated. 'May I see your licence, please?'

Mick swore. He felt in the pocket of his leather jacket and withdrew the licence in its plastic holder. Coates had checked and already knew that it had been endorsed twice for offences committed within the past two years, the second, for failing to stop after an accident, only six months ago. Under the totting-up procedure, Mick Harvey was going to lose his licence if Coates had his way.

'Your offside brake light isn't working,' Coates told him.

'Yeah, I know,' said Mick. 'I'm getting a bulb in the morning.'

Coates looked down at the tyre nearest him. It was very close to the acceptable limit of wear; he inspected another and saw a bald patch, which meant he could charge Mick for that. He noted it down and told him.

'I'd like to see your insurance certificate and your MOT certificate, please,' said Coates.

'I haven't got them on me,' said Mick.

'I see. Then they'll be indoors, won't they? Why don't we go inside and get it over with?' asked Coates.

'It's not convenient,' Mick said.

No, thought Coates, because you haven't got them.

'Well, in that case, I give you notice to produce them within five days at any police station. Merston here is the nearest.' He took a form out of his pocket and began to fill it in. 'Shall we make it Merston?' he said.

'Make it where you bloody like,' said Mick, who had been called upon to obey similar requests before.

Coates handed him the notice.

'Within five days, then,' he reminded Mick. 'And get that brake light and the tyre seen to.'

As he made his report before going off duty, Coates spared a thought for Harvey's poor pale wife, who might now be a scapegoat for his own small success, but he did not intend to let go. He recalled his colleague's query as to whether Mr Patchett knew about Mick's driving record. Mr Patchett would hardly be keen to employ a driver who might involve the firm in trouble. Coates decided to carry the matter on, but first he would give Mick a chance to produce the car's papers.

He was again on late shift when he returned to The Buildings a week later to discover why Mick had not complied with the law's requirements.

Beverley opened the door, and looked startled when she saw who was there. The bruise on her cheek had faded and a yellow stain marked her face. She wore no make-up and her hair needed washing.

'Evening, love,' said Coates. 'Is he in?'

Beverley nodded towards the living-room. Coates walked through and found Mick on all fours on the floor, playing with Cliff. Three toy cars were arranged on the brown and orange patterned carpet, and Mick, making loud roaring noises, was pushing another towards Cliff. The child grabbed it and pushed it back towards his father, but Mick had seen the constable and stood up, scowling.

'You haven't brought along your insurance and MOT certificates,' Coates stated.

'No – well, I haven't got them, have I?' said Mick. He stood in an aggressive posture, hands on hips, legs apart, a defiant expression on his face. He and Coates were about the same age.

'You admit you haven't?'

'Got to, haven't I?' said Mick, and then rage swept over him. 'I know why you're harassing me like this. It's because of those two bloody women,' he said, and angry colour flooded his face.

'Ah – so you were driving your own car on Thursday night, then?' Coates pounced.

'No, I wasn't,' said Mick.

'How do you know it was two women who laid a complaint against you, then?' asked Coates.

There was a short silence as Mick tried to think of a way out of this.

'Well?' prompted Coates.

'I wasn't driving dangerously,' Mick muttered.

'Two witnesses say that you were,' Coates replied. 'And it's an offence to drive a car more than three years old without a valid MOT certificate and any car without insurance cover, as I'm sure you know.'

'If you have me up, I'll lose my licence,' Mick said.

'You will,' said Coates with satisfaction. 'You should have thought of that before.'

While they were talking, Beverley had come into the room and quietly removed Cliff, closing the door. The constable could hear Radio One playing in the background as Mick glared at him.

'I'll lose my job,' Mick said. 'I'm a delivery agent.'

That was a grand description of his employment, Coates thought.

'It's down to you, mate,' he told Mick. 'You can tell the magistrates. Perhaps they'll be sympathetic.' Magistrates often made curious decisions.

'But there's the kids,' Mick said. 'What about them?'

'You're making me cry,' said Coates. 'You'll receive a summons in due course,' he added. The insurance offence was grave and carried a minimum penalty of four points, enough by itself to take Mick over the top. Even if the women did not go ahead with their charge, or if it failed, there was no doubt of his fate.

Coates went away well satisfied. An irresponsible driver would be off the road for a time, at least; perhaps he would learn some sense before his licence was restored.

The radio was still playing as he left The Buildings and he did not see Beverley or the children again.

As soon as Coates had gone, Mick called Beverley. Someone had to answer for what had happened.

No one came in response to his summons. He went into the kitchen where the radio was playing to an empty room. Swearing, Mick looked in the other rooms for his family, but the flat was empty and the pushchair had gone. So had their outdoor clothing.

What did she think she was doing, taking the kids out at this time in the evening in November? They should be going to bed. And where had she gone? It couldn't be to her friend Pat, who lived in the next block; she wouldn't have taken the pushchair all down the stairs for that little distance.

Mick stormed round the flat pulling bedclothes from the bed, wrenching the coverings from the children's cots, and flinging a plate across the kitchen to shatter in pieces.

She couldn't stop out all night. Soon she'd be back, and by God, she'd pay for this little lot: for not being there when he needed an outlet for his anger and for going off without his permission when it was her duty to be at home making his supper. Mick retained enough control not to wreck the whole flat but he was wound up, adrenaline coursing through his system. He couldn't just stay here waiting for her ladyship to turn up. Mick flung on his jacket and ran down the stairs. He paused beside the car: better not chance it tonight; it would be just like that sodding copper to be waiting round the corner ready to catch him again. He went to the Cricketers; a few drinks would make him feel better.

Mick was acquainted with a number of people but he had no real friends. His brother and sister had moved away from the area and his mother had remarried; his father had left home when Mick was twelve years old. Boys he had known at school had either married and settled down by now or had moved away. A few tearaways were some-times in the pub, and Mick knew details about one or two jobs that had been done in the district which would have interested the police. He did not want to belong to a gang; he still did the odd bit of thieving on impulse if he got the chance, but he did not want to be part of anything organ-ized where he would have to conform to other people's rules. If you didn't look out for yourself, no one else would, so why should you think about them?

Mick had never been very articulate. Most girls he had met were swift with ready answers and verbal put-downs, often meant as a form of challenge, to which Mick had never been able to respond in the same key. Beverley was the exception; she was quiet and timid. Both these characteristics appealed to him; he felt no threat where he knew he could create fear, and with her there was no need to talk. Thus it was that Cliff had been conceived, mundanely enough, in Beverley's small schoolgirl-like bedroom one evening when her parents were out. Mick had been angry. Wasn't she on the pill? He thought all girls were. But an abortion was out of the question: the kid was his, wasn't it? Something really his own, to which he had a right. A flicker of spurious affection for Beverley carried him through the brief engagement and hasty marriage which, under the circumstances, her parents insisted upon, although they had hoped for better things for their daughter. Mick, at that time, had felt strong and confident. He was earning good money working on a building site, but then the firm employing him went into liquidation and soon after the wedding he was out of a job. He had found another as a grocery warehouseman, but he did not like being indoors. Besides, when orders came from retailers, it was boring having to find the goods specifically ordered. He took to despatching what was easiest – ready-cooked rice in tins instead of raw in packets, coconut cake-mix instead of Victoria sponge, and the nearest perishables – instead of rotating the stocks so that they moved within their proper shelf lives. After complaints he was sacked, and his next job was as a milk roundsman. That didn't last; he didn't care for the hours, he did not like trundling round at a snail's pace, and he did not enjoy repartee with his customers. He had had a spell out of work before he was taken on at Patchett's, and during that time he had clocked up his driving offences, being caught – as now – with a worn tyre, and more seriously, failing to report an accident. Some busybody had taken his number and reported him when he'd brushed against the kid and knocked him off his bike. The kid wasn't hurt – just his leg cut a bit where the bumper had caught it; he'd dived for the ditch and banged his head – got concussed, it seemed. His mother had carried on alarmingly, saying the child might have lost a leg. Mick had been lucky to escape a charge of careless driving; as it was, he had been fined and had his licence endorsed. He'd have got away with it without the interference of the witness. There was usually someone about prying into things which were not their concern.

But no one had been around the night the girl died.

Mick had seen the job at Patchett's advertised in the local paper. He had been asked for his licence, but he had said it was away having a speeding endorsement removed after the three years' period necessary for working it off. He'd bring it in as soon as it was returned, Mick had said, using on Mr Patchett the smile with which he had once, so briefly, charmed Beverley.

Mr Patchett had approved Mick's frankness in confessing to the small misdemeanour; he'd been going at forty miles an hour where the limit was thirty, Mick had admitted. It wasn't a question of belting along to the public danger; there had been scarcely anyone around at the time, just a copper with one of those ray gun things they point at you – they were very unfair. By the time he might reasonably have been expected to have received his amended licence, Mick was giving satisfaction and the matter was never referred to again; old Patchett had obviously forgotten all about it, as Mick knew he would, the silly old fool.

In the Cricketers, Mick's spirits improved. If he could fix his insurance and the MOT before the case came to court, the charge would lose its force and he might get away with only a fine. Those two women, though, were something else. If he knew who they were, he'd soon scare them off. They'd been in a blue Golf with a B registration, and Mick reckoned he could remember the number, near enough. All he needed was a policewoman pal who could check it out for him. But even to save himself, Mick was not going to go out looking for susceptible policewomen; they didn't exist, he was sure; it was a most unnatural job for any female to want to take on, but that showed how things were these days, with women trying to make out that they were as good as or better than men. He'd never let Beverley have any ideas like that; she'd soon learn who was boss if she tried anything on.

He'd deny everything, if the charge was brought. He'd convince the court the women were bluffing to cover up some fault of their own. That was it; he could say they'd been all over the road, blocking his path, and that they'd become hysterical. He'd manage. Mick successfully pushed the problem away, but he must do something about the car. Apart from the tyre and the light, there were a few other things which might hold up its MOT. The bill for putting it right could easily come to more than a hundred pounds, even if he got a bloke he knew who did repairs in his spare time to fix it. Then there was the insurance. How was he to find the cash? Most of his pay packet went on the rent and what he gave Beverley for food and to keep the kids nicely dressed, not to mention the shirts and jeans he needed himself, and his new leather jacket had cost a bomb. He forgot about his beer, and the price of petrol.

There was Beverley's nest egg.

Cliff, in his innocence, had revealed it one day when they were in the flat alone together. It was while Mick was still out of work, before he had started at Patchett's. Beverley had taken Mandy round to the doctor for a routine injection, and Cliff and Mick had been crawling about on the floor pretending to be lions and tigers. As they romped, the leg of the settee had caught in the carpet which was loose in one corner of the room. Cliff had tugged at it, exposing the boarding below, digging with small fingers at a plank. The sounds he made were not easy to understand, but Mick heard the word 'Mum' and then the child laid a hand on his lips and shook his head, solemnly enunciating 'No say.'

Mick soon saw why. Under the flooring, in a green

Marks and Spencer's bag, was an envelope containing over a hundred pounds.

At first Mick had been furious. He'd sat there looking at the notes, thinking of her deceitfulness, and with him on the dole, too. He could use that money. He was too generous, that was the trouble, if she had been able to put all this by. Then he calmed down; perhaps it was a holiday fund she meant to surprise him with. He wouldn't mind a week in Torremolinos. He'd say nothing, not yet. He knew where it was, and meanwhile the amount stored away would no doubt increase. He'd take it when he was ready, or when he needed it badly.

Like now.

Beverley and the children were still out when he returned to the flat. Mick took the money, taking care to replace the carpet neatly. Then he went back to the Cricketers; there was nothing here to stay for.

4

Fleeing with her children, Beverley had acted instinctively. Mick must have done something bad last week when the policeman came round, and they were going to get him for it. She'd been with him when he'd cut in close to a cyclist just to force him off the road, and there'd been that kid he'd hurt when he'd done the same thing not so long ago. She hated going out with him in the car; he seemed to expect everyone else to get out of his way.

Now that copper had come back again. She did not want to be there when he left, for Mick's rage would rebound on her, as it had before. She had no long-term plan in mind as she bundled the children out of the flat without waiting to fasten them into their outdoor clothing. She tucked their proofed zipped suits under her arm, seized the pushchair and hustled them on to the landing. Somehow she managed to transport her load downstairs in one journey, the pushchair hooked over the arm with which she held Mandy, Cliff clutching her skirt as he took the steps carefully, one at a time. Beverley had put on her own padded coat but had not taken time to change her shoes and had on only a pair of worn down-at-heel pumps. She dressed the children in the lobby by the main entrance and had finished before the policeman came down. She wheeled the pushchair away, tugging Cliff by the arm. Puzzled by this sudden dash in the dark, the little boy soon began to grizzle. At the end of the street Beverley turned to the left, away from The Cricketers. She was not thinking in any rational sense but some inner compass steered her in the opposite direction to Mick's known haunts. She hurried along an alley between two rows of terraced houses, an area where, in the ordinary way, she would never have gone at night, but now there was no worse terror than Mick to dread. She scuttled along between the high walls and emerged at the end into a residential street. Here, the houses were set behind low fences or railings and inside them people were safe, with curtains drawn, meals on the table and television sets flickering companionably. There were cars parked alongside the pavement outside most of the houses, and a steady flow of traffic went by as she trudged onwards. A bus passed, and Beverley tried to interest Cliff in it as his protests developed into determined crying. He dragged at her hand, unwilling to walk any further, and Beverley was forced to gather him up in her arms.

'It's fun going out at night,' she told him. 'Look at all the lights.'

Cliff's sobs subsided as his mother struggled on with one arm round him, the other hand pushing Mandy. If only she'd got a twin pushchair, she thought; she needed one as Cliff was still so small, and she'd meant to try to pick one up, secondhand, using some of her hidden savings, but one way and another she hadn't got round to it. Beverley spent a great deal of her time regretting the past. Trying to relieve her aching arm, she tucked Cliff against her hip.

Luckily Mandy was quiet; she had just been fed before the policeman called and had now dropped off to sleep.

People were still returning from work and a few passers-by looked curiously at the young woman and two children, but though it was unusual to see a mother and children out at this hour in the winter, it was not late enough for them to attract much attention. The trio went on, Beverley's pace soon slackening, and at last she had to set Cliff down again. They came to the park, and she paused at the entrance; it was very dark inside and there would be no shelter except in the toilets. Beverley turned back and went on down the road with Cliff whining again. He couldn't go much further, and neither could she. Without a rest, she could not even walk back to The Buildings, and she certainly dared not do so until Mick had had time to cool down. If only she'd had the chance to get at her savings: then they could have made a run for it, but where would they have gone? If they'd taken a taxi across Merston to her parents' house, would her mother have let them stay? Perhaps for a night, if she'd made up some tale about having locked herself out and Mick being away, but Beverley knew there would be no lasting help there, and it never occurred to her that if she found a taxi now, they would pay the driver.

Anyway, there were no taxis in this part of town and she had no coin for a telephone call.

She was walking beside a solid stone wall beyond which was a graveyard. The church might be open; weren't they always? She'd seen some film where this man took refuge in one. Beverley opened the wooden gate and propelled the pushchair up the tarmac path between rows of gravestones. The street lamps gave enough light for her to see her way to the door.

'Now we'll soon be warm and dry,' she told Cliff. They could spend the night in the church, then go home after Mick had left for work, take the money, pack a few things and leave. She'd find them a room somewhere. Reaching this decision, Beverley felt quite brave.

The church door was locked. Nowadays, menaced by

vandals and thieves, churches no longer provide the sanctuary they once afforded.

There were ledges on either side of the porch. Beverley sank down on one, drawing Cliff close beside her. She had half a tube of fruit gums in her pocket and she gave him one, pulling him on to her lap. Heavy against her, sucking the sweet, Cliff drowsed off. Beverley leaned back against the cold, unyielding wall. In spite of her padded coat, she shivered.

Laura never bothered Tom with trivial concerns, so she had not told him about the nocturnal adventure. He was at home, however, when a police sergeant called to check up on some details a few days after the incident. She learned that the offending driver had been traced and that he would be served with a summons for several offences against the Transport Act in addition to a charge of careless driving if she and Mrs Quilter went ahead. Mrs Quilter was still prepared to proceed. Was she?

'Yes,' said Laura.

Tom prised the story out of her after the sergeant had gone.

'What a wretched thing to happen,' he said. 'How frightening for you. It was a good thing you got his number. Now the police have these other charges to bring against him, you can forget the whole business.'

'But we can't! He might do it again to somebody else,' said Laura.

'Didn't you say the sergeant told you they'd got enough against him already to make sure he loses his licence?' said Tom. 'That's the main thing – to get him off the road.'

'He'd be off it a bit longer, with a careless driving offence chalked up against him,' said Laura.

'Don't be so sure. He might get a pat on the head from the magistrates and a warning to take more care in the future,' said Tom. 'Whereas if I'm caught doing eighty miles an hour perfectly safely on the motorway, I'll get clobbered. It would be an awful ordeal, darling, being in the witness box, and there might be some unpleasant publicity. It wouldn't be a nice experience for you at all.'

He looked earnestly at her as he spoke, running his hands through his disordered thick dark hair. His tie had slipped to one side and the top button of his shirt was undone. He looked more like an overgrown schoolboy than a successful entrepreneur.

'I'm sure Marion won't want to give it up.' Cravenly, Laura used her friend as a support for her own feelings.

'Melt her,' instructed Tom. 'You can melt anyone.'

'He shouldn't be allowed to get away with it,' Laura insisted.

'He won't, if the police press other charges,' said Tom. 'If you do go ahead and he gets a wily lawyer, he could make you and Marion seem quite foolish. Women drivers and all that, you know.'

'But there are two of us. The court would believe us,' Laura said. 'We both saw him go round the roundabout the wrong way.'

'It would be different if there'd been an independent witness,' said Tom. 'Please, darling.'

He caught her to him, holding her against his thick, sturdy body. Laura loved to feel his strength, the steady thump of his heart, the contrast between his physical vigour and his gentleness.

'I'll talk to Marion,' she promised.

After nearly two hours in the church porch, Beverley had to move. Cliff had woken up and was grizzling again, and she was too cold and stiff herself to remain still any longer. She could see no alternative to going home, but by now surely Mick would have gone out? He went to the pub every night, leaving her with the ironing and the television. Now she was always glad when he left, though at first she had protested. He'd said there was nothing to keep him at home.

Once, she'd found him smashing, with his bright eyes and curly hair, and the long soft moustache which had

40

tickled her face the first time he kissed her, and he walked with such a swagger. They had met at a disco, to which Beverley had gone with a friend, and she had been astonished when he had wanted to take her home. One thing had led to another, and though at first, when she found she was pregnant, she was dismayed, and her parents were shocked and angry, it had all worked out, or so she had thought at the time. She had been briefly happy then; to be married at eighteen was the major achievement of her life, and then there had been Cliff, so sweet and appealing, but soon such a disturber of peace. She'd had no idea a baby could be so demanding.

They had been lucky to get the flat. The council kept a few for newly-weds, and they had had to live with her parents for only a few weeks. Mick had gone out most evenings then, but when they moved he often stopped in, working hard at painting the flat and getting it straight; he was good at that sort of thing. Her morning sickness had passed and she had been willing enough to make love. If they had a row – and they did, when Mick called in at the pub instead of coming straight home – making up had been quite exciting. And he was a good father. In fairness, and despite her present misery, Beverley had to admit that he was good with the children, especially Cliff, in whom he took so much pride. Mandy was still too young to appeal to him much.

If they went home, at least she needn't fear that he'd hurt the kids. Some fathers took it out on them, but she was the only one who would suffer from Mick's anger. It began to rain as she dragged her way back through the streets. She carried Cliff some distance, but had to set him down again. The rest of the fruit gums kept him quiet for a while, but he was crying when they arrived at The Buildings. It was too much to hope that the neighbours wouldn't hear him.

She opened the door of the flat to find the vengeful chaos wrought by Mick. Beverley had to remake the children's cots before they could be put to bed. Cliff was shivering, so she made him some hot cocoa which settled him down, but by now Mandy was awake and crying. Beverley sat down by the fire in the living-room to feed her. Her own head was reeling with fatigue and nervous reaction, but at last she felt warm again. She fell asleep with the baby held in her arms.

More than an hour later, Beverley woke. She had not even begun to clear up the flat and Mick would be angrier than ever when he returned to the mess. Carefully, she got to her feet and carried Mandy into the children's room, tucking her into her cot without waking her. Then Beverley started to restore order. With brush and pan she cleaned up the kitchen; she tidied the rooms and straightened the furniture. In the living-room, under the carpet in the corner, was her passport to freedom if things became too bad to bear.

They could get a divorce. If that happened, Mick would have to give her some money.

Facing the thought of so drastic a solution frightened her. Perhaps this wasn't all Mick's fault: perhaps the police had made a mistake and if so he had every right to be angry. Because he had wanted her to say he had been at home when he wasn't did not mean he'd been doing something wrong. Once this particular business blew over, things would settle down and they would be happy. She might treat herself to a home perm, try to make more of herself. She'd been pretty once; a boy called Danny had said so, before she met Mick, who never made that sort of comment. She'd try to keep the place better, too, and take more trouble over the cooking.

Holding fast to this positive attitude, Beverley made ready for bed and lay waiting for Mick to return.

But he didn't come home that night.

Police Constable Coates went to see Mr Patchett.

The furniture shop was a narrow old-fashioned interruption in the flow of multiple stores flanking the High Street in Fordbridge, and both its neighbours were impatient for its lease to be up, when they would compete to devour the

42

premises. Meanwhile Mr Patchett, who lived in a flat above the shop, the only private resident for some distance around, continued to provide old-fashioned personal service on ever-dwindling profits. At night, upper-storey windows nearby were dark; they belonged to insurance offices and building societies. Mr Patchett knew he would have to go in the end, obliged at last to accept the march of progress and his own increasing age, and retire to a bungalow in Worthing as advised by his son; but when that happened, it would mean final defeat. There would be no poir.t in further struggle. If Doris, his wife, had not died all those years ago, things might have been different, but as it was, the shop was what had kept him going though he regretted that the business would no longer be worth handing on. Still, that didn't matter; his son had never wanted to join him and was doing well in computers.

The previous evening, Mick had left The Cricketers with a thirty-five-year-old woman who described herself as a single parent; he had spent the night with her. When Coates called at Patchett's, he was already out delivering goods, and Mr Patchett, between customers, was making up the books. From time to time in the past police officers had called at the shop inquiring about stolen goods, but Mr Patchett had never been offered a table or chair or three-piece suite that had, as it were, fallen off the back of a lorry, and so far he had not been robbed. He paid his takings into a night safe at the bank along the road every evening after he closed, and was confident that his presence above the shop deterred thieves.

Coates ascertained that Mick Harvey worked for Mr Patchett.

'Are you under the impression he's got a clean driving licence?' he inquired.

Mr Patchett repeated what Mick had said about working off an endorsement.

'I forgot to ask about it later,' he admitted.

Coates frowned. He did not like to see the shopkeeper being taken in.

'Look, I'll tell you, off the record, he's got a couple of

current endorsements and he's going to have another,' he revealed. 'He was stringing you along.'

'Oh dear,' said Mr Patchett. 'What did he do?'

'Well, for one thing, he failed to stop after an accident,' said Coates. 'A kid got hurt.'

'That won't do at all,' said Mr Patchett, who might have overlooked a minor misdemeanour. 'He's willing enough, officer. Likes his own way, mind you, but gets things done. Of course, he doesn't measure up to the last man I had, who was here for years until he retired, but I didn't expect it.' He sighed. When engaging Mick, he had deliberately set out to give youth its chance. 'He'll have to go. I see that.'

'How long has he been here?' asked Coates.

'Two months,' said Mr Patchett.

'No problem, then,' said Coates. 'That one has enough nerve to appeal against wrongful dismissal if he'd been with you long enough.'

'Has he had another accident?' asked Mr Patchett.

'No, but he's been driving his own car without insurance, which is a serious offence,' said Coates. 'Mind, I haven't told you that.'

'I'm glad you did,' said Mr Patchett. 'I appreciate it, officer. I must obviously get rid of him. He's not reliable.'

Mr Patchett gave Mick his cards, with two weeks' pay, when he returned from his rounds. It would be difficult to manage without a driver in the next few days but the Job Centre had promised to send along some applicants and if none of them was suitable, he would advertise. Meanwhile, his former driver might help out for a while.

When Mr Patchett spoke to him, Mick retaliated angrily.

'That copper's been here shouting the odds,' he said.

'You didn't tell me the truth about your licence, Mick,' said Mr Patchett. Respecting Coates's confidence, he had merely asked to see it.

'Well, what would you have done?' asked Mick. 'I needed the job. I've got a wife and kids.'

'You could have been frank with me,' said Mr Patchett.

'What – and have you turn me down? Not likely.'

'You're in more trouble now, though, aren't you?' Mr Patchett asked.

'I'd only got a duff tyre,' said Mick. 'That could happen to anyone, and I was going to change it, wasn't I?'

That wasn't Coates's version of events.

'I'm sorry,' said Mr Patchett. 'You'll have to leave.'

'But I've done a good job,' said Mick. 'You won't get another bloke as would carry all that stuff without help.'

'You've worked well,' Mr Patchett allowed.

'But I like the job. I like being out and about,' said Mick.

'There are other jobs in the open air besides driving,' said Mr Patchett.

Mick saw that his pleading was useless. He felt a surge of frustrated rage and an impulse to strike the old man, but Mr Patchett was not the cause of all this; it was those women who had reported him for what had been just a bit of fun. But for them, the police would have left him alone, he'd have worked off the points on his licence and become, in due time, a lorry driver.

He made a rare effort at controlling himself.

'Will you give me a reference?' he asked.

'I can say that you have proved honest over money matters,' said Mr Patchett. 'And a willing worker. But I can't say you're truthful. You'll have to be content with that, Mick.'

He went into the back office and wrote out a short testimonial which he gave to Mick, adding twenty pounds to what he had already put in an envelope because of Mick's wife and the children.

In working hours during the morning, Mick had paid the insurance with a large chunk of Beverley's savings. Now he could get the car seen to, as long as obtaining an MOT certificate did not involve too much outlay. Anyway, he could probably pay off the bill in instalments. The law would look at things differently if the certificates were in order when the case came up. Perhaps he could find some lawyer who would delay proceedings until there had been time to wipe out that first endorsement. Such things could be done.

Again, he wondered who those two cows were. The passenger had been just a dimly seen blob but he'd had a look at the driver as he swept past the Golf, and the shape of her head had been visible in his own headlights as he sat on the tail of the other car; she had that sleek sort of hair done up on her head, a bit like those ballerinas you saw on the telly. They might have come from anywhere in the country, but the chances were that at that time of night they weren't far from home.

He'd keep an eye out for that blue Golf.

5

The night before, Mick had been quite surprised when Rene – that was her name – had asked him for ten pounds before she would take off her clothes. He hadn't realized that she was on the game. Still, it had been worth the money, and afterwards she had said he could come as a friend next time. To Rene, a young man like Mick was a treat to enjoy in between the demands of her part-time job which helped so much with the social security. She had one regular client who came on Monday afternoons while her children were at school; he was a fifty-year-old accountant who paid well and could never stay long as he had to get back to the office, so it was easy money. Two more like that and she'd be able to go entirely private, she told the mesmerized Mick.

He was returning to her place tonight, but he would have to go home first to pick up a change of clothes; he liked to have everything clean each day. He'd borrowed a razor from Rene this morning, a ridiculous little thing it was, but he'd managed a decent enough shave and he'd trimmed his moustache with her scissors, peering at his reflection in her gold-framed bathroom mirror. The bath-room itself was like a jungle, full of plants in pots; and she'd been a bit like a tigress, he had thought as he clipped away, grinning at the recollection. It hadn't been at all like that with Beverley.

Beverley. She'd taken the kids out last night. Had she gone running to her parents? He didn't know if she'd taken her purse with her; he might have emptied that too, if he'd thought of looking for it. Where had they gone?

Looking up at The Buildings from the pavement below, Mick saw a light on in the living-room of the flat. It was a long time since he had run eagerly up the stairs but now he took them fast, working himself up into a renewal of anger against Beverley as the cause of his problems. If he hadn't been so bored at home, he'd have had no need to go off drinking and wouldn't have been on the road at the same time as those two cows. But no one could want to sit around with a whining bunch of bones like Beverley, especially when there were women like Rene available.

He opened the door of the flat and a smell of baking greeted him. Cliff ran forward with cries of 'Dad – Dad,' and Mick swung the little boy off his feet into the air.

'There we are, Cliff,' he exclaimed. 'Who's the big fellow, then?'

He lifted the child up to sit on his shoulders, astride his thick neck, and took him into the living-room where his gaze went at once to the corner in which Beverley had hidden her money. Did she know that it had gone? Well, it was his by rights, wasn't it? He set Cliff down again and turned on the television. Then he knelt on the floor and began pushing a toy car across the room for Cliff to chase. The child ran to and fro with ever more excited cries until finally he tripped and bumped his head on the corner of the coffee table, his cries now turning to yells of pain. Mick's attempts to console him had no effect and Cliff's crying grew even louder until at last Mick thrust the boy from him.

'Go and find your mother,' he said, and went into the bathroom.

Beverley heard the door close and hurried out to Cliff, who was soon pacified when given a biscuit. She had decided to pretend last night had not happened and had prepared a casserole for Mick's meal, adding fresh vegetables to a tin of stewed steak, and had made treacle tart, his favourite, using frozen pastry. She was resolved to give him no reason to find fault with her, hoping that then he would again become the young man he had been when they first met.

Thus had Beverley fortified herself against his return, but she did not see him at all. He left the bathroom and she heard him go out of the flat while she was still busy in the kitchen. Later, she saw the heap of soiled clothes he had left on the floor and found that he had taken several clean sets. His shaving things had gone, and the small holdall he kept in the bedroom.

Had he gone for good? Her first feeling was one of relief. Later, she thought about money.

Mick stayed with Rene until Sunday night, but then she said she must get back to work. Besides, if anyone stayed regularly she stood to lose her supplementary benefit, and indulging themselves wouldn't feed her kids. Mick had been rather shocked to find that she left them alone in the house while she went in search of clients. They were only five and seven, and he had some idea it was against the law. But she was never gone long, just as long as it took, and they slept soundly while she worked. They were nice little kids. He took them to school on Friday while Rene had a lie-in, and on Saturday they all went to a safari park for the day.

He'd had the car fixed, managing to get some part-used tyres from a written-off job and the rest of the necessary work done by a man he knew who worked in a garage by day and serviced vehicles in the road outside his house in his spare time. That was the way to do things, thought Mick: be your own master, beholden to no one.

He went to the Job Centre and he looked at advertisements in the local paper, but the only positions he fancied were connected with driving. He had no wish to be a warehouseman again or become a paint sprayer in a factory. He'd still got some of Beverley's money, and when he signed on, he'd get his unemployment benefit.

When he returned to The Buildings, Mick said nothing to Beverley about where he had been, but he told her he had lost the job at Patchett's and so there'd be no more money.

'Oh Mick! Why?' asked Beverley.

'Because of that copper, that's why,' said Mick. 'Told old Patchett I'd got some points on my licence, didn't he?'

'Oh dear!' Beverley had been so obsessed by her own problems that she had not considered wider ones which would affect them all. 'You'll soon find something else,' she said. After all, he had before.

'I'll not get a driving job,' said Mick. 'Not with that bloody copper gunning for me.'

'Well – ' Beverley cast about for a practical suggestion. 'Couldn't you set up on your own?' she suggested. 'Decorating or window-cleaning, for instance?'

He could, too. It was a good idea but he wouldn't tell her so. And it would depend on keeping his driving licence. Still, the summons, if it ever arrived, would not come for some time and it was never his way to look far ahead. All he'd need, if he was to become a window-cleaner, was a ladder and a roof-rack on the car so that he could transport it. There'd be cloths and a pail in the kitchen.

'Where's that free newspaper?' Mick demanded. Every week it arrived regularly through the letter-box and Beverley always read it eagerly – it contained recipes and fashion hints as well as scraps of local news among the financing advertisements. Mick wouldn't let her buy magazines; when he saw her reading one, he told her not to waste hard-earned money on rubbish like that and cuffed her across the face to make sure she didn't forget. She'd look at Pat's *Woman* sometimes, when she went round there; it was a pity, really, as it would have been nice to have a bit of a read when the kids were asleep and Mick was out.

Still, they had television; there was always that, if you needed to be taken out of yourself.

Beverley took the newspaper from under one of the cushions on the settee and gave it to him. Mick sat studying the *For Sale* columns intently, running his finger along the lines of print. He was in luck. There were two lightweight extending ladders offered, both here in Merston, and a roof-rack in Fordbridge. He'd go after them in the morning.

Mick left Beverley alone that night; he just didn't fancy her after Rene. She did not know whether to be glad or sorry; she had hoped for a reconciliation which would give her renewed hope for the future.

The next day Mick went off to acquire his equipment, taking Cliff along for the ride. He fastened him into the child seat. The vendor of the cheaper ladder was an old man who could no longer use it because of his rheumatism. Mick beat his price down, using the argument that as the ladder was still unsold it must be overpriced and the old man would be lucky to get rid of it at all. He lashed it to the roof of the car outside the old man's house; he ought to have got the roof-rack first, he thought, as he set out for Fordbridge.

When he reached the address of the advertiser who had a rack for sale, he found that there was no one at home. A neighbour told him that both husband and wife went out to work.

Mick boiled up with anger. He'd planned to be all set up and ready to work at once.

'Should have said evenings only in the ad, then,' he complained, and the neighbour told him that the wife worked only part-time and was usually back by half-past one.

'I'll come back,' said Mick. He could pass the time in a pub, he thought, and then remembered Cliff; he couldn't take the child into a bar. Instead, he drove into the town and past Patchett's. How was the old fool managing deliveries without him?

Ignoring the double yellow lines, Mick drew into the kerb some way past the shop. Then he lifted Cliff down and set off up the road with no plan beyond the vague notion of going into Patchett's and stirring things up with his former employer.

The pavement was busy and Cliff dragged at Mick's hand as he met a forest of advancing and retreating legs. Mick stopped to pick him up and blocked the way of passers-by, causing a woman to knock into him and drop a package she was carrying.

It was not in Mick's nature to apologize. He had started to say 'Do you mind?' in his most aggressive tones when he recognized the woman. He placed her at once, with her freckled nose and springy red hair. She'd been toasting buns with a kid by the fire when he took a corny old velvet chair to her place from Patchett's. He switched his reaction and bent towards the parcel, but Marion had already gathered it up. She, too, was annoyed by the collision, but when she saw that the young man was burdened with a small child, she softened. The way modern fathers shared in their children's upbringing was one of the better characteristics of their generation.

'You O.K., then?' Mick asked.

'Yes, thanks. No harm done,' said Marion. She had been to collect some books obtained for her by the good bookshop in Fordbridge; Merston had no bookseller other than a small branch of W.H. Smith. She was about to move on when the young man spoke again.

'How's the boy, then? Peter, was it?' Mick had a good memory.

Marion stared at the ingenuous face beneath the mop of curls. The long mouth below the moustache was stretched in a grin. Where had she met its owner before and how did he know Peter?

'Bet he likes that room you've fitted up for him,' Mick added, unaware that he had been, to Marion, easily forgettable.

His words gave her the key. Of course! The helpful delivery man.

'He's fine,' she said. 'Back in London with his father,

but I expect he'll be coming again before long.' Now it was her turn. 'This is your little boy, then?'

'Yes. Cliff's his name,' said Mick proudly. 'Say "Hullo" to the lady, Cliff.'

Cliff remained dumb, clinging to a tuft of his father's hair.

'Is Cliff helping with your deliveries today?' Marion asked.

'Oh, I've left Patchett's,' said Mick. 'I was only helping out there, temporary like. I'm on me own now. Got me own business.'

'Oh, have you?'

Why should she be surprised by this information? Why shouldn't he be his own boss? He'd got brains, hadn't he? Mick began to bristle.

'What are you doing?' Marion asked.

'Cleaning windows,' said Mick.

'Really? What luck I ran into you, then,' said Marion. 'I suppose you wouldn't think of coming out our way? People in Didbury badly need a window-cleaner and we can't get anyone to take us on.'

'Well – ' Mick's sudden hostility was deflected by the prospect of gain, but he wasn't going to make it sound easy. 'I might be able to fit you in,' he said. It was only a few miles away, after all, and he had to start somewhere. 'I'd need a full day's work to make it worth my while, because of the distance.'

'I'm sure you'd get one,' said Marion. 'For a start, I know Mrs Burdock at Clyde House would be delighted if you went there, and she's got a lot of windows.' Laura had to get the part-time gardener to do them and he hated the job. 'And there are plenty of other people who would be only too pleased, I'm sure, if you called on them.'

'Well, I'll see,' Mick said. 'Mind, I'm not promising.'

'No, of course not.' Marion understood the gambit.

Whilst they talked, pedestrians had eddied about them and they had moved towards the nearest shop front in an attempt not to block the pavement. Marion's parcel was growing heavy. If she didn't put it down soon, she would drop it again.

'Goodbye, then,' she said, and moved off.

'See you,' said Mick cheerily. The interlude had diverted him from his intention to harass Mr Patchett. Now he had something definite to do, a customer clamouring for his attention, and one with a bob or two behind her; that place of hers was worth a few quid, and she'd have friends to match who could be charged a good bit if he went all that way to oblige them. Mick returned to his car. By the time he had joined the stream of traffic, Marion had disappeared down an arcade which led to the car park where she had left hers. A traffic warden, on her way to write Mick a ticket and deprived of her prey, watched him go with regret.

Mick was now in an ebullient mood. He decided not to bother about the roof-rack. His best plan would be to trade in the car, now equipped with its MOT certificate which would last for a year, in exchange for a van. That would be much more professional and it would get the police off his back if they were looking out for the Maxi.

By this time he was thirsty, so he stopped at a pub on the edge of the town, taking some crisps out to Cliff, whom he left in the car in the yard behind the pub. He had intended to be gone only a short time, but after his first pint he needed another, and when he returned to the car the little boy was crying. Apart from being frightened, left alone for so long, he had needed to relieve himself and had messed his smart corduroy trousers.

Mick was disgusted. Cliff was too old for that now. He took the child home and went out again straight away to see what could be done about the car. The future was suddenly bright and he had forgotten that he would have to face a summons.

6

Among the books Marion had brought back from Fordbridge was a beginner's course in German which she had bought for Tom Burdock, who had been trying to learn the language solely from tapes played in the car when driving to and from work. He had large plans for mastering simple Spanish, too, since he had several outlets in South America; he already spoke schoolboy French. His business deals were conducted in English, but he thought wheels would be oiled and good will created if he could acquire some linguistic skills, though he had no natural ear nor latent ability. Marion felt that some grammatical knowledge had to come in the end, unless one was content merely to master various phrases parrot-fashion. She had offered to work with him when he had time; her own German was good enough to carry him well past the elementary stage and she read it with ease. They had spent an hour one wet Saturday afternoon working with the texts that accompanied his tapes and had made progress, but the dialogue was dull and Marion had sought out something more likely to catch his interest. Tom, however, was reluctant to study at weekends; in fine weather he worked in the garden, extending himself physically to compensate for hours spent in the office. A number of weekends were taken up with clients from overseas who wanted to see the country. Sometimes they stayed at Clyde House, giving Laura the chance to use her skills as a hostess. She had gradually transformed the once run-down small Georgian manor house into an elegant and comfortable home, and she was an excellent cook who enjoyed planning dinner parties. She kept her freezer well stocked so that she was never at a loss if Tom brought someone home for dinner without warning.

Didbury was a very small village without a shop or a pub. Its church shared the services of a peripatetic vicar who lived two miles away in Poppleton and was aided by a trio of lay readers. There had been some building in the past decade: a close of squat new brick houses had been built in what was once an orchard but unfortunately the developers had clawed out every tree so that no buyer had the pleasure of finding a mature specimen in his small plot. Apart from this spur running off the main street and a clutch of council houses, the dwellings included three Victorian villas and a row of terraced cottages high on a bank which dated from the seventeenth century. All had been modernized and equipped with central-heating systems. The owners worked either in London, which was within commuting distance, or in Fordbridge, Swindon, and even Reading. The cottages had once been homes for farm labourers; now, agricultural workers lived in new bungalows supplied by their employers. Most of the land round the village was arable, worked by three different families, one of them the Careys, who owned their farm and whose son Nicholas was a friend of Peter's. Between the Careys' land and that of the adjoining farm, which belonged to an Oxford college, was a bridle track leading to a small copse and on to a footpath across the fields to Poppleton. Chalk had once been dug from the copse, but only in a small way and the pit had never developed into a proper quarry; however, it was full of hollows. A tangle of trees and bushes had grown up unhindered in recent years, and villagers walked that way with their dogs at weekends and on fine summer evenings. Anyone who had noticed that a Morris Minor saloon had been dumped there had long forgotten to be annoyed about it as the undergrowth began to surround its rusting presence. There were other things in the copse, too: old cycle frames, and plastic bottles left by picnickers. No one seemed to lay claim to the land; some people thought it belonged to the council and others favoured the college: no one wanted the responsibility for it which would involve cleaning it up.

When Marion and George Quilter bought Lime Tree

Cottage, which had once been an inn, Clyde House was owned by an elderly widow whose family had lived there for several generations. She lived in some discomfort, gradually closing down more and more of the house as her fixed income covered fewer outgoings and as it became increasingly difficult to find effective domestic help. Finally, she had succumbed to a stroke and had died in a geriatric ward. The house had hung fire on the market; though the village was well-placed, close to a motorway, the house needed thorough renovation and the garden was a jungle. Marion had gone to the auction of the old lady's furniture and found it pitiful to see once cherished possessions come under the hammer in a draughty marquee on the erstwhile lawn. There were quantities of linen sheets and tablecloths, old hairbrushes, photographs in silver frames, and other once-treasured objects. She had liked old Mrs Waltham, admiring her forthright nature; she was a type familiar to Marion after years of service life, a woman accustomed to directing others, and enduring adversity without complaint. The Burdocks had been able to buy the house at a relatively low figure; they took down the wing added in Victorian times and restored it to its original simplicity, at the same time reducing it to a manageable, convenient size. Tom's business was now thriving, and last summer they had put in a swimming pool. George had had a theory that Tom's company owned the house in some tax-evading manner. Soon after the Burdocks had moved in, he and Marion had gone to Germany on his final posting, but after his retirement the two couples had become better acquainted. Tom had been a support to Marion after George's death. She had returned from a day in London to find him lying in the garden, his body already cool. He must have been there for several hours; the shock was appalling.

Marion had maintained contacts made during her months in London while George was stationed in Northern Ireland. In retirement, he had intended to find some occupation but she did not want to become over-involved with local fund-raising or other village activities, for she felt she had done enough welfare work during her years as a senior officer's wife. However, she had another reason. While she lived in London, she had met, in the course of her work, a research scientist with an appointment in Cambridge who came to London regularly. They had fallen in love. It had been as simple as that: neither had been looking for an affair and, at the beginning, both found it troubling, but soon it became so important and so mutually enriching that to abandon one another was unthinkable. Hugh now found he could manage his difficult marriage with far greater ease and had more patience with his teenage children, and Marion's life took on a new dimension. After George retired, she continued to meet Hugh; her work gave her an excuse to go to London. They were very discreet, meeting expensively in various anonymous hotels.

Marion felt such a burden of guilt after George's death that she ended the affair. Although the post-mortem findings were that he must have died instantly, she was obsessed with the thought that if she had been at home she might have found him in time for his life to be saved, or at least that he would have spent the day in some other way than digging the vegetable patch. Tom divined some of this; his sympathy was a great help to Marion at that time. He told her, then, about his mother's suicide and the shadow it had cast upon him. They shared a confidence, and Marion felt not only a genuine affection but some responsibility for the pair. When Tom was out of the country she kept in touch with Laura, and they would often spend an evening together during his trips abroad.

Soon after George's death, Hugh accepted an appointment at an American university; he had intended to turn it down because of Marion, and had not told his wife about the offer. His was the easier path; his children were now both at universities in England, and his wife took to campus life with enthusiasm. Marion, however, had suffered a double bereavement, and when her brother's marriage broke up, she was eager to grasp the chance to help him.

She had built a protective fence around herself, not wanting to let anyone come close to her again, but Peter had penetrated this defence. She loved his company and looked forward to his visits. During the recent summer, Marion and Peter had spent a lot of time at Clyde House where they had the freedom of the swimming pool, and she had seen Laura's affection for her nephew grow, evoking a response from Peter. She knew herself to be a prickly person: Laura was much softer, more obviously maternal, and Marion understood that the absence of a family was a sorrow to her. They had discussed it once, when Laura had suggested that Marion would have been comforted, after George's death, if they had had children.

'They'd have been grown-up by now and gone,' Marion had replied, a little brusquely.

'Even so,' said Laura. 'They'd marry and you'd have grandchildren.'

'Not necessarily,' said Marion. 'Marriage seems to be going out of fashion.'

'It won't really,' said Laura, and sighed. The sigh was a clue and Marion prompted Laura.

'I've never minded about not having children,' she said. 'We always thought they'd appear, in time. When they didn't, we thought about adopting, but neither of us was keen enough to try. We met plenty of other people's children, as it was.'

'I wanted a family,' Laura confessed. 'I went to doctors and so on. There was nothing wrong. I didn't want Tom to have tests in case they said it was him. He'd have minded so much.'

She'd made Tom her child, Marion saw. She did everything for him at home. He was very untidy, and when he returned from the office, already tousled, he would cast his belongings round the house, strewing papers and his briefcase on different chairs, throwing down his coat. Laura happily tidied everything. He depended upon her totally and theirs appeared to be a really complete relationship. Marion wondered if their physical communion brought them the ecstasy she and Hugh had shared; watching Laura rest a hand on Tom's arm, seeing the gentle hug the large, bear-like man would give her and the looks that they exchanged, she felt reassured. Perhaps children would have spoiled some of that intimacy; childbirth often brought sexual problems in its wake, not least the fatigue of the mother, and babies grew into teenagers who could be rebellious, rude, and worse; a baby in a cot was not a certain passport to bliss. But Laura was only thirty-eight; she might yet have a baby.

On her way home from Fordbridge, Marion called at Clyde House to deliver Tom's books and found Laura laying the table in the dining-room. Tom was bringing a client home for dinner and to stay the night. The man came from Oslo and had visited them before.

'He's nice,' said Laura. 'And all Scandinavians speak such perfect English. It makes it easy, having him to stay.'

'The table looks lovely,' said Marion, admiring the place settings and the bowl of late roses arranged in the centre of the long mahogany table. 'What are you feeding him on?'

'Typical English food,' said Laura. 'Roast beef. Tom says to keep off fish with Scandinavians because their own is so marvellous that we could never compete.'

'I've found us a window-cleaner,' said Marion. 'At least, I have if he remembers to come.' She told Laura about her encounter. 'He worked for Patchett's, so he should be all right,' she said. 'He was very helpful the day he brought my chair.'

'Let's hope he comes soon,' said Laura. She had not yet told Marion Tom's views on their traffic adventure. 'By the way,' she went on. 'Tom doesn't think we should go ahead with that court business. They've found whoever it was – it seems there were things wrong with his car so that they can prosecute him without our help.'

'I know,' said Marion. 'But that won't include reckless driving or whatever they call it these days. He ought to be penalized for that.' The man could be out at this moment, causing someone else to have an accident. Tom's attitude was typical, however: Joe Public wanting to stay out of trouble. 'I suppose they wouldn't have picked him up for his faulty car if we hadn't reported him,' she allowed.

'No.' Laura seized on this comforting observation. 'So we did our bit, really.' She looked at Marion anxiously. 'Will you agree to let it go?'

Marion certainly did not want to upset Tom or provoke friction between him and Laura.

'I suppose so,' she said, rather ungraciously. 'I wonder who he was?'

'Oh, just some tearaway. Does it matter?' Laura said.

'He probably makes a habit of that sort of driving and gets away with it every time,' said Marion. 'Still, George would have taken the same line as Tom, I expect. All right. We'll let it go.'

Mick called at Lime Tree Cottage the following week. In the interval, he had succeeded in selling his car to a youth he had met surveying vehicles on a used car lot where Mick himself was looking at vans. Impressed by Mick's production of a valid MOT certificate, the youth was well pleased with his purchase, and Mick, putting money down for a dark blue Morris Minor van which had begun life in the service of the Post Office, had some cash in hand. The van lacked the zip of the Maxi and its MOT would expire in three months, but by then he would have progressed with his business and would be able to buy something better.

He had already mentioned his new venture in The Cricketers, but without winning any customers. Local small tradesmen cleaned their own windows, and bigger concerns had contracts with an established window-cleaner. No housewife in the area would pay out good money for this job.

'You should get leaflets printed. Post them through people's doors,' Rene suggested, when he had cleaned hers in a dummy run to see how long it took.

'That's an idea,' said Mick, and they spent some time composing an appropriate advertisement. 'But how will customers get in touch with me?' he wondered as he finished printing his address on the page. 'I've got no phone and I reckon it would take for ever to get it fitted.'

'You could give my number,' said Rene. 'I don't mind you doing that till you can get it connected.' She needed the telephone for her private clients and she always left it off the hook when actively working.

'Thanks, Rene,' Mick said.

'Only till yours is installed, mind,' she said.

'Right,' Mick agreed.

He had rushed off to an instant-print firm and had had the leaflets produced, two reams of them on flimsy yellow paper. He bore them home in triumph.

'Look at these, then,' he said to Beverley, tipping the bundles on to the kitchen table.

'Oh Mick, whatever did they cost to print?' asked Beverley. 'Wouldn't it have been better to have gone round personally finding customers first?'

'No, it wouldn't,' said Mick. Trust Beverley to knock him. With a different woman, someone like Rene, for instance, with a bit of spunk, there'd be no limit to what he could do, but with Beverley it was like being chained to a zombie. 'This'll soon spread the word,' he told her.

'Whose phone number is it?' Beverley had been carefully reading the notice.

'A pal of mine,' Mick said airily. 'There's usually someone there to pass on messages.'

He went to the sink and opened the cupboard below, where Beverley kept her plastic bucket, a sponge and some rags. Mick took them all.

'What are you doing with those?' Beverley asked.

'What does it look like?' Mick replied. 'Borrowing them, of course.'

'Oh Mick! I was going to clean the floor later,' Beverley protested.

'Well, you'll have to use something else, won't you?' said Mick. 'Christ, Beverley, you're enough to send anyone up the wall – can't you ever find anything to say except "Oh Mick"?' He copied her whine. 'I've had enough,' he added, and went out of the flat.

He spent the rest of the day distributing leaflets in the better residential areas of Merston, and whilst doing so was asked by several housewives to call as soon as possible. Mick didn't clean their windows right away: he'd keep them waiting several days; it didn't do to seem too keen. People were lucky to get him.

When he went to Didbury, Marion was standing on a ladder cleaning leaves from a gutter. Mick walked up the path past the open garage in which he could see her red Fiesta.

'Like me to do that for you?' Mick asked her, staring up at her as she stretched upwards, her thin thighs outlined in jeans.

Marion had seen his blue van draw up outside. Mick had underestimated the length of his ladder and had to drive with the doors open, lashed together.

'Hallo,' she said. 'You're prompt. I didn't expect you so soon.'

'I changed my rota so as to fit you in,' Mick told her. 'Seeing as you were desperate.'

This was hardly how Marion would have described her situation; however, a window-cleaner on the premises was, like a bird in the hand, better than one *in absentia*.

'Good,' she said, descending the ladder. 'And I would be glad if you'd finish off this job for me, since you're here.' The ladder had seemed to move once or twice as she reached out to fish round in the gutter. A few tiles had slid from the roof and perched precariously on the rim.

Mick climbed up in her place and made a fair job of completing her task; he'd charge her extra for that. Then he set about the windows, filling his bucket with warm water at the kitchen tap. She made him a cup of tea while he was using Beverley's sponge. Because of the leaded lights, he could not wipe the windows off with the scraper he had bought and had to leather them with a chamois he'd borrowed from Rene.

Perched on the ladder, Mick peered with interest into the rooms beyond. He'd been in the kid's room already – fancy keeping it just for his visits! The woman lived here on her tod, that was for sure, otherwise her old man would have done the gutters. What a waste of all this space! She had quite a garden, lawns and flowerbeds. But Mick wouldn't want to live here; Didbury was a dump, with no life at all. Whatever did folk do here in the evenings? There wasn't even a pub.

He could see a double bed in the main bedroom. A sweater and skirt hung over a chair. She'd have jewellery, rings and things; they'd be there, in that dressing-table. It wouldn't be difficult to suss out a way to enter the cottage when she was out and there was sure to be plenty of stuff worth taking – money, radios, things easy to sell or handy to use. It would be stupid to nick something while you were working, but you could keep your eyes open and collect another time.

Drinking tea in her kitchen, answering Marion's questions about Cliff, Mick planned how he would rob her.

Marion was startled at being asked to pay eight pounds for her windows; it was about a pound a window. And he'd requested another two for the gutters; he'd put the dead leaves and other rubbish in the dustbin and noticed the larder window open as he did so; it wasn't very big, but Mick had squeezed through smaller openings.

After he had gone, Marion telephoned Laura to say that he was on his way, and warned about his prices.

Laura had taken some time to answer the telephone and Marion was on the point of hanging up when she heard the rather breathless voice at the end of the line.

'I've just got in,' said Laura. 'It's getting dark. He'd better hurry up.'

7

Every few weeks Laura made an expedition into the countryside beyond Didbury, explaining to anyone who was curious that she wanted to explore fresh areas and find new walks for Cleo. In fact, she went to inspect houses that were for sale.

They were always large houses with several acres of land. Laura pretended to herself that if ever she found one she liked better than Clyde House, she would persuade Tom to look at it and perhaps they would move, but in her heart she knew that she would not really uproot him, nor did she want to; moving would not cure her restlessness. The houses she saw were always isolated, standing in the midst of their land some distance from the nearest neighbour, their seclusion lauded in the selling agent's literature. Sometimes they were in poor repair, and Laura would mentally plan their restoration. She had no faith in her own talent for interior design and knew that her colour schemes at Clyde House were safe rather than striking, but she was practical and could plan structural improvements and the modernization of archaic kitchens with confidence. By this time she had seen a lot of houses, even a few mansions, but what Laura sought was contact with the family as much as she wished to see the building. Nothing was required of her except interest in the property; the vendor, on the other hand, was anxious to impress upon the visitor how suitable the place would be for her, and there would be, at the least, enthusiasm, sometimes even the brief illusion of friendship.

That morning, she had been to Grange Court, in the Cotswolds.

'We'll enjoy today,' she had told Cleo as they started out, the dog spreading herself comfortably on her rug, prepared for sleep. Laura meant to go to Burford on her way home, have lunch at a pub and wander round the attractive shops.

Grange Court, when they reached it, was as well-situated as its description promised – something that was not always the case, as Laura had discovered. There was no abattoir or silo close by, no small industrial complex half a mile away nor open prison across the fields. A short drive led between wrought-iron gates to the long mellow house constructed of the local stone, with roses, wisteria and clematis, all now in winter suspension, climbing up the walls.

Laura had given Cleo a good run earlier. Now she instructed her to be good, shut her in the car, and put herself into the frame of mind appropriate to a house-hunter as she approached the oak door which must have been there since the place was built. There was an ancient bell-pull beside it, and Laura could imagine the jangling within the house that it would produce, but she heard no sound.

She had been observed, however: the door was opened by a tall old man with a pale, lined face. He had thick, straight snow-white hair, neatly parted on the left, and very blue eyes with which he regarded her above the half-glasses perched on his long thin nose.

This must be Mr Masefield, the owner.

'Mrs Burdock?' he asked. 'I saw you arrive. Do come in.'

Laura stepped into the stone-flagged hall and was at once aware of an aura of dampness in the air, which she had noticed in other such houses where the heating was imperfect and no damp-proofing system had been installed.

'I'm afraid I'm a poor hand at showing people round,' said Leonard Masefield. 'The truth is, I don't really want to move.'

Laura found this lack of enthusiasm understandable.

'Have you lived here long?' she asked.

'Forty years,' he answered. 'My wife died last winter.'

'Oh, I'm sorry,' Laura had met widows selling up; this was her first experience with a widower in such circumstances.

'I can't manage on my own,' he said. 'I've tried house-keepers – girls with illegitimate babies, widows – ' here his voice trailed off. More than one had thought a permanent position might be secured and he had had, even at his age, one very embarrassing proposition. 'It's isolated, you see,' he went on. 'And there's no bus. A man from Birmingham

65

made an offer and I thought everything was settled, but it fell through. It happens all the time, the agent tells me.'

As he talked, he led the way into a large, untidy room. At one end of it stood a grand piano, the rack up and supporting some open sheet music. There were several easy chairs covered in faded Sanderson printed linen, all with piles of books and papers on their seats. The room was chilly, apparently heated only by two logs which smouldered unsuccessfully in the open fireplace. Laura surreptitiously felt a radiator by the wall; it was quite cold.

'What a beautiful room,' she said, as she mentally tidied it up. It was all she could do not to begin at once by folding the open newspaper that lay on the floor and attempting to revive the fire. Most houses, however uncomfortable or in need of renovation, were orderly on the surface when she went to look at them. Mr Masefield was clearly unable to deal with his own domestic muddle, just like Tom. For the first time since she had been making these expeditions, Laura felt shame at her own deception. She had no intention at all of buying this house and she ought to confess without delay.

But he had begun to talk about the music.

'My wife played the violin,' he said. 'I accompanied her. We were only amateurs, of course, but it gave us pleasure. We played in a small orchestra for a time.' He showed Laura a photograph of a dark-haired woman with a serene expression. 'I miss her,' he added, then went on more briskly, 'That explains why I'm selling. Let's move on and I'll show you the rest of the house. You'll see that it needs modernizing. The boiler is very old and uses a lot of oil. There's no damp course and there's a lot of land – fifteen acres – but a local farmer puts his sheep on it. That's not a problem. Maybe you want a paddock for ponies, as we did once. I expect you've got a family.'

'Yes,' said Laura automatically. That lie had begun in her first tour of inspection. She would tell houseowners that she had a son and a daughter. They had become quite real as she described them and the boy had gradually turned into Peter. She had given him a sister, Jane.

'We had three,' said Mr Masefield as he led the way upstairs. He showed her the ten bedrooms. In a large one facing the front there were photographs of school cricket and football teams, and in another she saw an old doll's house and a rocking horse. 'The grandchildren used to enjoy playing with them, but now they're grown up,' he added.

'Where will you go?' asked Laura.

He had put his name down for a flat in a mansion run by a non-profit-making association which housed the elderly. There was a warden, he told her, and a communal dining-room in which, he emphasized, each person had his own table and was not forced to share. There were large grounds, with whose upkeep the more active tenants helped. 'It won't be so different from here,' he added. 'I mean, with regard to the surroundings. Like home, but without the worry.'

'But your work – what did – do you do?' asked Laura. With all these books he must be a scholar, perhaps a professor.

'I ran my own business,' he said. 'In Birmingham. We made electrical components. We lived in the city at first, then moved out here when things went better and the children were arriving. I sold out twenty years ago and the firm went public later.' He laughed, a wry, mirthless sound. 'One day you're head of a thriving concern, an important man in your own small world, with power. Next day, you've become a has-been. But we were lucky – we loved living here, and were able to develop our musical interests. We didn't need a lot of friends nor want a busy social life. Beth had a few outside contacts and interests but I became a hermit, catching up with reading I'd not had time for when I was young.'

He'd made his early fortune in the war, manufacturing parts needed for aeroplanes, then switched his thriving business to wider peace-time use, realizing, when he sold out, what had seemed an enormous amount of capital, only to be caught by the later sudden soar of inflation when oil prices rocketed. Some of this Laura apprehended as she understood that Mr Masefield was no longer rich. She wondered how old he was: he looked at least eighty.

He showed her the large bedroom with the sagging double bed where he and Beth had slept in harmony through the long years of their marriage and where now he must lie alone. Laura always missed Tom's comforting bulk beside her when he went away; but he came back.

'Where do your children live?' she asked, and learned that one son was in Australia, where he had gone on a working holiday as a young man; he had married a sheep-farmer's daughter and now ran the huge estate himself; the other owned a hotel in Guernsey. Mr Masefield's daughter had married a doctor and lived in Scotland. None of the grandchildren had ever stayed long at Grange Court, though even those from overseas had made many visits. Here was a man who genuinely had a large family, yet no member of it lived near him. We are all alone, Laura thought, and felt fear.

'You're cold,' said Mr Masefield, noticing her sudden shiver. 'We'll have a glass of sherry, but first you must see the garden and what the agent calls the outbuildings.'

They walked all round the cultivated area, and he pointed out the extent of the land that went with the house. A mantle of neglect lay over what had once been well-maintained. Beth, it transpired, had been a keen gardener; she had been supported by a man from the village who still came at intervals.

'I'm not very practical, I'm afraid,' said Mr Masefield. 'I ran an efficient business, but that was years ago, before microchips and computers. I've forgotten all about it now.'

'My husband's like that,' said Laura. 'He has his own business, but he's not very handy about the place.'

'I expect you take good care of him,' said Mr Masefield. 'Come along. Let's go in and find the sherry.'

He offered her Tio Pepe. Laura drank it with enjoyment, ignoring the dust on the elegant Georgian glass in which it was served.

'You've got some lovely things,' she said. She was not very knowledgeable about antique furniture or porcelain, but, aided by her house-hunting excursions, her eye was improving. 'What will you do with them all when you move? You'll take some, I suppose?'

'Yes, and sell the rest,' he replied. 'My daughter may want a few things. If you and your husband would like any of it, you must let me know. You'll be bringing him to see the house, won't you?'

'I don't think he'd find it suitable,' Laura managed to say.

'Oh! Oh dear!' The old man's face fell. 'But you like it, don't you?'

'Very much.' And she would love putting it to rights.

'I'd like you to have it,' he said. 'I'd like to think of you here.'

'But I'm afraid it won't do for us,' Laura said firmly.

'Don't decide now,' said Mr Masefield. 'You might change your mind when you've had time to think about it. Come and see it again.'

Laura looked at his pleading eyes. He was old enough to be her grandfather, and he had no one here to help him sort out his affairs or dispel his isolation.

'You must let other people come and see it,' she insisted.

'I will,' he promised. 'But please come again.'

Laura had not been able to put him out of her mind as she drove home. She had had lunch in Burford, as she had planned, and bought herself a new pair of shoes. Then she had taken Cleo for another walk, but she kept thinking about Mr Masefield reading about the Dissolution of the Monasteries – she had glanced at some of his books and seen that they covered a wide range of subjects including that one – amid the ruins of his home. Beth's clothes still hung in the walk-in closet he had shown her, which he thought had been a priest's hole during the Civil War.

She would go again.

On his way to Clyde House, Mick stopped to post leaflets through doors that he passed. Even if only half the inhabitants of Didbury required his services, there would be enough work here for a couple of days, he decided, turning down the Poppleton road as directed by Marion. He saw the entrance to Clyde House on his right and drove up to the front door. Lights were already on in the house, long bright rectangles breaking the straight lines of the front. A blue Volkswagen Golf was parked on the sweep of gravel which separated the building from a wide lawn, and as Mick drew up behind it, a golden Labrador bitch came towards him, gently wagging her tail. Because he was looking at the dog, Mick did not notice the car's registration number, and was only subconsciously aware of its make.

He got out of his van and walked over to the front door, which was approached by a short flight of steps. Mick pealed the bell vigorously, and a woman opened it. She was almost as tall as Mick, with dark hair swept up in what seemed to him an old-fashioned style as he automatically gave her an appraising glance. She wore a loose green sweater over a cream-coloured shirt, and a pleated checked skirt in various muted shades of green.

'You're the window-cleaner,' she greeted him. 'Mrs Quilter said you were on your way. Will you be able to see? It's getting quite dark.'

'I'll manage,' said Mick.

Her hair reminded him of someone he'd seen recently. While he wondered about it, she was speaking.

'If you go round the back, I'll show you where the tap is,' Laura instructed. 'Through the yard,' she added, as he stared at her, apparently not understanding.

Mick had expected to enter by the front door, walk through the house having a good look round as he went, and so to the kitchen to fill his pail with warm water at the sink. The fact that he would carry dirt on his shoes through the passages, and that this was why Laura was sending him round to the back, did not cross his mind. He decided that she was a stuck-up bitch even before he identified the car.

She put it away while he was running water into his bucket at the tap in the yard. With a raincoat thrown on but not fastened, she opened the garage doors, then walked round to where the Golf was parked, the dog following. Mick was standing right behind the car as she drove it into the garage which was, he observed, large enough to hold three cars. He could see the neat head and the pale profile as she passed him, then the sleek rear view as the interior light came on when she opened the car's door to get out. He glanced down at the number-plate. He had found her.

Mick was still standing there, staring, when Laura, having locked the garage, came towards him.

'Everything all right?' she asked.

He was holding the scraper in his right hand, and he raised it. For an instant Laura had the notion that he meant to strike her with it. What a silly idea! She dismissed it as he answered.

'Yes, thanks,' he said calmly. 'I'll start here, at the back.'

Fate had delivered her to him, quite by chance: the woman who had shopped him to the police and caused all his troubles, and she was here at his mercy.

For once Mick controlled his impulse to act without thinking. Revenge needed careful planning. He took his time over the windows, incidentally giving them a very thorough cleaning which impressed Laura when she assessed his work. He examined all the rooms. It was quite a place. Her old man must run a Rolls, he decided, and there'd be plenty of loot here for the taking. But that wasn't enough. He needed to get back at her in some way which would hurt, and which would stop her from pressing charges. It wouldn't be enough just to threaten her, although he'd enjoy seeing fear on that pale, calm face. He watched her in the kitchen. She'd put a big apron on and was stirring something. There was a blue Aga cooker in the room, which was as big as his whole flat in The Buildings, Mick extravagantly estimated, slopping water on to the panes which separated them.

She paid him in cash from a wallet stuffed with notes, saying his hands must be very cold.

Might have offered me some hot water, then, bloody

cow, thought Mick, or tea, like that Mrs Quilter, who was a different type and not bad, in her way.

He stuffed the money into his jeans as Laura asked him how often he planned to call and he told her once a month. She assured him that there would be plenty of potential customers in the village but suggested that he was rather expensive.

'I done a good job,' he told her.

'Oh yes,' she agreed, deciding not to tell him that some of her neighbours, however desperate for his services would not be able to afford his charges. He'd find that out soon enough.

'I don't have to come all this way to get work,' he said. 'I'm doing it as a favour. Take it or leave it.'

'I'll expect you in about a month's time, then,' said Laura.

As she heard his van chug away, she wondered if he would come again. He had left her a leaflet which gave a Merston telephone number.

Calling Cleo in to be fed, Laura put him out of her mind. Soon Tom would be home and the best part of her day would begin. She still felt a lightening of her heart when she heard his car in the drive.

Mick drove on to Poppleton. There were no other houses along that road, which wound between fields until it reached the main road which led in one direction towards the motorway, and, if you turned right, to Merston.

He would be back.

8

When he went to see Rene on the way home, Mick found that there had been some telephone calls from people in Merston wanting their windows cleaned. Rene had written down each name and address with a green felt-tip pen on a pink piece of writing paper emblazoned with a violet in the corner. She soon sent him away, for she was expecting a client that evening.

He called in at the Cricketers before going home, his mood still good because of the varied successes in his day. When he arrived back at The Buildings, Beverley was cooking sausages and chips, and the smell as he entered the flat reminded him that he had eaten very little since breakfast. Subconsciously aroused by his unsatisfied contact with Rene, Mick went into the kitchen and beamed at his family. He homed in on Beverley, looming towards her, hands ready to warn her what would be required of her as soon as the children were in bed. He'd brought a bottle of red wine back from the pub. They'd drink it in bed; that would loosen up even Beverley. He'd learned from Rene about the pleasure of eating and drinking in bed; it was amazing where crumbs could be found.

Beverley's pale, pinched face showed apprehension and she moved away from him as his hand reached for her.

'Don't I get a kiss?' he demanded, but Cliff was shouting at him.

'Dad – Dad – ' He was always pleased to see his father.

To Beverley's relief, Mick's attention was diverted and they managed to eat their meal without overt discord.

'You got some work, then?' Beverley asked when he gave her five pounds. He could spare her that much: Cliffie must be fed.

'Yeah. Been busy all day,' said Mick. 'And I finished up at some rich bag's house over in Didbury. There's several there want me to call regular.' He wondered about telling Beverley who the rich woman had turned out to be, then decided to keep it to himself.

'You'll have to keep accounts,' Beverley told him. 'For income tax.'

He hadn't thought of this, and he didn't mean to pay any tax on what he earned; moreover, he planned to go on drawing unemployment pay – how could anyone check up? But it wouldn't do for Beverley to find this out.

'Maybe I should,' he said. 'Get me a notebook tomorrow, will you?'

He began drinking the wine while Beverley was settling the children, and in the end, after finishing the bottle, was too fuddled to do more than grasp at her with hot, heavy hands when they went to bed. She slipped away from him, taking a pillow and their only spare blanket, and spent the night on the sofa.

The next day he went off on his rounds. He had slept heavily and woken late, and Beverley had not disturbed him because she did not want him to realize that she had moved out of the bedroom during the night. She made some sandwiches for him to take to work, and filled a flask with milky tea. She'd do that as long as he gave her housekeeping money. After he had gone, she set off to buy a cash ledger in which he could record his earnings. She bought a second notebook, too, in which he could write down his expenses, and in it she entered the cost of these and of two ballpoint pens, one black, one red. She had once worked in an office where she had been in charge of the petty cash. She could keep the books for him, she thought, still faintly nurturing the hope that their relationship would improve.

That evening when he came home she showed him her purchases, and he did his best to remember where he had called since he had begun window-cleaning. The list of visits was far from complete; Mick meant to keep it that way, but his Didbury calls were entered. Mick halved the amount that he had earned when writing down the takings.

That evening Beverely was nearly happy, believing things would work out in the end. Shutting her eyes, yielding to Mick in bed, she could almost imagine that she was young and in love again. Almost.

The estate agent telephoned to ask Laura what she had thought of Grange Court. He always rang after her visits; this was a snag, but she was becoming adept at parrying his questions and inventing reasons for each house's unsuitability.

'Mr Masefield thought you would be wanting to see it again,' prompted Mr Feathers, who dealt with her file. Mrs Burdock seemed hard to please; since she had been on their books he had sent her to see more than a dozen houses, some in excellent repair and exactly fitting her specified requirements. Still, he was accustomed to difficult clients and recognized that many women wanted to move merely as a whim or from boredom and it was reasonable to expect resistance from their husbands. He had begun to fear that Mrs Burdock was such a customer. Nevertheless, his business was selling houses, and Grange Court would not be easy to unload at anything like a good price for the vendor.

'I might do that,' Laura acknowledged. When she did, she would make it quite clear – as, indeed, she had already tried to do – that she would not buy the house.

'Let me make an appointment for you,' offered Mr Feathers, who knew that many a sale had resulted from such an unpromising beginning. For one thing, Mr Masefield would probably settle for a good deal less than the asking price, which Mr Feathers himself had fixed.

'No – don't worry, I'll do it myself,' said Laura. 'Just give me the telephone number.' As Mr Feathers had made the earlier arrangements, she had not needed to know it; she would have rung his office if she had been forced to cancel her arrangement to view.

Mr Feathers repeated the telephone number to her, and Laura, who had been in the kitchen when he rang and was speaking on the extension there, wrote it down on the corner of the file in which she kept her own pet recipes, often culled from magazines, and which she had been consulting when Mr Feathers called.

She arranged to see Mr Masefield the following week, looking forward to it, planning what she would take for him, as if he were really her father or her grandfather. Laura's own father had died when she was fifteen. She had been kept away from school until after the funeral and when she returned people had shunned her as if she had a contagious illness. Courage had been required and expected; Laura exhibited a stiff upper lip and wept in private. The experience formed in her a habit of containment; she learned to bottle up her griefs and disappointments. When she married Tom, she had a good job as personal assistant to a company director; she had kept it on for some years, and her salary had given them a measure of security when Tom had launched out on his own. It had been Tom's joy to free her when they moved to Didbury; now he could repay her for those early struggles by giving her a lovely house and money enough for anything she wanted. He needed her talents as a hostess, but she knew that he wanted the satisfaction of being a successful provider. She loved him, and so she accepted her new role; there was a price for everything. She had Cleo, and she was involved with several charitable causes such as the local branch of the NSPCC, but she felt close to no one except Tom.

She liked Marion Quilter, who was an undemanding friend, and who had brought Peter into Laura's life.

Laura loved Peter. She saw a lot of him when he visited his aunt. They went for walks with Cleo. The little boy was interested in animals, birds and insects, and Laura, who was ignorant about wild life, learned from him. She had bought some reference books so that they could look things up. When he held out his small, grimed palm to display a caterpillar or two ladybirds, she would feel a sensual joy at his dry touch. He and Marion had spent hours in the swimming pool last summer; now Laura planned to reclaim the tennis court. She was only a moderate player herself, but Marion had been keen, and wanted Peter to learn the game. There had once been a grass court on the level lawn at Clyde House, and there could be one again. She would work at her own game, lose those extra pounds which Tom liked so much, and become quicker on her feet. If Tom, who played squash twice a week, became enthusiastic too, they might have a hard court laid. Peter could use it in the winter.

Mr Masefield was delighted to learn that Laura was coming again, and he invited her to lunch.

Laura accepted. She looked out some home-made jam to take to him, and she made him a sponge cake.

He was watching for her, and when she parked outside Grange Court, he came out to greet her. He had had his hair cut, she noticed, and was scrupulously shaved, his lean cheeks shining. The sherry glasses were clean today, and she saw dust-free islands here and there where someone – her host, perhaps – had attempted an improvement in the drawing-room.

He had laid two places at the big table in the kitchen.

'It's warmer in here,' he said.

'Yes – the Aga,' said Laura, smiling. 'We've got one, too.'

'Beth found it wonderful for stews and things,' said Mr Masefield. 'But I'm afraid I'm not much of a cook.'

His Aga still ran on solid fuel, Laura learned, so it fell to him to feed it and remove the ashes. He didn't mind, he told her; it gave structure to his day to have some necessary tasks.

'Don't you have any help at all?' she asked.

'Not now,' he said. 'A woman used to come twice a week from the nearest village, on her bicycle, but she gave up when I got a housekeeper. Took offence.'

'Couldn't you get her back now?' Laura suggested. If Mr Masefield belonged to a different social level, people would be busily obtaining the services of a home help for him. No doubt he qualified, in any case, because of age.

'I haven't asked her,' he responded.

'I think you should,' said Laura firmly. 'If she can't, or won't, she might know of someone else. And whoever buys the place will need help. It could be a selling factor.'

He smiled when she said that.

'Clever woman,' he said. 'All right – I'll try her.'

There was cold ham and a baked potato for lunch, with Stilton to follow, and he opened a bottle of claret.

'Tell me about your children,' he said.

Now it came so easily.

'Well, Jane's eight and Peter is ten,' she said. She told him about Jane and her pony, attributing to this fictional child what she knew about the Carey girls. Then she talked about Peter and how he liked swimming and cycling and was interested in zoology. She became animated; her face, which in repose had looked heavy, became almost pretty as colour washed her cheeks.

After lunch he gave her a book for Peter: Ernest Thompson Seton's *Wild Animals I have Known*.

'My father gave me this when I was ten,' he said. 'I loved it. I won't be able to take all my books to my old folks' home. We'll find something for Jane next time you come.'

They arranged it then. She would come before the school holidays began. She'd bring another cake, and more jam; he'd been delighted by these gifts.

'You must bring the children in the holidays. See how they like the place,' he said. 'Then perhaps all three of you can work on your husband. I'd so much like to think of you all living here.'

'We won't be buying it,' she told him, her hand resting on his thin arm in the tweed jacket. 'We really won't.'

But she would come again. She'd managed to tidy up some of the books while he was searching for what he wanted to give Peter, and by degrees she might be able to help him sort things out a little.

Laura had enjoyed her day and drove home happy.

As soon as the envelope arrived, Beverley knew what was in it.

Mick had already gone when the post was delivered. Even on wet mornings he left promptly, though he couldn't clean windows if it was raining. As long as he was out of the flat, Beverley didn't mind where he went but he must have been finding work because he gave her five pounds every so often. She could save nothing now, and she would need to dip into what she had put by to get Christmas presents for the children. She had planted some bulbs from the market in a bowl for her mother; they were in the airing cupboard, just beginning to sprout among the piles of garments. Beverley never seemed to stop washing clothes and nappies, and the air in the flat was always damp. If she dried things in front of the gas fire in the living-room, the windows steamed up. They needed a tumble-dryer but it would be wrong to use her secret fund for that; Mick would wonder where she had got the money, and besides, she might need it more urgently if things went wrong again. He wasn't keeping his records up; several times she had brought out the ledger and asked him if he would like her to do it for him, but he'd snapped back at her, saying it was his business and he'd see to it when he was ready.

She had almost forgotten the policeman's two visits, but when she saw the envelope, she remembered. This was a summons. She'd seen one before.

She put it by his place when she set the table for their meal. He opened the envelope and glanced at its contents; then, swearing, he pushed at the crockery, sweeping some of it on to the floor, the full teapot just missing Cliff as it overturned and spilled all over the carpet.

'Oh Mick!' Beverley cried, but he took no notice, storming round the room in a destructive rage seeking things to break or hurl about. He grabbed a book from the settee; it was a manual on infant care she had been lent by a girl she had met at the clinic. Mick threw it out of the window, breaking the glass into smithereens.

While Beverley watched in horror, Mandy, wedged into the high chair, began yelling and Cliff started to cry.

'Get out of my way, you stupid bint,' Mick snarled at Beverley, pushing past her, his hand on her chest.

Beverley cried out in pain as she stumbled back, knocking into Cliff who was coming towards her looking for comfort. Mick snatched up his jacket and rushed out of the flat. Beverley, at the broken window, saw him emerge below into the yellow light from the street lamps. Rain was pattering down as he got into the van, started it up and drove away with exhaust fumes pouring out at the back.

Well, at least he had gone.

Beverley ran downstairs to retrieve the book, taking Cliff with her but leaving Mandy in the high chair. Mr Duke opened his door and watched her progress, whilst in other flats curtains twitched at windows. Most of the neighbours knew that things weren't right between the Harveys, but they were not the only quarrelling couple and some people thrived on rows. It didn't do to become involved.

The book was soaked. Beverley carried it upstairs and laid it to dry on the radiator. Cold air was pouring in through the shattered window. Most of the glass had fallen outwards, but there was some inside the room and spiked shards framed the large hole in the pane. Cliff stopped crying and marched towards it, hands outstretched ready to grab at one of the interesting shapes, and Beverley saw him only just in time to snatch him away before he reached it. She scolded him, and his tears flowed again. Mandy had not stopped crying since her father's outburst began.

It was all too much to bear. Beverley gave way to her own distress for some minutes before she attempted to console the children. Then she started to clear up the mess, sorting out broken crockery, picking the margarine off the floor, scraping jam from the carpet. The children were in bed before she read the letter Mick had received. Mick was to appear in court early in January. She did not bother to read the charges; she knew he was guilty of whatever offence had been alleged.

Eventually she pulled herself together enough to try to do something about the window, through which cold air and rain were steadily pouring. She found some drawing pins and fastened several sheets of the weekly free paper across the gap. She would have to find someone to mend it, unless she took the children and left. Then Mick could do what he liked.

Beverley swept up the splinters of glass from the floor and arranged a chair in front of the window to keep Cliff at a distance from it. Then she went to the corner and raised the carpet, telling herself that she'd need some of her savings to pay for a repair when all the time she had another purpose.

She lifted out the green plastic bag. It felt very light. Panic swept over her as she patted it, punched it, then opened it.

It was completely empty. All her money had gone.

9

Mick ignored the police summons, but he did not stop trying to think of ways to intimidate Laura. He went to Didbury again and cleaned windows at the house nearest to the Burdocks, where in conversation with Rosemary Wilson he learned that Tom Burdock drove a BMW, not a Rolls, and was often away on business. Mick watched Rosemary leave the back-door key under a water butt when, after paying him, she went to fetch her children from school. She deserved to be done, he thought, looking through the windows at the Wilsons' good furniture, large television set and video recorder. He could tip someone off and take a share of the proceeds without touching the actual robbery.

Unaware of Mick's aspirations, Rosemary Wilson departed without a qualm while he finished off her windows. Because he had been to the Burdocks and to Marion Quilter, he must be all right.

How could he frighten that woman? What would scare her enough to make her withdraw her charges against him? Mick considered entering the house one night when her husband was away – he could easily watch the place until a time came when the BMW did not return – with a stocking over his face. He could threaten her with a toy gun, tie her up and leave her like that until somebody found her. He didn't want to rape her; he didn't fancy her one little bit and where was the fun in that? It would scare her all right, but it wouldn't be any joy for him. Kidnapping her and shutting her up alone to starve would be satisfying, but was impractical. Where could he hide her? And he'd have to leave her there, wherever it was, to her fate, when he wanted to witness her fear.

Time was passing. Soon the whole nation, as it seemed, would be on holiday from Christmas until the New Year and her husband would be about. Mick himself had Cliff to think of now, and Mandy. He took home a small tree which he had cut from a plantation he had seen on his rounds.

They went to Beverley's parents' house on Christmas Day. Beverley was pale and had dark circles under her eyes which her mother chose to ignore, but her father felt some concern at seeing his daughter looking so wan. The children were clean and spruce, and Mick remained sober throughout the visit, though he and his father-in-law got through most of the wine provided. Beverley's mother made sure everyone understood the hours of preparation that had gone into the meal, its cost in money and the fatigue of her labours. Beverley was on edge lest her own difficulties became obvious to her parents; if she let them know the truth, her mother would only tell her that she had made her own bed and must now lie in it, the literal interpretation of her plight.

She had not dared to mention the theft of her money to Mick.

On Boxing Day they went to Leicester, where Mick's mother lived in a pleasant suburb with her second husband. This was an easier day for them all. Mick's mother made a fuss of the children, and his stepfather was genial, willing to put himself out for the acquired family as long as it was only for a brief period. He liked a bit of fun himself, and was taking Betty off to Brighton for a few days in the New Year. Betty was great when she'd had a few drinks.

He had had doubts about the boy, who seemed to switch jobs too often, and whose wife was a pathetic little thing. It was hard to fathom what Mick saw in her, but still waters ran deep, and if Mick was like his mother they doubtless had much to enjoy. He knew that they had had to get married, but that was a common enough event, even now. Of course they were short of the ready – what youngster wasn't, especially with two kids to support? Frank, a generous man, gave the boy a tenner when they left.

Beverley had put the summons safely away in a drawer. Such an important document mustn't get lost. As Mick had received them before, he must know what had to be done about it.

She was so shocked by the loss of her money that she was unable to think beyond the next minutes and what task must be done in the day's routine. Her friend Pat's husband mended the window for just the cost of the materials. Beverley was very upset, saying that she had broken the window by knocking against it, but Pat was certain this wasn't true. Maybe Cliff had done it, barged into it with a toy or something, and she didn't want Mick to know, though Pat thought that Beverley could have told her the truth.

Mick made no more entries in the accounts ledger, and he did not replace her pail, but he was getting work. A cleaner already established in the town had broken his wrist and Mick moved in on his territory. He had to charge the same price as his rival, which restricted his profits in the town, but he discovered that people in the country areas were so thankful to have anyone call that they accepted high rates, though they asked him to space his visits wider apart than he suggested. He did the work adequately. It wasn't hard, though dipping one's hands into cold water wasn't pleasant. Some of his customers asked him to clean the insides of their windows; while he did that, he was warm, and had a chance to look round. Once, he took ten pounds from a handbag he saw in a bedroom. There were over sixty pounds in the woman's purse and he did not think the owner would miss one note.

Peter returned to Didbury the day after Boxing Day. His

father brought him over from Suffolk, where they had all spent Christmas with Caroline's parents. David was going back to London alone for the rest of the week, then rejoining his wife and baby daughter for the weekend until after the New Year. His office could not cease all activity during the long holiday period.

Marion was pleased to see her brother, who looked tired but content. There were wings of grey in his hair above his ears, and she thought he was beginning to look distinguished in his middle age. He confessed that the thought of a few nights' unbroken sleep was attractive. Sarah rarely slept for more than four hours at a stretch.

'Well, you're certainly experiencing life to the full,' Marion said. 'Most people start contracting out of things as time goes on, but you haven't.'

'Have you?' David asked.

'To some extent,' said Marion.

'You never know what – or who – is round the corner,' said David, who thought his sister too young to bury herself in the country, although she was far from idle. He did not know how he and Peter would have managed without her support in the months after his first marriage broke up, but now, with that translation work which was a solitary occupation, she must spend most of her time alone.

'When do you want Peter back?' Marion asked.

'Can we play it by ear a bit? Have you anything fixed when you want to get rid of him?'

'Not a thing.'

'It's difficult for Caroline now, with Sarah,' David said. 'She won't have much time to take him anywhere in any part of the holidays that's left.'

'You don't have to explain,' said Marion. 'He can stay here as long as you like. I'm counting on quite a long visit this time and there are lots of things we can do. Nicholas has been counting the days till he got here.'

'Mutual, as you saw,' said David. Peter had already gone out on his bike. 'That's fine, then.' He was relieved. The blending together of his new family with the old was not easy and needed to be gradual.

84

While they were talking, Peter was making a detour on his way to the farm. He went through the copse, anxious to make sure the Morris Minor was still there. It was undisturbed, just as he had left it, the crisps and a tin of Coca-Cola still in the boot. The comics had become rather soggy and damp.

He went on down the track and joined the field path to the farm. It was a sunny day but there had been a frost in the night and the ground was still firm. He pedalled onwards, singing.

Peter had told no one else about the car. It was his own special place and he meant to keep it secret.

The day appointed for the hearing of the charges against Mick Harvey came and went. Mick had made no answer to the summons, and he did not appear in court.

The next day PC Coates saw him leaving the Cricketers. He was with a woman – not that thin little wife, but a henna-rinsed, smartly dressed older woman whose arm was linked in his.

Coates drew in to the kerb and wound down his window.

'Didn't turn up then, did you?' he remarked.

Mick stared at the uniformed figure. What did he mean?

'In court,' Coates said. 'If you don't next time, there'll be a warrant out,' he warned.

'What's all that about?' asked Rene, when Mick had led her past without replying.

'Some parking bother,' Mick said lightly. 'I was meant to go to court and I forgot.'

'Didn't you plead guilty by post? That's the easiest way,' said Rene comfortably. 'They're going to get you, whatever you say.'

'I wasn't guilty,' Mick said.

Rene gave him a knowing look.

'Oh yes?' she grinned. 'Who says?'

'I say,' said Mick, scowling.

'Well, Mister Tough Guy, you'll hear more of that,' she told him, laughing.

Rene wasn't afraid of him and Mick felt no need to alter that. He had met his match in her.

'That bleeding copper's got it in for me,' he said.

'Better go and say you're sorry, and pay up next time,' Rene advised. 'It's only money, isn't it?'

But it wasn't, not for Mick. If he lost his licence and went on driving, that sodding copper would hang about waiting to catch him. Mick didn't know if you could be sent down for driving without a licence. Quite probably you could; you couldn't do a thing these days without someone having it in for you. Why couldn't people mind their own business?

He went to Didbury again the following day.

Peter liked being at Lime Tree Cottage. Aunt Marion was always the same, always cheerful and brisk, always fair, and never in a grump. Mummy and Daddy had had grumps, but Dad didn't these days, only he was always so busy. Often he wasn't back from the office till quite late, and sometimes he brought papers home. Mummy hadn't liked that, and Caroline didn't either, but now she had Sarah to keep her busy in the evenings so perhaps she wouldn't mind so much in future. Peter occupied himself with his collection of dead insects or his Lego, or watched television. But at Lime Tree Cottage there wasn't any competition; he and Marion were alone together with no one else requiring her attention and there was order to their days. They had breakfast at eight every morning, and Peter was expected to help wash up and to bring in logs for the sitting-room fire. He had to make his own bed – not difficult, as it simply meant pulling the duvet straight and shoving his pyjamas under the pillow. He often played with Nicholas. The boys rode about the neighbourhood on their bicycles. There was little traffic in the lanes around the village apart from first thing in the morning and again at night when people were on their way to or from work, and both Marion and the Careys thought the boys were old enough to be granted a certain amount of freedom.

Marion tried to clear her desk during Peter's visits, but sometimes there were urgent translations that had to be done, or work that she had not managed to finish as rapidly as she had hoped. On a day when Nicholas had to go to the dentist and she had to rush through a piece on hypnosis which had appeared in a German medical journal, Peter pedalled up to Clyde House to see Laura.

He went straight round to the back door, as he always did, took off his boots and walked in. There she was in the kitchen, an apron on and a strand of her hair wandering over her cheek. They beamed at each other, each feeding a fantasy, for after his mother's flight Peter had developed a long-running serial story in which Tom died – not painfully, but as the result of some debilitating illness – following which David comforted Laura and in due course married her. This dream withered whenever Tom was present, because Peter liked him and did not really want him to die. He might go off and marry someone else, like Mummy, Peter scripted in a revised version of his soap-opera. When Caroline entered their lives, his original scenario had to be scrapped, but Laura's importance to him grew.

She came forward now to kiss him. She'd never done that to start with. Unknown to Peter, she had felt shy and awkward in his company, unused to children and afraid of oppressing him. Boys had to be trained to be men and have stiff upper lips; kissing was out and soppy until they were old enough to tangle with girls, Laura had believed. Things changed one afternoon when Peter was helping her peel vegetables for a casserole; she had cook-ins, as she called them, when she prepared dishes for the freezer, and Peter enjoyed being her assistant. His task now was to scrape carrots before slicing them in the food-processor. The knife he was using slipped and he cut himself quite badly. It hadn't hurt a lot; his yelp was due to surprise more than pain, but Laura was very upset. She comforted him not only with first aid for the wound but by hugging him. She felt all soft and nice, and she had a special smell, partly flowery, which Peter liked. He hugged her back. She

87

had taken him to the doctor in case the cut needed stitches, and the doctor had clipped it together. Laura blamed herself for this injury; perhaps he was too young to be entrusted with a knife. She had returned him to Marion with distressed apologies. On this occasion, Peter had been spending time with her because Marion had to go to a memorial service. Nicholas and his family were away.

Marion had reassured her. Peter must learn to use knives safely and to respect their dangers, she declared. People shouldn't always be protected.

Parting then, Peter had lifted his face to Laura to be kissed and had wrapped his arms around her, clinging to her. Watching them, Marion had felt a stab of what she was honest enough to recognize as jealousy. She loved Peter; she was his aunt, but they did not kiss in this warm way. It was her fault; she had always been undemonstrative. Only with Hugo had she found true emotional release. Perhaps Laura and Peter needed each other, Marion thought. She had not needed Peter when he started to play so large a part in her life; he was a duty which had to be undertaken, but now when his visits ended, she felt desolate for several days.

Today Laura came forward and hugged him.

'Peter, how lovely! How's everything?' she said. 'How was Christmas? Would you like some hot chocolate?'

Peter had never had it until one day she had made him some. It had become his special treat and Marion had bought a tin, too.

Laura put the milk on to boil, made coffee for herself, and they sat at the table with their mugs while he told her about his visit to the house where Caroline's parents lived. He and Dad had gone to the coast on Boxing Day and walked by the sea while everyone else went to sleep. He had seen various types of gull and other birds not found in Putney or Didbury. He had played billiards with Caroline's father, which was fun. There were bats in a barn there, and you were not allowed to destroy them, which annoyed Caroline's mother who said they were filthy. She was in favour of exterminating all of them and paying the resulting fine.

'I've some sympathy with her,' said Laura. 'I've always believed they get tangled in your hair, if it's long, like mine.' She smiled.

She looked pretty when she smiled. Her eyes went all twinkly.

'Endangered species must be protected,' Peter stated.

They discussed seal culling and whales, and the shooting of elephants by ivory hunters. Peter found Laura's views on these subjects to be satisfactory. When they had finished their drinks she took him through to the hall, where a tall Christmas tree dressed with tinsel and glass baubles stood in the stairwell. The star on the top was level with the upstairs landing; it was as high as the tree in Caroline's parents' house. There were two parcels still beneath it, both wrapped in festive paper. Laura gave them to him.

'This is a book a friend of mine gave me for you,' she said. 'I'd told him how fond you are of wild creatures. It's very old, because he's old and it was given to him when he was ten.'

Peter unwrapped the book, carefully turning the pages and studying the illustrations. There was a name neatly written on the flyleaf.

'Is that your friend?' asked Peter. 'Leonard Masefield?'

'Yes.'

The book was printed on very thick paper and the pages had uneven edges. It was full of stories about different animals, and though old-fashioned, it looked nice. After a lengthy inspection Peter opened the other parcel. It contained flipper feet, a snorkel mask and an electronic game.

He was ecstatic. Dad was taking them all to Corfu in the summer; he'd be able to hunt for coral and piranhas.

Peter had a present for Laura. He'd made it at school, in crafts; it was a dog modelled in clay and fired in the kiln.

Love for Peter gave Laura the insight to recognize the subject.

'It's Cleo!' she cried, delighted. 'Oh, Peter, how lovely! Thank you.'

Peter had been at Didbury more than a week when Mick, on impulse, returned there. He had no plan. It wasn't a month since he had cleaned that Burdock woman's windows so she wouldn't be expecting him; besides, a fine rain was falling so it wasn't the weather for work. He might just go there and see how the mood took him, maybe threaten to carve her up.

Whipping up his fury, pressing the van to greater speed, Mick was irritated by its sluggishness as he headed towards the country. A mile out of Merston it began to misfire and splutter. He cursed as he saw that the petrol gauge registered empty. Bloody thing! Filling the tank cost money, and at Patchett's Mick had had things organized nicely. While buying petrol on Mr Patchett's account, he would fill a couple of cans for himself. Old Patchett never queried the bill. Mick drew in to the verge. There was no filling-station ahead for several miles; he would have to go back to town. He crossed the road and stood at the kerb, thumb extended, a can in his hand; he always had an empty one in his vehicle on the chance of milking a tank. It didn't occur to him to walk; he had a right to a lift.

In the end, he got one from a lorry driver who took pity on the figure standing dejectedly in the drizzle and delivered him at a self-service station in the outskirts of Merston. Mick filled his can and paid in the shop. He stayed there chatting up the girl attendant and watching how she switched on the pumps while he waited for a customer who would give him a ride back to the van. The morning rush was over and business slack. Mick had developed the habit of staying in bed late himself these dark days; it was one of the advantages of being self-employed.

A small Fiat drew up at a pump. The driver was a blonde in a fur fabric coat. As she got out and prepared to fill her car, Mick sprang forward wearing his most alluring smile.

'I'll do that for you, love,' he said. 'How many do you want?'

'Oh, thanks! Fill her up, please,' said the blonde, who was a market researcher on her way to Swindon to explore people's detergent-buying habits. After Mick had filled the tank and while she was paying for the petrol, he began cleaning her windscreen with a rag he had in his pocket, so that when he asked for a lift up the road she could hardly refuse to give him one. His mood had improved by the time they parted, but when he opened the van's door he discovered that his transistor radio had been stolen. You couldn't trust anyone these days.

He could replace it with a radio from Clyde House; he had seen one in the main bedroom and another in the kitchen. If that cow was out he could turn the place over. No one would be able to see the van if he parked it round at the back where that cold tap was, in the yard. On the other hand, that wouldn't scare her, and her old man probably had plenty of what was needed to replace what he took.

He wanted to see that stuck-up face fold in terror.

He'd delay his visit. He'd think about it a bit, cast about for a good idea, and first, he'd pick up a radio; he could not face the day in silence.

Mick kept straight on, through Poppleton towards Flintsham and the motorway junction, turning over in his mind various acts of vengeance against the woman who had become the focus for his hatred.

On a hilltop he paused at a fork in the road; to the left lay Flintsham, to the right, a minor winding lane led through fields and past a lonely farm towards some hamlets. He turned left. In Flintsham, an expanded commuter village now bypassed by the feed road to the motorway, he parked in a lane and went ahead on foot. He carried a sheaf of his advertisements, an excuse for his presence as he looked for an unattended house.

He soon found one where the back door had been left

open for the expected plumber. A note instructed him to lock up and leave by the back door when he had finished. Someone else's emergency had delayed the plumber, and Mick had plenty of time to take the portable radio out of the living-room. He wore his thick driving gloves so that he left no prints. After that spell in Borstal he'd got a record.

Whilst he was there, he had a look round. He found fifty pounds in a desk but he didn't risk going upstairs in case the plumber arrived. He'd be the one to get blamed when the householder came home and found things had been lifted. Mick liked that idea.

It was the woman's turn next.

10

It was still drizzling as Tom drove home that evening. His mind ranged over the day's events – telephone conversations with clients in Bahrain and Cairo, and plans for a visit from potential buyers in Saudi Arabia who wanted to see the factories where some of the products Tom handled were made. He would act for anyone who wanted his services and had agents overseas selling a variety of goods from small electrical gadgets to patchwork, all of whose producers were in too small a way of business themselves to employ their own export staff.

Sitting in a queue at some traffic lights, Tom listened to German dialogue on a tape, hoping to absorb the useful phrases by some form of osmosis. He could already understand more of what went on at business meetings in Hamburg and Munich than when equipped only with the limited technical vocabulary he had acquired as he dealt with catalogues and telex messages. It would be pleasant to converse easily with his agents, he thought, sliding the car into gear and forming in his mind the phrase, *Ich möchte nach Hause fahren.* It was good practice to think up short sentences of such a nature, as Marion had taught him. They must ask her to dinner as soon as Peter had gone. Tom admired Marion and planned to offer her a job when his business had taken the next expansive stride he foresaw. He could do with a dependable personal assistant with linguistic skills. His secretary, though capable, did not speak even schoolgirl French. He wondered if Marion would consider tackling Arabic; that curious flowing script would present a challenge. If she would join him in the business, even part-time, he might be able to take Laura away for a holiday at last. He felt guilty because it was so long since they had had even a weekend away together. He would have to agree that Marion could have as much time off as she wanted, to free her for Peter's visits; it would be worth his while to offer her the job almost on her own terms. Tom had Laura at home to complement him; Marion would fulfil the same need at the office if she could be persuaded to take it on.

Driving on, he began to anticipate his return to Clyde House. Every evening he looked forward to the moment when, if Laura had not already heard the car and come out to meet him, he would enter his warm, comfortable house and be enfolded in her arms. How lucky he was! He might have gone through his entire life without meeting such a woman, so warm and soft, so certainly his. At this moment she would be preparing for his return, seeing to dinner – she somehow managed to have all preparations done before he arrived so that only last-minute assembly was required – and listening to his tale of the day. He pictured her switching on the outside lights; the fire would be burning cheerfully in the drawing-room and the sherry decanter and glasses would be on the tray.

He turned off the motorway, a contented man. The beam of his headlights pierced the darkness ahead as briefly he considered the contract just agreed with a firm who supplied children's clothes cut out and ready to sew. He planned to market them throughout Europe and had begun by successfully selling them in France through a magazine offer. Women gained the creative pleasure of making the garments without the problems of cutting or design, and every pack contained motifs which they could appliqué to the finished item if they wished, thus completing a decorative as well as a functional item at a moderate price. Phrases from the promotional literature occupied his mind as he reached Poppleton and took the side lane for Didbury. He met no other car as he travelled along its narrow, slightly humped surface. To the left, as he approached the village, lay his own land, the two fields now let to Bob Carey who ran sheep in them.

He turned between his own entrance gates and drove up the gently curving approach to the square house which delighted his eye whenever he returned to it.

There were no lights showing. Tom frowned. Laura had said nothing about being home late; she almost never was, but it happened just occasionally if she went somewhere with an Arts Appreciation group she had joined, or to a theatre matinée. As he slowed the car, a shadowy figure moved towards him from the side of the house. It was Cleo. That was odd; Laura usually took her with her in the car, or, if she were going out for some time, shut her in the house. He drove on into the yard, the dog following, trailing her tail.

The garage doors were closed. Laura left hers open if she went out for only a short time, and she would open his before he came home.

Tom stopped the car and got out, turning off the lights. Cleo came up to him and snuffled his hand, her tail now waving gently.

'Where's your missus, then?' Tom asked her, fondling her ears. 'Why hasn't she taken you with her?'

What had happened? Nothing very important, or Laura would have telephoned him before he left the office. She never bothered him with trifles but she would have rung if there had been some emergency.

The back door was locked. Tom let himself in and put on some lights. Then he looked for a note which would explain where Laura was. They kept a wipe-off message block in the kitchen, but there was nothing written on it.

Cleo was whining. She wanted her dinner, of course. Normally Laura had fed her by this time. How was it that the dog had been roaming about outside? Now admitting his unease, Tom went through the house turning on more lights and calling Laura by name, but the place was empty. The silence, broken only by the ticking of the long-case clock in the hall, echoed back at him.

Next, he went to the garage. Laura's Golf was there, neatly parked.

She must be somewhere in the village. Perhaps she had gone on foot with Cleo, who had run off and returned alone. Probably Laura was now hunting for the dog. It was very unlike Cleo to behave in such a way, but perhaps she had come on heat and was acting in a wayward fashion.

He went back into the house and found a tin of Chappie and some dog biscuits which he mixed up in Cleo's bowl.

'There you are, old girl. It lacks your missus's touch, I know, but you must put up with that,' he said, setting it down in the corner of the kitchen where Laura always fed Cleo.

Cleo sniffed at it, sampled a few morsels and then turned away.

'Well, be like that, then,' said Tom. She'd eat it if she were really hungry.

He felt upset and disgruntled. The scenario for the evening was being rewritten and he did not like the new version, where he was not in control and had not read the script. Surely Laura would realize that Cleo had found her own way home and would come back? He'd better go and look for her, he thought, but decided to wait for a while in case, knowing he would soon be home, she telephoned. To fill the time, he lit the fire in the drawing-room. It flared up quickly, the wood and strategically situated lumps of coal soon catching. Tom was no good at laying fires himself.

After this he paced restlessly about, then decided to do some telephoning himself. He rang the Wilsons and asked

Rosemary, who answered, if Laura was there. Learning that she was not, he asked if Rosemary had seen her during the day, but she hadn't. Tom explained the circumstances and Rosemary said that she knew Cleo never left Laura.

'But there'll be a reasonable explanation,' she added quickly. 'She'll turn up or telephone any minute.'

'Yes, of course,' said Tom.

Next, he telephoned round the village, asking everyone he could think of if Laura was with them or if they had seen her that afternoon or evening. No one had. There was no reply from Marion's number, and Tom nourished the hope that the two had gone somewhere together, perhaps taken Peter to the cinema. Yes, that was it. But why had Laura left no message, and why was Cleo wandering about?

He wrote a note to Laura on the message pad, in case she returned before he tracked her down, and propped another on the hall chest where she would see it if she came in through the front door. Then he went out to search for her. He left Cleo behind; and lights on in all the downstairs rooms with the curtains still undrawn.

Tom drove slowly round the whole village. It did not take him long. There was no one about; the inhabitants were either having their evening meal by now, or had settled by their firesides. When he reached the lanes beyond the houses, he stopped constantly and got out of the car to call Laura's name. The night air was raw and the faint drizzle still descended from the heavy skies. The sound of his voice was thrown back at him but there was no other answer. In the end, Tom had to return home alone.

On the way, he passed Lime Tree Cottage. It had been in darkness when he passed, but now lights were on there, so he stopped, buoyed up again with hope. They had been on some excursion and Marion's car had had a puncture or a break-down, he decided, walking up the path expecting to find Laura in the house.

He pealed the bell.

Marion answered the door promptly, and from her surprised expression at finding him there, he knew Laura was not with her.

'Why Tom, whatever's wrong?' she asked.

Tom's thick, dark hair was untidy; he had loosened his tie which had slipped to one side, and there was a smear on his face where he had rubbed a hand made grimy by his efforts with the fire. Tom often looked dishevelled at home, but Marion had never before seen him distraught.

'I can't find Laura,' he said. 'Have you seen her? Is she with you?'

'No. I haven't seen her all day,' said Marion. 'Peter and I have been to Swindon. We went swimming and had lunch and then went to the cinema. We've only just got back.'

'I telephoned and got no answer. I thought Laura might be with you,' Tom repeated.

'I'm afraid not,' Marion said. She'd thought of asking her to join them, but had selfishly decided to keep Peter to herself. 'She can't have disappeared, Tom,' she added.

'Well, I know, but it seems she has,' said Tom.

'Come in and tell me,' Marion said, taking his arm and leading him into the house.

'I'd better not – she might be trying to telephone from somewhere,' Tom answered.

'Fill me in quickly,' Marion urged.

As succinctly as he could, Tom told his tale.

'Did you check if her coat had gone? Her boots?' Marion asked him.

Tom hadn't thought of that.

If it was anyone else but Laura who had vanished, Marion would have been suggesting he should look to see if she had packed a suitcase.

'I'll go and look,' he said, pleased to have a task. 'Do you think I should call the police?'

It was dark, cold and damp, a winter's night, a time when all citizens who could be were indoors.

'Yes, I do,' said Marion. Laura might have had an accident when out with Cleo; she could be lying in a field somewhere with a broken leg, or she might be ill. Even women as young as Laura had been known to have heart attacks or strokes, and George had died like that. 'Would you like to telephone from here?'

But Tom thought he'd go home first. She might have come back.

'Right.' Marion patted his arm again. 'Ring me if I can be useful, and let me know when she turns up.' She gave him an encouraging smile. 'I'd come back with you,' she said, 'but there's Peter. He's in the kitchen having his supper. If you do need us, we'll both come.'

'Thanks,' said Tom, and left.

When she had closed the door behind him, Marion turned to find Peter standing at the rear of the hall looking like a little ghost. He had heard their conversation.

Marion reacted briskly.

'You heard Tom, I expect,' she said. 'Laura seems to have got lost somewhere, but she'll soon turn up. Let's get on with supper and by then Tom will have rung to say she's safely home.' She gave Peter a hug. 'She'll be all right.'

But why hadn't she telephoned, if her absence had some trivial straightforward cause?

Tom telephoned half an hour later to say that she was still missing and that the police were on their way.

'Can't we go and look for her?' Peter demanded. 'I know all the walks she goes on with Cleo.'

'I don't think we'd be much use in the dark,' said Marion. 'Tom will ask us to go up there if we can do anything.'

She almost wished he would do it right away, for Peter had turned grey with anxiety. Waiting was always the hardest thing to do at such a time. She and Peter had already discussed every reason they could think of for Laura's disappearance, but the one that made most sense was that she had met some misadventure while out with Cleo and was lying helpless in a field, exposed to the weather and unable to summon aid.

'You'd think Cleo would have guided Tom to where she is,' said Peter, who had read stories in which faithful hounds did just that.

'Yes, you would,' Marion agreed. The police would have dogs. She told Peter that. 'They'll show a police dog something of Laura's, for the scent, and she'll soon be found,' she said. 'She can't be far away, after all, if she walked.'

They rationalized the puzzle together by the fire. Marion wondered at what age you could give a child a slug of brandy to pull him round. She gave herself one, and offered Peter some of it. He swallowed it and made a face. Then Tom telephoned again to tell them that the police were going to search the fields and footpaths where Laura was known to walk. They had already searched the house and all the outbuildings; a waste of time, he'd thought, but they had said it was routine. They had torches and searchlights. A police dog was coming, and some of the neighbouring men were being asked to help because their local knowledge would be useful. Tom wanted to go with them. He asked Marion if she would come to the house so that someone was there if Laura came back on her own. A constable, he mentioned, would not be quite what she would be expecting. The searchers would go out in several groups. Bob Carey was guiding one lot over his land and two other farmers would do the same on theirs. Laura's raincoat and her boots were missing, but she had not taken her handbag. It was in the hall.

Marion and Peter were both glad to be part of the action. Laura would soon be found now, Marion insisted, as they went out to the car.

At this stage no one, not even the police, thought that any third party was involved with Laura's disappearance.

As well as searching the land around Clyde House and along the various footpaths, inquiries were made at houses in the village, but as Tom had already discovered, no one had seen Laura.

'We can't do more until first light,' said the inspector in charge of the operation.

His men had been through the copse. They had sent probing beams from their powerful torches into ditches and hollows. One officer had even investigated the Morris Minor in its nest of brambles.

Marion had made up the fire in Laura's drawing-room, and she and Peter had sat there playing Scrabble – Peter knew where it was kept. Neither of them had spirit for the contest and they soon gave up. Marion turned on the television set, where there was an old adventure film showing. Watching it, Peter's eyelids began to droop and at last, as she had hoped, he fell asleep. She lifted his legs up on to the sofa, where he was sitting, and fetched a blanket from one of the bedrooms to tuck round him. Then she turned all the lights off except one lamp by her chair. She left the television on, the sound turned low.

What could have happened to Laura? People did disappear – children on paper rounds and at fairgrounds, even walking home, had vanished, never to be seen again and probably murdered. But could such a thing happen to a grown woman, and in a place as quiet as Didbury?

Tom came in at last. She went to meet him in the hall.

'The police have gone home,' he told her. 'They'll start searching again as soon as it's light, if we've heard nothing by then.'

'What can we hear, if she isn't found?' asked Marion in surprise.

'They seem to think that she might have been kidnapped,' said Tom. He stared at Marion, his eyes almost glazed with shock and fatigue.

'Oh!' Such an idea had never occurred to Marion.

Tom made a curious sound, an attempt at a laugh.

'I wouldn't have thought I was quite in that financial league,' he said.

Marion considered the suggestion.

'You live in a large house,' she pointed out. 'I suppose that qualifies you in some people's eyes.'

'The police thought it might,' said Tom. 'If so, we'll soon hear something. Otherwise, they wondered if she'd gone off with a lover.'

'Not without a suitcase and her handbag,' said Marion.

She gave Tom a little shake. 'Of course she hasn't done that. What a stupid theory.'

'The whole thing's like a nightmare,' said Tom.

'Yes, it is, but like a nightmare, it will pass,' Marion assured him. 'Tom, you're soaked through and exhausted. Have you had anything to eat since you got home?'

'I couldn't swallow a mouthful,' Tom said.

'You must have something,' Marion told him. 'Let's go into the kitchen – Peter's asleep, we must try not to wake him. What about a sandwich and a good stiff whisky?'

The whisky part sounded all right to Tom. He shed his wet raincoat, letting it fall on a chair in the hall; he still had on his muddy boots. Marion bit back the reproof that rose to her lips as she saw the trail of footmarks he had left on the pale carpet in the passage. What did a little dirt matter now? As they passed the Christmas tree a shiver seemed to pass across its branches and a scatter of needles dropped almost silently on to the floor.

In the kitchen, she made him a toasted bacon sandwich which he ate absent-mindedly whilst drinking the whisky. He had just finished when the front door bell rang.

Tom sprang up at the sound, sending the chair he had been sitting on flying. He barged into the door, banging his leg, as he hurried out of the room. What a clumsy bear he was, Marion reflected as she followed, pausing to retrieve the chair. She closed the drawing-room door upon the sleeping Peter as two men entered the house. One was the uniformed inspector who had been in charge of the search for Laura; the other, younger man was in plain clothes. Both looked grave.

Marion heard the younger man telling Tom that a woman's body had been found on the railway line near Hickling Halt, which was over twenty miles away. The description given of Laura and of the clothes she was presumed to be wearing tallied with details of the dead woman. The plain-clothes officer showed Tom something in a polythene bag. It was a Victorian brooch, made of pearls set in a starburst. Tom had given it to Laura years ago and she almost always wore it. At the sight of it,

Tom gave a howl of pure agony that was almost primeval. Marion never forgot that sound.

11

Policemen came and went in the next minutes, while Marion and Detective Superintendent Grainger, the plainclothes officer who had produced Laura's brooch, waited for Tom to regain his self-control. He went alone into his study and closed the door. Grainger had been unable to tell him how Laura had travelled to the place where she was found.

'Do you really not know how she got there?' Marion asked him. She had taken the two officers into the kitchen, reluctant to admit this horror into the small sitting-room which was Laura's own, where she kept her desk and sewing.

'Not yet,' said Grainger.

Inspector Ford from Merston was remaining until the dead woman's identity had been confirmed, since her disappearance was on his patch, but it seemed that this would be a mere formality; the investigation into what had happened would be Grainger's responsibility as she had been found within his area.

'I just don't understand it,' Marion said. 'Hickling Halt is so far away. She couldn't have walked.'

'No,' said Grainger. He looked at Marion. 'She was badly mutilated by a train which ran over her,' he told her. 'Someone's got to identify her formally.'

'Tom?'

'Well, yes.' Grainger glanced at the closed study door.

'He'll do it,' Marion decided. 'He'll get himself together in a minute.' If she took this duty from him, he would later feel that he had failed Laura in some way.

'They'll make her look as tidy as they can,' said

Grainger. 'But her head was severed. He'll find that out in time.'

'Oh, my God!' The train wheels, of course.

'He found no note, did he? Mr Burdock?' Grainger was asking.

'No.'

'It's usual, with a suicide,' said Grainger.

Suicide! The idea was appalling.

'But why should she kill herself?' Marion asked. 'She was happy. They were both happy.'

'You're certain?'

'Yes, as far as one can be about anyone else. Who can really know the truth?' she answered.

'You're a close friend of them both?' Grainger pursued.

'I suppose so. Yes. I saw a lot of them,' Marion said.

'That's why you're here now?'

'Yes. Tom asked me to be here while he went out with the search parties, in case Laura turned up or telephoned,' she said.

Grainger nodded.

'I see,' he said.

'I'd go with him to the mortuary, only I can't leave Peter. That's my nephew. He's asleep in the drawing-room,' she said. 'He's only ten.'

'We could leave it till the morning,' Grainger said. 'But the sooner we get on with things, the better.'

'I doubt if Tom will sleep, whatever happens,' Marion observed. 'I'll go and see him now,' she added.

She left the room, returning in a few minutes to tell Grainger that Tom was going upstairs for a wash and would be with them shortly.

'Anything going on between them, do you think?' Grainger asked Ford.

'Between her and Mr Burdock?' Ford looked surprised. 'I wouldn't know.'

'Hm.' She was considerably older than the bereaved husband, but that didn't mean a thing. Grainger's experience during his police service had taught him to suspect everyone and everything. He could, however, still be shocked, and the sight on the railway line had sickened him. The driver had braked when he saw an obstruction on the line ahead, but the train was travelling too fast to stop before passing over it. The police surgeon had said that the woman must have been already dead, for there was very little blood. Death could have been due to a fall from the bridge above the line. The circumstances were obscure, and might prove to be suspicious. Before she was moved, the Home Office pathologist had come out to the scene to view the body in position. Trains had to be stopped, bus diversions arranged for passengers; and the area was cordoned off while the photographers and the scientists were working. A video of the area might help them later, after normal communications were restored, which must be done as soon as possible.

Meanwhile, if there had been foul play, the husband's part in what had happened must be ascertained. However, it was too soon, yet, to call it murder.

Tom came downstairs and said he was ready to go with them to the mortuary. He had changed his crumpled shirt and had on a clean white one, and a black tie. His hair was slicked down tidily and he looked, to the officers, composed. Marion diagnosed his condition as one of stunned disbelief; he was moving like an automaton.

'I'll be here when you get back,' she told him. She couldn't leave him to return to an empty house.

She looked in on Peter after they had gone. He was sound asleep, his mouth a little open, his breathing almost silent. She tucked the blanket round him; there was no point in waking him and taking him upstairs to one of the bedrooms. She and Tom would not be going to bed that night. The police would have to try to piece together what had happened and were sure to have a lot of questions. They had been extremely kind when George had died, but then there was no mystery.

In a crisis, people needed food; you could do without sleep, but only if you ate. She made sandwiches, thawing out a sliced loaf from the freezer by spreading it around the Aga top, and put on the coffee percolator.

The little party returned after just over two hours. Tom was white-faced; one look at him confirmed what Marion had already accepted as the truth. Inspector Ford was not with them; he had been replaced by another man whom Grainger introduced as Detective Inspector Masters from his own division. The two police officers gratefully accepted sandwiches and coffee, and Tom managed to drink the small mugful which Marion gave him, having laced his with whisky. Then Grainger led him off to his study to be questioned. Masters went with them, but after a time he returned to the kitchen, where Marion had been clearing up. He asked how she had spent the afternoon and when she had last seen Laura.

She had already told Inspector Ford all this. Perhaps demarcation between areas forbade him from telling his colleague what he knew. Trying not to sound tetchy, Marion repeated what she had said.

'How long have you known Mr Burdock?' Masters asked.

'Since they moved here. That was about four years ago,' said Marion. 'I met them briefly then.' She explained about the cottage and George's retirement, followed so soon by his death.

'You were all friendly – the three of you?'

'Yes. And Laura was very kind to my nephew, who spends a lot of time with me. She let him use the pool. She was very fond of him, and he of her.' Marion paused, her eyes filling and a lump blocking her throat, a very rare experience for her. She blinked hard; now was not the time to weep for Laura. 'She was a good, kind woman, and this is a terrible business,' said Marion, convincing Masters in that instant that she was in no way emotionally involved with the husband. He went on questioning her, however, for he had to answer to his chief, and at last Marion caught the drift.

'My God,' she exclaimed. 'Is that really what you think? That I was having an affair with poor Tom? Good heavens, inspector, I'm at least ten years older than he is and I've never gone in for cradle-snatching. Besides, Tom adored

Laura; she meant everything to him. You've seen how he's been pole-axed. All this was for her – the house – the business. He slaved his guts out for her – to give her total security. Theirs was as nearly a perfect marriage as I've ever seen.'

Masters told her he believed her. He rejoined the superintendent in the study, where Tom had supplied the time of his departure from the office and the names of his staff who could confirm it.

The precise time of Laura's death had not been established. It was not known how long she had lain on the railway line; there was an hourly service at that time of night, so she could not have been there longer than an hour, or the previous train would have been the one to be involved. She might have been there only a few minutes, but the pathologist thought from her body temperature and making due allowance for the coldness of the night that she had been dead for at least half an hour before discovery. More would be known after the post-mortem, when the contents of the stomach and the degree of digestion would give further indications as to what had happened. The dead woman's clothes had gone to the lab for testing. There were stains on her coat and a button was missing. If she had been attacked, she might have clutched at her assailant and traces of what he wore could have adhered to her short string-backed leather gloves. There was no obvious sign of sexual interference; the post-mortem examination would reveal if there had been recent intercourse.

She wore no watch. Grainger had remarked on this to Tom, who said she always did. She had a little gold one on a gold bracelet which he had given her. As far as he knew, it was working properly – not at the repairer's – and even if it were, she had an old one she could use. He checked in her bedroom; the old one was in her jewel case but there was no sign of the other. She might have left it by a basin or the sink and forgotten to put it on again, he supposed. Grainger ordered a search for it; it might be important.

'I just don't see how she could have got there,' Tom kept repeating. 'Her car's in the garage. She must have been kidnapped, as Inspector Ford thought.' Poor Laura, how terrified she must have been! Perhaps she had fought and struggled, and that had caused her captor to kill her.

'You noticed no signs of a forcible entry?' Grainger asked.

'No.'

'Well, we'll be examining the house,' said Grainger.

It was unlikely that Laura, if a kidnap victim, would have gone off in her wellington boots. Instinct told him that the man was what he seemed to be, a shocked grief-stricken husband who had loved his wife, but the intellect had to reach the same conclusion. Many a guilty man had, in the past, put on a most convincing act, and there was only Tom's word that the dog had been wandering about outside when he came home.

At the moment, the area round where the body had been found was being searched minutely for any evidence it might yield and for the watch. Searchlights were deployed upon the scene, and the work would go on in daylight, when something missed earlier might be discovered. The bridge above the line was being examined. If Laura Burdock had jumped over or been pushed, there might be traces on the stonework – fibres from her clothing, scrape marks from her boots. And if she had been carried there by someone who had dumped her, possibly unconscious, on the track, crushed grass or even footmarks, since it had been drizzling at the time, might be found.

The case had only just begun. Before it ended, much would be laid bare. House-to-house inquiries in Didbury would begin first thing in the morning. Someone would know how Laura Burdock had spent her day; someone must have seen her, somewhere.

Tom and Marion killed a quantity of whisky between them as the long night wore on. Grainger and Masters left at last, but not for long, they warned.

The house was warm. Marion had earlier adjusted the central-heating clock to stop it from switching off, and the electric fire was on in Tom's study.

'Do you think she killed herself?' Tom asked.

'No,' said Marion firmly.

But any other answer was so melodramatic that it was impossible to contemplate.

'I don't know how I'll live without her,' Tom said. 'She saved me from the wilderness. Do you understand?'

Marion reckoned that she did.

Poor Tom's a'cold, she thought, and felt her heart would break for him. And what about Peter? How was she going to tell him that Laura, whom he loved, was dead?

Whoever was responsible for this dreadful thing would have a lot to answer for: there must have been some outside agent, some unknown villain out there in the night, who knew the truth.

At last Tom's eyes closed and he dropped into an uneasy slumber. Marion curled up in the big leather armchair and leaned her head back, trying to relax her tense muscles; eventually, she, too, dozed.

Mick had waited until after dark to get rid of the body.

He'd had his wish – frightened her, seen a look of pure terror on Laura Burdock's face. It had happened just like that first time, and had been as spontaneous, only then he had left the girl in the ditch and driven away.

That afternoon, when he had left the pub at closing time, he had gone to Didbury. Driving down the lane from Poppleton towards the village, he had seen the woman and her dog climb a stile into the road ahead of him. Because of the dog he recognized her, delivered up to him like this as if to order. She paused on the grass verge as he approached, waiting for him to pass before she and the dog crossed over. Her eyes stared at him beneath the pulled-down brim of the rain hat she wore as he drove straight at her. He wasn't sure if she screamed, but she put up her arm in a vain attempt to protect herself and her mouth opened wide in a big O of fear.

Just as last time, there was a considerable bumping effect on impact. Last time, Mick had stopped at once and dumped his victim in the concealing ditch nearby. Now he drove on, shouting aloud in delight. Then he braked sharply. She knew his van and would have recognized him. What if she wasn't dead? He'd best make sure. He slammed the gear lever into reverse and roared back up the road to where the dog was sniffing at the inert bundle which lay half on the tarmac, half on the grass verge. Mick got out and stood over her. She gave a faint moan, but her eyes were closed. He glanced round wildly. At any moment someone might come along and he would have to say that he had just stopped, too. It wouldn't do if the bloody woman talked. If he said she'd stepped out in front of the van giving him no time to stop, she would deny it.

There was no wide ditch here in which to dump her. Mick opened the van and bundled her inside, putting a sack over her to hide her before lashing the doors together upon the ladder which protruded. Then he leaped in and roared away. Glancing in the rear view mirror, he could see the dog standing in the middle of the road, mournfully gazing after them. There was no other soul in sight.

Mick drove on, temporarily sobered up, his heart hammering. What now?

There were no sounds from the woman. He must get rid of her, put her in a lake or river. If she wasn't already dead, that would silence her for good and serve her right. She'd do no more harm. Some ten miles on, he stopped and switched on the radio he had stolen earlier. A few mewing sounds came from behind him, so he turned the volume up. He looked over his shoulder at the mound behind him; it was unmoving. Mick felt no further need to feed on her fear; his immediate lust had been appeased and now all he wanted to do was to make himself safe from the consequences.

He moved on, turning westwards when he reached the motorway and driving along the slow lane at a steady fifty miles an hour, about the best the van could do except downhill. He might tip her over the embankment along here and let someone else get the blame for a hit-and-run. But there was traffic about; he dared not do it in daylight, when he might be seen.

At the next slip road Mick turned off, seeking minor roads and isolated areas. He seldom went anywhere on foot and knew no footpaths or field walks. He tried to think of quiet roads that passed near rivers. A quarry would do, or a gravel pit, if he could find one. It was while he was trying to remember where there was one that he passed over a railway bridge.

There was his answer! He stopped and got out of the van. The light was fading now, but looking over the bridge, Mick could see the twin metal tracks stretching into the distance. Put her over there and the next train would finish her off, hiding all signs of earlier injuries.

While he stood there a train went by beneath him at some speed.

Mick went back to the van and drove on. He did not want anyone to remember seeing his van in the area if questions were asked later; people were so quick to blame you for things that weren't your fault. Turning north, he passed through the plantation where he had found the Christmas tree and pulled in to a little-used lay-by. Here he was, to some extent, concealed. He did not like the tall dark trees that lowered oppressively over him, and he did not like having to stay still. He turned the radio up and, while he waited, ate the sandwiches that Beverley had made him for his lunch and drank the tea from his flask.

Slowly the light ebbed from the winter sky and then Mick realized he must wait even longer. People would be going home from work now; there would be traffic in the quiet roads around the bridge and slow commuter trains would stop at Hickling Halt.

He could leave her here, in the forest.

No, because she might not yet be dead and someone else might find her. The bridge was better.

Waiting, tuned in to Radio One and high on alcohol followed by euphoria and tea, Mick passed the time.

His petrol gauge showed empty again as he drove into Merston that night. Mick had put only the two gallons from his can into the van that day. He stopped to put in five pounds' worth at a different filling station from the one he had been to earlier. This old van seemed to drink the stuff.

The children were both in bed and Beverley was ironing when he reached home. Her face was white and set and she did not look up as he entered.

'Well, don't I get a kiss?' Mick asked. His mood was ebullient; he had taken care of everything and his troubles were over.

Beverley's timid heart was racing. He didn't know that she had discovered the theft of her savings. She would go on pretending that she hadn't while somehow she collected more money. When she had enough, she'd decide whether to leave. Meanwhile, she did her best to steer away from trouble. She did not know how to read Mick's current mood.

'I brought you a present,' he told her grandly. 'Seeing as you didn't get a lot at Christmas.' She'd had nothing from him then, in fact.

Mick had noticed the watch when he heaved Laura out of the van. Though still alive, she was unconscious; her arm had dropped limply away from her body and he had seen the gold bracelet glinting between her sleeve and the short gloves she wore. It seemed a pity to let that go. He'd planned to give it to Rene, but, governed as usual by impulse, changed his mind. It was Rene's bad luck for being out; he'd called there on the way home and found the place empty.

Beverley was astounded. The watch was beautiful, so small and neat.

'Oh Mick,' she said. 'How lovely. Thank you,' and she

would not listen to the silent voice which told her it had been bought with her own money.

That evening he was almost the old Mick. Beverley forgot to be afraid; she even began to think there might be a brighter future for them after all. They had sex that night. Beverley no longer called it making love, for it wasn't; for her it had become a test of endurance. But for once he wasn't really rough and it hardly hurt at all.

It was only later that she wondered where he had got the watch. Surely he wouldn't have gone and bought it specially for her? He hadn't taken her money just for that.

Cleaning windows, he'd see things lying about. It was probably quite easy to take something if the window was open, and you could reach inside without entering the room. People left their watches on window ledges or shelves when they took them off for washing.

He must have thought of her, though, even if he'd stolen it.

12

Marion woke at a sudden sound and took some seconds to remember where she was, and why. It was very warm in Tom's study, the electric fire still glowing; across the room, in another chair, Tom sprawled, his head turned to one side, his shoulders hunched.

Peter was standing in the doorway taking in the scene. Marion got up, wincing at the stiffness in her legs. She put a finger to her lips, indicating Tom, and hurried over to the boy, leading him out of the study.

'Have you just woken up?' she asked.

'Mm. Fancy being up all night,' said Peter. Then he added, 'She isn't back, is she?'

'No.'

'It's getting light,' said Peter – optimistically, for it was only six o'clock. 'We can go and look for her now.'

Marion had taken him back into the drawing-room, where the blanket that had covered him was neatly folded on the sofa. Such tidiness pierced her control and she felt tears prickle. She bent to the fire, put on some logs and blew at the embers with the bellows from the hearth. Soon a flame began to flicker among the ashes. She sat back on her heels and turned to face him.

'Come here, Peter,' she said, and stretched a hand towards him.

Peter moved forward and stood close to her. Marion circled his thin body with her arm. There was no way to spare him and bad news was best imparted fast and straight.

'She's been found, Peter,' she said. 'She had an accident and I'm afraid she's dead.'

She felt him grow rigid against her arm and he half turned away. Marion was ready to release him: some people managed sorrow best alone; but she felt him tremble and instinct took over as she drew him to her. Peter sank against her, not crying, his face pressed into her sweater. She held him close. It was the first time she had embraced anyone for a very long time.

'She couldn't have known anything about it,' Marion told him in the kindest of lies. 'She can't have suffered.' She was getting cramp in her leg but would not move. 'It's awful,' she added, hugging him.

It was some time before Peter asked her what had happened. Marion decided to tell him as much of the truth as she could without adding horror to shock, for he would hear later, from village gossip, when the news got out, and if he knew she had lied to him, he would suffer in another way. She explained that Laura had been found on the railway line at Hickling Halt but that no one yet knew how she had got there. The police needed to trace her movements during the previous day as then they might be able to find out if someone had driven her there against her will.

'Not that it seems very likely,' Marion said. 'Didbury isn't the sort of place where things like that happen.' Yet such incidents did occur in the most improbable spots, and had she not warned Peter never to talk to strangers or go off with anyone he didn't know, however plausible the reason given for him to do so might be, even in Didbury?

'Perhaps someone told her Tom was ill and he'd take her to see him,' said Peter. 'To trick her.'

He had evidently taken in her lesson.

'Perhaps they did.' It was as likely as anything else.

A few tears slid quietly down Peter's face, and he sniffed. Marion, reluctant to let him go, gave him another hug. Her leg was agony and she did not want to encourage morbid speculation, so she released him.

'Let's get some breakfast,' she said. 'We must make Tom eat something, so we'll have to, as well, whether we want to or not.' She sat squarely, pulling her toes up towards her shin. 'I've got cramp,' she said. 'This is a cure.'

'Is it?' Peter was interested.

'Mm. There, it's beginning to go,' said Marion. 'Give your poor old aunt a hand up, Peter, there's a dear.' She levered herself to her feet, holding his arm as he bent solicitously towards her.

The two went out to the kitchen.

'Now, you know where Laura keeps things, don't you?' Marion said. 'Do you think she's got some Weetabix?' This was Peter's current favourite cereal.

She hadn't, but there were bran flakes and sugarless muesli from a health food shop. Laura had been trying to cut down on fats and sugar and add fibre to their diet.

They had just finished setting out china and cutlery, and Peter had found the marmalade, when the front-door bell rang.

'That will be the police,' Marion told Peter. 'They said they'd be back early.'

Peter nodded.

'I'll go and let them in,' said Marion. 'You watch the toast.'

Detective Inspector Masters stood on the doorstep with

two other men, whom he introduced as Detective Sergeant Norris and Detective Constable Woods. The sergeant gave a quick glance at the Christmas tree as he entered. What an incongruous sight it must seem in a house visited by sudden and violent death, Marion thought, resolving to dismantle and remove it as soon as she could.

Tom, woken by the door bell and the sound of voices, appeared from the study. He looked grey and haggard. Masters greeted him in a sympathetic manner and introduced his colleagues. The inspector looked tired; Marion wondered if he had been to bed. The police might have been working all night at Hickling Halt, she supposed; they were more likely to find clues as to what had happened there than anywhere else.

'Breakfast's ready, Tom,' Marion said. 'We'll be in the kitchen.' She led Peter off so that the policemen could talk to Tom on his own. What would they want to know? What secrets would they learn in this silent house?

Soon Tom, tousled and unshaven, came into the room.

'They want to go through all Laura's things,' he said. 'Her desk and upstairs – all that. I've had to agree, but – ' he shrugged. 'I don't know what they expect to learn that way.'

'They've got to start somewhere, I suppose,' said Marion. How would they ever discover what had really happened? 'Have some coffee.'

To set an example, she put muesli, which she loathed, into a bowl for herself, and gave Peter some. Manfully, he spooned it down, copying her, both chewing hard, their throats reluctant to accept the gritty mixture.

'I thought I'd go to the office,' Tom said, somewhat sheepishly. 'I don't see what I can do here and I might as well keep out of the way while the police help themselves to the house. I won't go for long, but there were things arranged for today and I must cancel what I can.'

'Oh!' Marion was startled, but she understood his need to cling to routine; besides, he had clients depending on him. She hoped he wasn't so tired that he would wrap his BMW round a lamppost on the way. 'Good idea,' she said.

Work was an anodyne and could help him through the next hours. 'Will they let you?'

'Oh yes.' They'd be checking up on his movements the previous afternoon, too: Tom and Marion both knew that. 'They'll know where to find me, if they want me,' he said.

'The Christmas tree, Tom,' said Marion. 'Shall we take it down?'

'Oh, would you?' Laura had always left it until Twelfth Night. Tom knew he could not bear to face the task himself.

'Of course we will,' said Marion.

'You won't be able to get it out of the house,' said Tom.

'Well, if we can't, you can help us when you come home,' she said.

At this moment Detective Inspector Masters came into the room. He glanced at Peter, who was trying without much success to get through a slice of toast and honey, having abandoned the muesli. Masters spoke to Tom.

'Could I have a word, please, Mr Burdock?' he requested.

'Yes, of course.'

Tom rose and left the room with the inspector. He soon returned, alone.

'It was about what she was wearing,' he said. 'They're going round the village asking if anyone saw her, and they're doing the same thing over at Hickling.'

'But you've already told them,' said Marion. 'And anyway, they must know.' For surely Laura had been dressed when she was found?

'I suppose it was just to confirm it,' Tom said. 'That blue skirt and sweater – that's what she had on when I – when I – ' He changed what he had been going to say and went on. 'Her raincoat and boots.'

'And her hat,' said Peter. 'Don't forget her hat – that waterproof one. It was raining a bit – she'd have had that on if she was in her raincoat.'

'Yes,' said Tom. 'Good boy. You're right. I forgot the hat.' It was an expensive one, plaid-lined, and matched the coat. 'Inspector Masters had better enrol you in his team, Peter. You're very observant.'

A little colour came into Peter's face at these words. He put the last piece of toast in his mouth and ate it up without noticing what he was doing.

'I'll go and tell the inspector,' Tom said. 'Then I'm going to have a bath and shave.' He moved to the door, then turned and added, 'Marion, I couldn't have coped without – '

'That's all right.' Marion cut him short. 'Glad we were around,' she said gruffly. 'And count on us to do what we can to help.'

Peter nodded vigorously at these words. He looked more himself now. Poor child, he had only just adjusted to his mother's defection and now he had this to face, the loss of a substitute figure immensely important to him. Whatever the cause of Laura's untimely death, its consequences would affect not only Tom. And Marion would miss calm Laura more than she had yet had time to estimate.

A thought surfaced in her mind. She should telephone David and tell him what had happened before he heard it on the radio or read about it in the paper. Unless the mystery was cleared up quickly it was sure to attract attention. Today was Friday: David was due back in Suffolk that night for the weekend to collect Caroline and the baby. Because of a cold which had developed over the New Year, Caroline had remained at her parents' home while he returned alone to London. He might decide to take Peter away from the scene of the tragedy.

Marion did not know what would be wisest for the boy. Like everyone else, he would have to work through his grief. She would ring his father later, when she could do so without Peter hearing her conversation. Perhaps by then the police would have concluded their investigation, she thought, with optimism born of ignorance.

Masters returned to the kitchen while she was washing up with Peter drying and putting things away.

'Well, young man, I hear you've noticed some important details about Mrs Burdock's clothing,' said Masters. 'I came to thank you. It could be important.' He smiled at the boy. Some lads decided at no older an age to become

117

coppers, and all should be encouraged to see the police as friends. 'Describe this hat, please.'

Peter did so. It was shaped rather like a fisherman's hat and he mentioned the lining.

'We must look for her watch,' said Masters. 'Maybe she put it down somewhere while she was washing. Have you seen it?'

Neither of them had.

She could have been mugged and dumped just for the watch, but, out in the country that wasn't likely. Until the pathologist had given the cause of death and described the dead woman's injuries, the police did not know what they were looking for except a straw in the wind. Suicide, at the moment, seemed the most likely solution. She had suffered some sort of breakdown, made the journey to Hickling by a means not yet known, and jumped from the bridge whilst in a confused condition. This was the conclusion Grainger and Masters had reached when they discussed the case at headquarters but it would have to be proved.

Masters was no longer so sure that things were as simple as that.

During the night the drizzle had stopped and the weather had turned much colder. It was freezing when the police went round Didbury early that morning making inquiries about Laura's movements, just as they had the previous evening when she was first reported missing. By now some villagers had heard a report on the local radio station which said she she had been found dead on the railway line near Hickling Halt.

A few people were found who had been missed on the earlier survey, and one of them, a retired man, said he had seen her VW Golf leaving the village at about ten o'clock, when he was out walking his dog. He supposed she was going to Merston, shopping. You couldn't manage in Didbury without a car, not really, he said; there was a bus only on Wednesdays, market day in Merston.

This was the first lead as to Laura's movements the day

118

before. Now someone else must be found who had also seen her.

Meanwhile, Tom had left for the office, planning to be back in three or four hours' time.

'I'll expect you for lunch,' said Marion. 'I'll sort something out for us all here, if that suits you.' There was bound to be plenty of food in the freezer. 'I'll have to go home for a bit, but I'll come back.'

Tom made no protest. He might not return at all if she wasn't here, he thought; there was no future now and it would be easy to run out of road. But first he wanted to know the truth about what had happened.

Masters and Detective Constable Woods were in the small sitting-room going through Laura's papers, and Norris was upstairs in the bedroom looking through her cupboards and drawers. While they were occupied like this, Marion and Peter set to work on the tree. Peter was standing on the stepladder trying to reach the star at the top when Mrs Rigby, Laura's cleaning lady, arrived. She had lain awake most of the night wondering where her employer could be, and had heard the radio news before a constable called to see if she could add to what she had said the previous night. Mrs Burdock often went out in the car, but Mrs Rigby had not known of plans for Thursday.

'Still, I wouldn't, would I?' she had said. 'Not necessarily. If I was there and she went out, she'd say she was off to Merston, or was taking the dog for a good walk away from the village. She did that sometimes.' Mrs Rigby had gone on to say that she gave Mrs Burdock three mornings a week, Monday, Wednesday and Friday, and went to Mrs Wilson the other two days. Mrs Burdock usually did a big shop each month and lesser ones weekly but she did not stick to a definite pattern if something cropped up that she wanted to do, like go off on one of those art trips to a museum.

Mrs Rigby had been asked to come up to Clyde House as usual. She had every intention of doing so, for how Mr Burdock was going to manage she didn't know, and she must help the poor man now, for his wife's sake.

She was somewhat nonplussed to see Marion apparently in command.

'Ah, Mrs Rigby, good morning.' Marion came down the ladder and led the neat, grey-haired woman away so that they could accord the tragedy proper recognition. Marion said that she was anxious to distract Peter, whom Mrs Rigby knew had been attached to Laura.

'Thought the world of that boy, she did,' said Mrs Rigby.

'We felt the tree should go,' said Marion.

'Yes,' said Mrs Rigby. 'Makes a proper old mess, doesn't it, but she would keep it till the right day. Still, it isn't in keeping now, is it?'

She went to fetch the boxes in which the baubles were kept, and then Masters asked her to step into the study.

Sad but gratified, Mrs Rigby obeyed.

While Marion and Peter completed the undressing of the tree, DC Woods was dusting for fingerprints all round the hall. He told Peter his would be taken later, to be eliminated from those found.

'Why? Do you think someone broke in and took her away?' Peter asked.

'We're not sure, son,' said Woods.

She might have come in from her walk and surprised an intruder, Marion thought. If she had faced him, he might have struck out at her and killed her, then dumped her to mislead the police. It was a much more bearable theory than suicide and would mean that, as Marion had assured Peter, she had truly not know what had happened.

Eventually Peter, Marion and Mrs Rigby had their prints taken. Another set was found that was probably Tom's; overlaid among these were more which were, Woods was sure, those of Masters and the chief. He sighed. They hadn't touched much but it did confuse matters.

A uniformed officer had come to the house with a message for Masters about his investigations in the village, which had produced no more news of sightings. Before he left, Masters asked him to take Peter out to the car and show him how the radio worked.

This was a good diversion. Peter returned looking

flushed and excited, and had persuaded the officer to help them take the tree out of the house and into the garden where they deposited it near the bonfire spot.

Mrs Rigby was allowed to sweep up the needles and to make Tom's bed and clean the bath, but then was asked not to do any more cleaning that day.

She would come on Monday, she promised Marion, who understood that the police were still hopeful of finding something to help them here in the house.

'And before, if he wants me. He has only to say the word,' Mrs Rigby declared.

Masters sent her home in the police car.

13

After Mrs Rigby had gone, Marion and Peter went back to Lime Tree Cottage. The post had arrived, and the letters included one for Peter from his mother. Marion had one with an American stamp, too. Seeing Hugh's handwriting on the envelope gave her a shock. She put it aside to read later, and while Peter read his, went up to her bedroom to telephone the Careys. They had heard the news. Marion explained that Tom had gone briefly to the office and that she wanted to be at Clyde House when he returned.

'I'm surprised he could go at all,' said Janet.

'I think he can hardly bear to be in the house without Laura,' said Marion.

'That's probably it,' Janet agreed. 'Shall I have Peter? He's better out of all this. How's he taking it?'

'It's been a sad shock,' said Marion. 'But I hope he won't need to know the grim details.' Maybe Janet didn't, yet. 'Would you have him for lunch?

It was arranged that he would go over shortly on his bike, and that both boys should be back in their respective houses well before dark. Horror had struck the village and nerves were on edge.

Peter was quite willing to go to his friend's house. He would be able to boast about his initiation into the mysteries of the police car. He spoke cheerfully, but Marion was not deceived.

'Mummy all right?' she asked.

'Mm. She's going to Bermuda for a holiday,' he said.

'Lucky old her,' said Marion briskly.

She watched him ride off on his bike. She had told him that she would be at Clyde House until some time in the afternoon. If he returned to the cottage first, he should telephone and she would come straight home.

Marion locked the back door and put the key inside the empty tit box attached to a cherry tree so that Peter could let himself in. They would have to find a new hiding-place if the box were used in the spring, she thought, going back into the house by the unlatched front door.

Peter had pedalled out of sight.

Before she telephoned his father, Marion read the letter from Hugh. He was returning to England, and he asked her to meet him for lunch in London the following Tuesday. He would wait for her in a restaurant where they had often met before until half-past two. He hoped she would come.

When she returned to Clyde House, Detective Inspector Masters beckoned Marion into Laura's sitting-room where the contents of the dead woman's handbag were spread out on a small table. The police had found her cheque book, with a stub made out the previous day to Sainsbury's, and Marion saw, neatly aligned, two ballpoint pens, a clean, uncrumpled handkerchief and some tissues, three old car park tickets, her purse and notecase, a comb and lipstick, and a blue leather engagement diary with her initials on it. What an orderly collection, Marion thought; her own handbag would not stand up so well to inspection.

Masters showed her the diary where, among straightforward entries like *Dentist, 10 a.m.*, and people's names –

Marion's appeared more than once – were two dates under which the initials *L.M.* were written.

'What could that mean?' Masters asked her. 'Do you know anyone whose name fits those initials?'

Marion did not. The initials appeared on a date in December and were entered under today's date, January 4th, in the follow-on section at the end of the diary.

'She'd got a new diary – we found it in her desk – but she hadn't started to use it,' Masters said.

This flaw in her friend's efficiency reassured Marion. There was no entry for Thursday, 3rd.

Masters explained that as Laura had been to Sainsbury's, checks were being made with the store to see if they remembered her visit and if she had seemed in any way distressed. He was going back to headquarters to confer with the chief superintendent, who had received the preliminary post-mortem report.

'What did the pathologist find?' Marion asked.

There was no harm in telling her what little he knew himself.

'Death was due to the fall from the bridge,' Masters said. Grainger had told him over the telephone that there were terrible injuries, but a skull fracture had been the fatal one.

'You think she jumped over,' Marion said. 'You do think it's suicide, don't you?'

'It's a possibility,' Masters acknowledged.

'But how would she have got there? All that way, without her car?'

'She might have taken a taxi,' said Masters. 'Or got a lift. We're making inquiries.'

'Laura go hitch-hiking? Never,' said Marion. 'And if she wanted to kill herself, she'd take sleeping pills, not do it like this.'

But would she? Would she lie dead where Tom would find her?

'She wasn't herself, don't forget,' Masters reminded her. The word *menopause* flitted through his mind, to be dismissed; Laura Burdock had been too young for that, but she might have had a miscarriage, lost a child, had some other genuine cause for depression. He asked Marion if she knew of such a reason.

'No. There was nothing like that. She was disappointed not to have children but she wasn't obsessed about it, like some women are. She got on with her life,' said Marion.

'Those initials – could they refer to a doctor? Perhaps she thought she had a serious illness,' Masters suggested.

'Wrong initials,' said Marion promptly. 'She goes to Dr Bartholomew in Poppleton, like everyone else in Didbury.'

'She could have visited a specialist privately,' Masters said.

'If so, she'd have written out cheques to him – or her,' said Marion. 'Has she done that?'

While they talked, Detective Sergeant Norris was sitting at Laura's desk on her Chippendale chair with the tapestry seat which Laura had worked one winter, going through the neat piles of her records. She would have no secrets left.

'No, she hasn't,' Masters replied. 'We've been through all the old cheque books we found.'

'Well, I've no idea who they refer to,' said Marion. 'It might be a place. Long Marston, for instance,' she hazarded somewhat wildly. She and Peter had been reading about Charles II's adventures, a subject which seemed to have passed him by at school. 'It's all so dreadful and hard to take in that whatever you discover isn't going to help very much.' How was Tom going to feel if it were proved that Laura had deliberately taken her own life?

She would never do such a thing to him, even if she were deeply unhappy. Not if she were in her right mind.

Masters left. He would soon be back, he said, and probably with the chief, who would want to see Mr Burdock when he returned from his office.

Marion went out to the kitchen, glad that there was plenty to do. Should she provide lunch for the various policemen about the place, she wondered, or would they have sandwiches with them? There had been a guard on the gate when she came in; the young constable had radioed through to ask if she might be admitted. The press, it seemed, had decided to take an interest in the case and he was at the gate to keep them away. He successfully protected her from the lone reporter hoping for an exclusive interview.

Her brother, when they talked on the telephone, had decided to leave Peter's plans unchanged. He understood his son's distress at the shocking thing that had happened, but removing him from the village would not stop him thinking about it, and whilst Caroline's parents would certainly make him welcome, he was much more at home in Didbury. Marion had told him she had a lunch date in London on Tuesday and would drop Peter off in Putney on the way. She had replaced the receiver with a wry smile.

'Over to you, aunt,' she told herself. 'David doesn't want to cope with this one.'

It would have been easier for her to help Tom without the boy to consider, but she was glad to have the responsibility and it would prevent her from taking total charge of Tom, which would not be for his ultimate good. Other people would want to help him, and they must, people nearer his age, his men friends. But had Tom any friends? He and Laura had not seemed to need anyone else.

He returned at last.

'I couldn't do a great deal but I've postponed some appointments,' he said. 'The police have checked up that I really was in the office yesterday.' His tone was bitter.

'Oh Tom, I know it's awful that their minds work like that but consider these terrible things one reads in the papers,' she said. 'If it's murder, it's often done by the husband or wife.'

'But it isn't murder, is it?' asked Tom. 'On the other hand, if that isn't the answer, what is?'

She wasn't going to tell him.

The pathologist's investigation had confirmed his early opinion that Laura had died less than an hour before her body was found. The stomach contents had been sent for analysis; shreds of lettuce had been found, and other indications that she had eaten a light meal which included grapes and an apple some hours before death. The lab would confirm this and routinely test for drugs in case the coroner wanted to know if Laura Burdock had been under the influence of any particular substance.

She had sustained multiple injuries, some of which were compatible with her fall from the bridge, but it seemed that she had lain across the line in such a way that the train wheels had missed her torso, running over her neck and her right leg. There was a great deal of internal bleeding which must have been in progress for a considerable time before death, and the chest was badly crushed; the pathologist deduced these wounds were received in an earlier episode, possibly as the result of collision with a car. The ultimate cause of death was, however, the severe skull fracture which had occurred when the deceased struck the railway line. Small fragments of grit from the track were embedded in the depressed wound above the hairline. These pieces were quite unlike those used for road surfaces but the laboratory would confirm the match. Marks already noted on the dead woman's coat could have been made by a tyre, and there were stains that looked like oil. Paint particles had also been found. Analysing all these substances might give a lead to the truth.

'So we are after a murderer,' Grainger said. 'She might – just might – have survived if she'd been treated after the original incident.'

Masters was glad to learn that this was not, after all, a case of suicide, though it was still a terrible business.

'It could have happened in Didbury, then,' he said. 'Someone ran her down and panicked. Decided to dump her.'

'Looks like it,' said Grainger. 'And coolly waited to do it till things were quiet.'

Both officers were briefly silent as they reflected on the callous conduct of an individual who could run someone down and then summarily dispose of their victim in a manner which turned manslaughter into murder.

'No sign of her hat or the watch, I suppose?' Masters asked. 'Or the button?'

'Not a thing. We'll have to look for them in the village now,' said Grainger. 'And skid marks – broken glass – the usual. But the accident may not have happened there.'

Grainger had dispatched a constable to tell the train driver that the woman was already dead before the train struck her. He had been deeply distressed at the incident. Grainger knew that drivers involved in fatal rail accidents sometimes never recovered, even when they were quite without blame.

'We must look for a vehicle seen in the area between that train and the one before,' said Grainger. 'Anything suspicious during that hour. And better check round the cars in Didbury – look for bumps and scratches.'

'We've got a few things to look for now, at least,' said Masters.

'And a villain,' said Grainger. 'If he'd left her wherever it happened she might have stood a chance. Someone would have come along and found her.'

'Maybe she knew whoever it was,' Masters said. 'Maybe she recognized the car.'

Tom sat at the dining-room table where various objects were now arranged on its gleaming surface. He had inspected Laura's cheque book, in which he had duly noted the stub relating to Sainsbury's, and he had been shown her pocket diary with the mysterious initials. There were also some letters from estate agents which made it clear that Laura had been actively house-hunting for more than a year.

'You didn't know about this?' Grainger asked when Tom, questioned about plans for removal, stared at him blankly.

'No,' said Tom. 'We had no plans to move. We meant to live here – well – indefinitely.'

Grainger and Masters exchanged glances.

'And you've no idea who or what the letters L and M stand for?'

'None at all,' said Tom.

'Mr Burdock, forgive me, but I must ask you this,' said Grainger. 'Could your wife have been having an affair? Perhaps planning to leave you and set up house with another man – this L.M.?'

'No. Oh no!' Tom spoke firmly but his tone seemed to Masters, listening, to be as much a plea as a denial.

'Mr Burdock, sometimes the husband is the last to find out this sort of thing,' Grainger said.

'You didn't know Laura. She wasn't like that,' Tom declared.

'How well did you know her yourself?' Grainger asked.

Tom stared at him.

'I knew her very well,' he said. But he had forgotten about the hat she wore with her raincoat; he had not known she had been driving around England looking at houses that were for sale. Could she have had a lover without his knowledge?

If that were so, their life together had been a sham.

'She could have been planning to leave you for somebody else,' Grainger said cruelly, not adding, for somebody even richer. The houses she had looked at were bigger and had more land than Clyde House. Perhaps she was greedy: throughout the ages women had used men for material gain.

'No,' Tom insisted.

'Well, Mr Burdock, we'll be following this up with the estate agents,' Grainger said. 'They may be able to throw some light on whoever else was involved.'

'Yes. I see that you'll have to do that,' Tom said wearily.

He had been relieved to learn that Laura's death was not suicide – if you could call it relief, when any alternative was equally unthinkable. Now here was another shock.

'She might have met her lover yesterday. There could have been some sort of tiff ending in an accident,' Grainger theorized. Suppose the lover wanted out, he thought, and

Laura became hysterical, threw herself in front of his car, for example? It was a tenable notion.

'First you thought I'd killed her – then you thought she'd committed suicide – now you say she was having an affair that somehow caused her death,' Tom burst out. 'Make up your damned minds, for God's sake.' He stood up, pushing his chair back so roughly that he knocked it over.

Masters stepped forward and righted it. He didn't blame Burdock for losing his temper, but the chief had to press him, though the poor guy must be almost out on his legs.

Masters opened the door for Tom.

'Mrs Quilter's in the utility room,' he volunteered, having seen Marion in there ironing Tom's shirts. Burdock was the sort of clumsy, bear-like man who aroused the maternal in women, thought Masters. Perhaps that had been a fault in the marriage and had led the wife to look for a different kind of relationship.

Down at the farm, Peter and Nicholas discussed the topic which was, at the moment, foremost in the minds of their elders. Nicholas did not know Laura well. He was shocked by her sudden death, but people did die: they got run over or shot by bank robbers. He felt sure Laura had been held up at gun point for ransom. Then the kidnappers had panicked. This solution made sense, for Tom was extremely rich.

His sisters, Fiona and Sally, had been out on their ponies that morning and had heard village talk; they knew that a train had run over Laura and caused dreadful injuries. Hearing this, Peter felt sick, and clung to Marion's assurance that she had known nothing about what had happened. If Nick was right, she might have been drugged.

'Let's go out on our bikes,' he suggested after lunch, during which Janet Carey had forbidden all mention of the tragedy.

Nicholas was agreeable. His mother gave them each a Penguin biscuit to assuage any hunger pangs they might experience and told them not to go further than the boundaries of the village, to watch the time and return well before dark.

They set off eagerly, riding down the farm track and so through to the copse. As they passed above the ridge, Peter was tempted to show Nicholas the car, but he resisted the urge. There was a great pain in his chest, like the one he had had when his mother went away. Then he had wanted to go off on his own, and he thought now that it would be quite nice to get away from Nick and sit quietly in the old car by himself.

They emerged into the lane and paused to decide which way to go. You could get up a good speed on the Poppleton road, which was very straight and where there was seldom much traffic. In summer, Nick's father's tractors chuntered up and down there with hay and silage.

Nick leading, they went that way, and soon saw ahead two uniformed policemen slowly walking along by the verge, both stopping to examine the tarmac surface and the grass by the roadside.

'Let's go and see what they're doing,' said Nicholas. 'They must be hunting for clues.'

Not here, Peter thought: it happened at Hickling.

He followed Nicholas, who was riding on fast. The nearest constable, not sorry to straighten his aching back, looked up as the boys approached. To Peter's disappointment, he was not the man who had entertained him in the patrol car earlier that day.

'What are you looking for?' asked Nicholas.

They were not seeking a murder weapon, so an inch-by-inch search had not been ordered, and the missing hat was large enough to be fairly easily seen. The search had already attracted attention from other passers-by and the constable saw no reason to dodge the question.

'A hat and a button,' he said, and anything else of interest. He decided not to mention the watch. It was likely that the three items would be found, if at all, near each other.

'But didn't – wasn't she – I thought the accident happened near Hickling,' said Peter.

'The poor lady was found there,' said the constable. 'But she left home on foot with her dog, didn't she? We want to know which way she went.'

There were no skid marks on the road, no broken glass, nothing to show that in fact they were quite near the spot where Laura had been knocked down.

'Wasn't she wearing her hat, then?' asked Peter. 'When she – I mean – '

'No, lad. It fell off,' said the constable bluntly. 'And a button had come off her coat. One of those round leather ones,' he added. 'And from what we hear, she wasn't the sort to go round with a button missing. She'd sew it back on.'

'Yes, she would, right away,' said Peter. She'd once stitched back a pocket that was beginning to rip from his jeans.

'Ah – you knew her, then?' The officer made a clicking sound with his teeth, and when Peter nodded, told them to keep their eyes open. Excellent results could accrue from appeals to the public.

'Yes,' said Peter, and turned his bike round. He did not want to be part of this.

'We'll look somewhere else,' said Nick, and followed as Peter rode back towards the village.

They might see something yet, the constable thought: they had young, sharp eyes and were constructed so that these organs were nearer the ground than his own. Still, the sergeant might not approve of them as official recruits.

Peter cycled through the village as fast as he could and went on to the boundary sign beyond which they were not allowed to go without special permission. He slowed down, the ache in his chest, which had intensified during the talk with the policeman, now easier. Nick rode past without his hands on the handlebars, making sounds like a police siren. He went on in token defiance for a hundred yards or more, and then waited for Peter, whose eyes were watering but that was, of course, due to the cold weather, to catch him up. They turned and rode more slowly back through the village, past Lime Tree Cottage, then the row of terraced cottages on the high bank. For a change, they went down the lane to the church.

Nicholas halted at the gate to the churchyard.

'I suppose she'll be buried here,' he said, looking with interest towards the tombstones.

'I suppose so,' said Peter, who had not thought of this part of the business. 'Uncle George is,' he added.

'Oh, is he? Where?'

'Over there somewhere.' Peter waved towards a clump of yew trees at the north side of the old Norman church.

'Let's go and look,' said Nicholas.

The boys propped their bicycles against the churchyard wall and went through the gate and down the path. There was one recent grave, the turf replaced unevenly over the mound of earth. Some withered flowers rested above it. Holly wreaths still lay on others.

'That's old Robson,' said Nicholas, indicating the new grave. 'D'you remember him? He used to walk to the pub in Poppleton every day and get drunk and stagger home singing in the afternoon.'

'Did he?'

'Mm. Not lately, though. He got so that he couldn't go anywhere and was a fair old misery.' Nicholas quoted old Robson's son, who worked on the farm. 'Funny to think of him under there. Do you believe in the resurrection of the body?' Nicholas danced a small jig in front of the remains of old Robson. 'Do you think old Robson will rise up at the last day and be given an endless supply of beer?'

'I don't know.'

Peter stared round. There was Uncle George's grave, the plain off-white stone already slightly discoloured. Inscribed upon it were his full name, the dates of his birth and death, his Army rank and the OBE he had been given by the Queen, and the name of his regiment. A holly wreath lay above where Peter supposed Uncle George's chest to be. They did put the stone at the head end, didn't they? Was Uncle George now a bundle of bones? How could he be restored to his body for Judgement Day?

'Maybe they have chats at night,' said Nick. 'Old

Robson, for instance, and your uncle. They'd have known each other, probably. Perhaps they rise up when the moon's full and have ghostly gatherings.' The idea appealed to him and he uttered a banshee wail. 'It'll be nice for Uncle George to have Laura to talk to,' he added.

'People get cremated,' said Peter. 'So how can they be resurrected?' What if Laura was cremated and left with no body to be raised again? Could a miracle happen? If Jesus appeared now, could he make her alive, like Lazarus?

'We ought to come here at midnight on Hallowe'en,' Nicholas said. 'When the spirits of the dead rise up. We might see them all then, having a party together.'

If they did, would Laura be there? Would she turn into a ghost whom he might see?

Peter didn't really believe in ghosts, but he wouldn't mind seeing one of Laura; that wouldn't be at all scary. Only she wouldn't be real. She had gone for ever.

And Mummy had gone away too.

14

On that cold Friday morning, Mick went off in his van as usual. He decided to visit the up-market part of Merston where the bank managers and more prosperous tradesmen lived, and people who commuted further afield. He had had some success here when he first called a few weeks ago and expected a welcome from his new clients.

He did not receive one. Two women let him do their windows but as they paid they complained about his high charge, more than double that of the previous cleaner, and said he need not return for two months; the others refused his services.

Mick did not give way to dismay. Stuck-up cows, he thought; there were plenty more folk only too glad to have him call and as it was he had made fifteen pounds in less than an hour, with no tax to be paid. It was too cold to go on working, so he went round to see Rene, willing to pay if she insisted, but she refused to co-operate while her children were around. She told him she was expecting a friend that afternoon and the kids were going up the road to her mother, who during the school holidays often took them off her hands for a couple of hours, though she did not know what activity it was that her daughter, thus released, undertook.

Annoyed, Mick called in at the Cricketers where he washed down the sandwiches Beverley had made him with several pints. Then he went home.

When he arrived, Mandy was asleep and Beverley was drawing pictures for Cliff on the back of an old envelope. She had been quite good at art at school and enjoyed making him laugh with sketches of animals and people. She had not expected Mick back until that evening, and her heart sank at the sight of him.

Cliff, as always, forgot her as soon as his father appeared and ran forward, ready to be swung into the air and admired.

'What – stuffing indoors on this lovely day?' Mick cried. 'Come on Cliffie – get your coat on and I'll take you down to the swings.'

Cliff obediently toddled off to fetch his padded suit. Mick helped him into it, zipping it up, tickling the child and making him shriek with excited laughter.

'We'll leave the girls, eh?' Mick said jovially, taking Cliff's hand as they went out of the flat.

Beverley stood at the window watching for them to emerge. Mick hadn't fixed any sort of child seat in the van; it wasn't possible to fit one, he'd said, and anyway Cliff was a big boy now, and sensible. He must sit quietly on some sacks that were in it. She saw Mick take the ladder out of the van and prop it up against the side wall of the block. He was a good father, she had to concede; he had never raised a hand to either child, no matter how much they cried. After being nice last night, Mick had cursed her this morning when she had accidentally got in his way as he was going to the bathroom. She had been bringing him a mug of hot tea which had spilled over her stomach and thighs, scalding her through her nightdress. He hadn't meant to hurt her, of course, but he hadn't said he was sorry and it just showed how little he thought of her. His good mood of the previous evening must have been due to something that had happened during the day to please him, but now he'd forgotten about whatever it was and she could expect more rough treatment.

She examined the watch he had given her. It looked as if it was made of real gold, and if so it must be worth a lot of money. It was the only really nice thing he'd ever given her.

She bundled Mandy into her outdoor clothes and went off to sell it.

Mick quite enjoyed himself down at the swings. It wasn't far to the park, where the children's playground occupied an area beyond a small ornamental pond. Mothers of lively children had to pursue them to make sure they did not fall in and drown among the fat, lazy goldfish. There were no other fathers about today and Mick saw himself as a magnet to the feminine eyes around him. He recognized one of the mothers; she had a baby in a pram and a little girl much Cliff's age. He'd noticed her looking at him on a previous visit so today he put on his best smile and said 'Hi, there,' as he pushed Cliff forward to lead her daughter up the steps of the slide.

From below, the two parents encouraged their children to embark on the long descent.

'I don't like this slide – it's too high,' said the girl.

'It's quite safe,' said Mick.

'It's all set in concrete. What if they fell?' said the girl.

Mick found her anxiety touching, though he had mocked Beverley when she had worried about the same thing.

The children came coasting down.

'There – she's all right, isn't she?' said Mick as the mother was reunited with her daughter. 'Doesn't do to make her nervous, you know,' he added cheerily, but to humour the mother he told the children that now they were to go on the swings. There, side by side, pushing the two toddlers with Mick for once limiting the range of Cliff's arc, he learned that the girl, whose name was Sharon, was on her own. Her husband had left her just after the baby was born and she was living on social security.

'Awful what some blokes will do,' said Mick. 'Fancy leaving a nice little family like yours.'

He took her and the children home in the van, the small girl wedged in with Cliff in the back, the pram beside them.

'It's ever so kind of you,' she said.

He had told her that he and his wife had split up. They'd divided the children, Mick said, and he'd kept the boy. That was why he had started his own business. Often Cliff came with him, he fabricated, and at other times a neighbour looked after him. It made a heart-rending story and touched Sharon deeply. She'd have liked to ask him in for some tea, but her mother was coming round later.

'Well, I'll see you again,' said Mick.

'Yes,' said Sharon, feeling pleased. He was so cheery, with that smile and that long soft moustache and his curls. She sang to herself as she set out the tea after he had gone and her mother was delighted to find her in such improved spirits.

Sharon's small girl had been clutching some object in her hand when her mother took off her coat. It was a large, round, brown leather button.

'Where did you find that?' Sharon asked, but the child lacked the vocabulary to tell her that Cliff had picked it up from the floor of the van and had given it to her.

It might come in useful, thought Sharon, though it matched nothing of hers. She put it in a small bowl full of odds and ends which she kept in the kitchen.

There had been a hat in the van, too, under some sacks. The children had not found that, and Mick had not noticed it either.

*　*　*

Leonard Masefield had been looking forward to Laura's visit. She was coming to lunch that Friday and would arrive at about half-past twelve, in time for some sherry first. His life had become so much a matter of simply struggling through the days that he had forgotten the pleasure of anticipation. He had taken her advice and gone in search of domestic assistance, securing temporary help from a cheerful girl who was expecting her first baby and was glad of a short-term part-time job.

The house was now a great deal cleaner, and today Jessie, who felt sorry for him, had assembled an Irish stew which was gently simmering in the low oven. But his guest never arrived, nor was there a message to tell him she would not be coming.

He waited until two. Then he ate a little of the stew. He did not know her address or telephone number to get in touch with her direct, though of course he could contact her through the estate agent.

He was a silly old man. She had not wanted to buy the house and she had told him so, very honestly. He had pressed her to return, and she had agreed out of pity, when no doubt she was busy and had other, more pressing things to do. They'd made today's arrangement with the excuse that Mr Masefield would seek out a book for her daughter, and indeed, he had found an early edition of *The Secret Garden* for her.

He told himself that Laura was too nice a woman not to ring up with some excuse if she had decided not to come after all, but perhaps she had simply forgotten all about it.

He had, however, seen her make an entry in her diary.

Very unhappily, Mr Masefield put on his coat and scarf and went out for a walk. A pop star had made an offer for the house and he had intended to tell Laura about it, ask her advice, make sure she really would not buy it. The thought of jangling electronic music and wild parties in these surroundings sacred to Beth and her Steinway was almost too much to be borne. Lonely and sad, Mr Masefield walked on through the bright winter day where a few clouds floated high in the pale sky and at last the sun sank like a big fiery ball over the distant hills.

Throughout the day the police continued their routine checking, gradually eliminating ossible leads. No taxi driver had collected a fare from Clyde House the previous afternoon, and Laura had been alone in Sainsbury's, where she was a regular customer known to several of the check-out staff. She had been wearing her raincoat and matching hat; an assistant had noticed it because she looked nice. Her manner had been as usual, pleasant and friendly, and she had not seemed upset in any way.

The various estate agents whose papers were found in Laura's desk had no record of any appointment made on her behalf since late November, when she went to Grange Court, some ten miles from Burford. During the winter people lost interest in house-hunting unless they were forced to move at once; there was a seasonal revival when the days began to draw out and the bite of winter left the air. She had never been to see any of the agents; all communication had been by post and telephone, and no one else had been in touch with them on her behalf.

'That's a great help,' said Grainger, learning this from the day's reports. 'The bloke's kept his head down, then.'

'Patient, too,' remarked Masters. 'If they'd been looking for somewhere for such a long time.'

'Maybe he was stringing her along,' said Grainger. 'Say he'd got a wife already, and kids. Perhaps he'd said, right, you find us a place and then I'll quit.'

'There can't be all that many men able to pay for a place of the sort she seemed to fancy,' said Masters.

'You'd be surprised,' said Grainger.

'What? And keep their wife in suitable style, too?' said Masters.

Grainger shrugged.

'It's been done,' he said.

'She doesn't sound that sort of woman,' said Masters.

'What sort? Ruthless?'

Masters sought about for the right description.

'Grasping,' he said. 'No one's yet said a bad word about her.'

'They will,' said Grainger.

Some of Friday's newspapers referred briefly to the tragedy but it was not mentioned in *The Times,* the *Daily Telegraph* or the *Guardian.* Several tabloids had paragraphs on inside pages which said that a woman's body found on the railway line near Hickling Halt had been identified as that of Mrs Laura Burdock, 38, of Didbury, who had earlier been reported missing. One paper mentioned terrible injuries but no hint was given, at that point, that her death might have been due to murder.

By nightfall the police had advanced no further with their investigation. They had finished going through Laura's possessions without uncovering further secrets, and Grainger had told Tom that inquiries would continue until the truth was discovered.

'It will be, in time,' he said. 'We're waiting on the lab reports. They'll tell us something but tests can't be done quickly.' The lab was always so busy, too, with other important material already in the queue for attention.

A check had been made with the dead woman's doctor. She had not consulted him for nearly a year and then her visit had been to request medication for a stubborn throat infection. She had never sought his advice on contraception and was a healthy woman. This was borne out by the post-mortem findings which had described her as well-nourished.

No strange cars had been seen in the village on Thursday, nor any unknown person; there were only two hundred and twenty people living within the boundary so it was not like hunting for a stranger in a town, where it was easy to be anonymous. Here, an unknown would be noticed immediately.

Marion went home soon after three o'clock. She found Peter and Nicholas in the kitchen drinking hot chocolate and eating fruit cake. They both had pink cheeks from being outside in the cold air. Marion found them some biscuits to round off their snack; they had already eaten the Penguins provided by Janet Carey.

When Nicholas had gone, Marion and Peter played Racing Demon and then Scrabble. It wasn't the moment for Cluedo. Peter was very quiet and he did not eat much for supper, but he had seemed to enjoy his chocolate and cake earlier, which Marion hoped meant he was getting over his shock. They watched television for a while and then it was Peter's bedtime. After he had had his bath, Marion went upstairs to say goodnight to him and was rewarded by an enormous hug. She did not refer to Laura because she had no solace to offer. She must take him off somewhere tomorrow, attempt to divert him.

Bob Carey was going round to see Tom that evening. Tom could hardly refuse to admit him if he turned up on the doorstep, Bob had said, declaring that tonight should be his turn of duty and somebody else would take on the next. Marion accepted this decision. A man's company might help Tom now. She feared the weekend would seem long.

She was exhausted, having had almost no sleep the night before, and she went to bed herself soon after Peter was settled. He lay reading, his door ajar. Marion looked in on him once more and found that he had fallen asleep over his book. It was the volume of stories about animals which some old friend of Laura's had given her for him. He seemed to like it.

Marion turned off his bedside light and smoothed his dark hair as she drew the duvet up around his shoulders.

She was soon asleep herself.

Before he went home that night, Detective Superintendent Grainger looked through the detailed post-mortem report again. It seemed that every possibility had been anticipated. Although the dead woman had worn gloves, so that nail scrapings were unlikely to yield useful information, they had been taken by the careful doctor who did not want to be placed in a position where later he could be accused of an incomplete investigation. He had examined the brain, so severely injured: there was no trace of disease. No secret malignancy lurked in the body; Mrs Burdock had borne no child and was not pregnant.

Some people gambled or drank; some collected *objets d'art* or stamps; some had lovers, some took up religion. Most people needed crutches of one kind or another to help them through life and Laura Burdock had been no exception. She had had a lover and she had planned to leave her husband. Perhaps the fact that they had no children was Tom Burdock's fault and she wanted a family before it was too late. Grainger developed the theory that she had met her lover yesterday afternoon, perhaps in the country somewhere at a point she had walked to with the dog. They had quarrelled. The man, in anger, had got into the car – or perhaps they were both already in it and Laura had got out of it – and driven off. She had thrown herself in front of it in a hysterical gesture if not a definite suicide bid. The lover had picked her up, perhaps thought she was dead, panicked, and dumped her to avoid being involved in an open scandal. The dog had eventually found her own way home.

If there was a lover, someone would know. They would have been seen together somewhere, some time. The man would be found in the end, and his initials would prove to be L.M.

At a press conference that evening, Grainger had appealed for help from the public, asking anyone who had seen the dead woman the previous afternoon to come forward. He wanted to know about cars seen in the area of Hickling Halt then or in the hours of darkness, and anything in the least suspicious, however trivial it might seem. Information often came as a result of such appeals, though cranks wasted a great deal of police time with faked tales of sightings. The inquest had been arranged for Monday. It would be short, for formal identification of the victim, and adjourned till a later date to allow the police time to complete their inquiries, but Grainger hoped that he would have something definite to tell the coroner by then.

He was just leaving his office when the telephone rang. It was the forensic scientist from the lab who had been at the railway line.

Paint particles found on Laura's clothing indicated that she had been in contact with a vehicle which had been painted blue over its original scarlet. A curly brown hair had been trapped in the belt buckle of her raincoat; although much the same colour as the dead woman's, it was not from her head. It was all rather vague at present but there would be more precise information soon.

This was evidence. Grainger went home content.

15

Saturday's tabloid newspapers featured stories about Laura's macabre death; details were revealed about her dreadful injuries – none of these released by the police but discovered by zealous reporters who had tracked down passengers on the train which had caused them. Villagers in Didbury had described the dead woman as quiet and kind. Mrs Rigby had been questioned and when it was suggested to her that her employer might have regretted having no children, thought that this could be so. The resultant headline, SILENT SORROW OF CHILDLESS WIFE, implied that Laura's death was suicide. The quality papers gave briefer, more factual accounts of the affair when printing Grainger's plea for help.

Laura's photograph had been shown on the local late television news programme the previous night, and Beverley had seen it. Hadn't Mick cleaned some windows in Didbury? Maybe he'd met the woman. She did not mention it to him. He had come in late, when she was already in bed and feigning sleep. This time, he had allowed her to get away with it. He'd taken a fancy to Sharon and planned to see her again the next day.

The morning was fine and sunny, with a sprinkling of snow lending the roofs of Merston a sparkling luminescence, and even Beverley responded to the dry, crisp air with a feeling of invigoration when she set off to the shops with the children. Mick was still in bed and had not announced his plans for the day; she could not face the morning in the flat if he was there. She had a little money now. The watch had brought in fifty pounds, more than she expected, and she had put by another twelve. There was the child allowance, and she would be able to get supplementary benefit. Single mothers managed. She could get a divorce. The idea was alarming but at the same time exhilarating. If she was really determined, she could escape. Pat would help. She had been married before and so had her husband, Jim; they would know what she was entitled to in the way of aid. Of course, Mick wouldn't give up the children altogether. Cliff meant a lot to him and a boy needed his father but something could be arranged. Heady with hope, Beverley bought sweets for the children at the newsagent's shop; then, seeing the *Daily Mirror* with its picture of Laura Burdock on the front page, she bought that.

She whiled away more than an hour, buying a loaf and some biscuits, and a tin of spaghetti shapes. When she returned to the flat, Mick had gone out.

Beverley's holiday mood remained with her for most of the day. She'd take the kids to the park later on, she decided as she gave Cliff a drink of blackcurrant juice to tide him over till dinner-time. Then, with Mandy's lips attached to her own nipple, she read the account of Laura's death. It sounded much worse written down like this than it had on the telly. Later, Beverley opened the drawer where Mick's work ledger was kept. He had made no entries since those first few days, but there, clearly recorded, was *Burdock, Clyde House, Didbury, £6*. Beverley could not know that Mick had not noted down the total amount he was paid, but had adjusted the sum to a reasonable figure for the information of the curious.

She replaced the ledger in the drawer and put the paper under the cushion on the settee. It might be wise not to mention the subject to Mick.

Mick had decided to take Sharon and her children out for the day. It would be a real treat for her to go somewhere nice. He would tell her that Cliff was spending the weekend with Beverley and then she'd be sure to invite him to stay overnight. She must have been missing it, after all: she wasn't like Beverley, always too tired. Frigid, that's what Beverley was. It wasn't natural. Women should be like Rene.

He was thinking about Rene and wondering how Sharon would compare with her while he scraped the frost off the van's windscreen, and had quite a shock when a police patrol car drew up alongside and PC Coates addressed him through its window.

'Got this one insured, have you?' he asked.

'I have,' said Mick, scraping on.

'Hm. What are you doing now, then? Bit of painting and decorating?'

'Window cleaning,' said Mick.

'You won't be able to do that when you've lost your licence,' said Coates.

'I won't lose it,' said Mick.

'You will, pal,' said Coates.

'Dead, isn't she? That one who made the complaint,' said Mick. 'Done herself in.' This had been the opinion expressed in the Cricketers the previous evening, where because of its local interest the affair had been discussed.

'Didn't you read that summons? I know you didn't answer it, but I thought you'd at least have seen what it said,' said Coates. 'Mrs Burdock and Mrs Quilter weren't pressing their charges. Of course, Mrs Quilter may go ahead now; it was the dead lady that didn't want to proceed.' Coates looked at Mick standing there in the clear winter sunlight, his curls standing out round his head, his breath showing cloudy in the cold air. 'You'll soon be smiling on the other side of your face, matey.'

'Get stuffed,' said Mick.

Coates drove on, confident that Mick's day of reckoning would not be long delayed. It took a few moments for Mick to understand that the policeman had handed him, as if on a plate, the name of Laura Burdock's companion on the night when all this persecution began. Mrs Quilter! That woman he'd been so kind to, taking that chair up to the kid's bedroom while she'd sat like a duchess making toast. And he'd cleared out those gutters for her, too, which wasn't his work as a cleaner of windows. Mick quite forgot that Marion had paid heavily for this favour as he resolved to settle the score with her. She'd been behind it all; she was responsible for the harassment he'd been receiving, her with her airs and her cups of tea.

Mick was so angry that he nearly abandoned his plans for seeing Sharon to go out to Didbury there and then. He thumped the bonnet of his van and, when he started it up, revved the engine to its limits, setting off round the corner with a squeal of tyres. Anyone getting in his way today had better watch out.

Didbury had been deserted on Thursday, when the weather was poor and it was a working day. Today, what with the sun out and it being a weekend, there'd be kids about and so on. Mick didn't consider that the police would be active in the village; he had put the matter of Laura's death quite out of his mind; but he decided that it would be safer to wait for the night.

Marion awoke early, beset by one of life's recurring problems: a conflict of duty. Tom was alone, bereft and wretched, but he was a man. Peter was also shocked and sad, but he was a child and so his need for diversion was more important than Tom's for support. She would stick to her plan for taking him off somewhere for the day. The sky was clear, but there had been a light fall of snow overnight and it might be wiser not to head for the Cotswolds, where there was a wild life park he had not yet seen; the weather was often more extreme there than in the Thames Valley. They would go to Windsor and look at the Castle. It was too cold for a river trip, even if the pleasure boats ran at this time of year, which she doubted, but there was plenty to see in the town and a number of suitable places for lunch.

Peter approved the plan, but without much enthusiasm. When Marion asked him if there was anything else he would rather do, he said no, it was a great idea. She suggested that he might like to invite Nicholas to go with them.

'Great idea,' said Peter again, but his voice was still flat.

Marion, glad of a way to repay some of Janet Carey's kindness to Peter, went to telephone her. They could spend the whole day in Windsor, she explained to Janet; there was a mass of armour to look at, which should interest the boys, and they could visit the carriages in the mews. They could go for a walk beside the river and look at the ducks and other birds, and they could even go to the Safari Park.

Janet, accepting for Nicholas, said that Bob had found Tom calm the night before. The Wilsons were going to keep tabs on him today; he wouldn't simply be left to get on with it by himself.

Before leaving, Marion telephoned him. He said there was no more news but the newspapers were driving him mad, telephoning constantly. He was thinking of leaving the telephone off the hook.

Marion asked him to put it back that evening as she would ring when she and Peter returned from their outing.

While she was on the telephone, Peter had opened the garage doors and cleaned the car's windscreen.

'Want to get it out?' she asked.

'No, thanks,' said Peter.

Usually, he jumped at the chance. Marion had taught him how to start the car and manoeuvre it in and out of the garage. He could just reach the pedals and there was space for him to move it up into second gear here, and he had driven up and down the drive at Clyde House.

It was dark when they returned from their day out, during which Nicholas had been cheerful and chatty but Peter had had little to say. He had shown sombre interest in the tombs of the kings and they had brushed up on some historical facts forgotten by Marion and never known by the boys. Both boys had eaten a good lunch washed down with Coca-Cola, while Marion had a large gin and tonic. Later, the boys had consumed enormous ice-cream sundaes. Marion suspected that Peter was forcing himself to swallow his but then wondered if she was being hyper-sensitive about him.

She was proved right, however, when after they reached home he rushed into the house and just managed to get to the cloakroom before he was sick. He was never car-sick. It might be a germ, Marion thought, although she knew in her heart that it wasn't. How could she administer comfort? There was no consolation for this sort of pain.

Sharon thought it was nice that Cliff was visiting his mother. It was hard on a brother and sister to be brought up apart. Would Mick and his wife ever get together again?

Mick didn't think so. There was this bloke she'd been seeing, he told her. He embroidered away, marvelling at how easy it was to spin a yarn while Sharon said 'Oh,' and 'Um' in sympathy.

He took them all to a country pub where the canal ran through the garden and there were swings and slides for the kids. It was here that he'd picked up that girl, all those years ago; he drove right past the spot where he'd barged her with the stolen Marina. The sun was bright but there was no warmth in it. Mick went into the pub for drinks and something to eat. Sharon had asked for soup and a roll as that was quite cheap but Mick wouldn't take her money; he bought some crisps for Emily, the little girl. Sharon had brought a bottle for the baby and a flask of hot water which she poured into a jug to stand the bottle in so that it warmed through. Mick, eating pork pie and chips, thought her very well organized. The baby was good and soon went to sleep but Emily had developed a cough which was irritated by the cold air. The sound got on Mick's nerves. She became rather whiney and lost what charm she had had for Mick, but he tried to mask his impatience as he put everyone back into the van. Emily was wedged into the rear beside the folding pram. There were rags and sponges and a bucket there, too, two empty petrol cans, and something else: a hat. This distracted her from her woes and she put it on. It came down well over her ears and she looked comic in it, her two little bunches of hair sticking out beneath the brim.

Mick recognized it when they stopped outside Sharon's house. The frame of Laura's face in those last moments, eyes staring under that very same brim, was a vision which he was sure would always fill him with pleasure whenever he called it to mind. The hat must have dropped off when he dragged her out of the van on the bridge. She had been surprisingly heavy when he hauled her out and managed to heave her, fireman fashion, over his shoulder and to the parapet. He took it from Emily, crumpled it up and stuffed it into his jacket pocket.

'I need that to keep my head warm on the ladder,' he quipped.

Sharon made tea and he sat in her lounge watching television while she fed the children and put them to bed. The news came on and he saw Detective Superintendent Grainger appealing for anyone who had seen Laura Burdock on Thursday afternoon to come forward. He asked also for anyone who had seen a car parked on or near the railway bridge near Hickling Halt to get in touch with the police, and to report anything suspicious that might have been noticed, including strange cars in Didbury.

Mick enjoyed seeing this, confident that no one had seen him at Hickling; and he had not driven into Didbury at all. They were looking for a car, weren't they? He drove a van.

The fact that they were looking for any sort of vehicle

caused him a brief frown. Hadn't they accepted it as suicide? Perhaps they were looking for whoever had given her a lift to the bridge. Yes, that was it.

Mick felt comfortable again, but he hadn't forgotten Mrs Quilter. He would have to get rid of her, too. She deserved the same fate. Then he'd get hold of one of those clever-dick lawyers who could delay things at court, get the hearing postponed until he'd worked off most of the points on his licence. Such things could be done. He might even get the rest of the charges dismissed so that no more points would be entered against him. He would get his HGV licence in the end, and until then he would go on cleaning windows. It was easy money: you could do a semi in ten minutes; people didn't complain if you left the odd smear. He'd get to know the country districts where there was money about and folk weren't too fussy about how they locked up. He'd be able to pick up quite a bit on the side, if he went back after dark.

Meanwhile, there was Sharon. She smiled a lot and was pretty, not like Beverley with her sulks. If he moved in with her, he could say he had decided to let Cliff remain with his mother and sister. Beverley would have to let him see Cliff whenever he wanted; it was his right.

The jeweller who had bought Laura's gold watch from Beverley had been surprised when she accepted fifty pounds for it without asking for more. He had asked her where she got it and was told it was a gift from her husband and that now they had parted. It was a very expensive watch and she did not look as if she would have the sort of husband to match it, but appearances could be deceptive. All the same, it might be wise to make sure it was not on any police list of stolen goods. He locked it away in his safe; Monday morning would be soon enough to attend to that.

He was out of the shop on Saturday when a constable called with a description of Laura's missing watch. The assistant he spoke to said he was sure that no one had brought it in, but he would check with his employer, just to make sure. The assistant forgot, remembering only when he reached home.

It could wait.

Detective Superintendent Grainger spent some time with Tom on Saturday morning.

There was a stubble of beard on Tom's chin and huge dark circles under his eyes, and the pallor of his face was tinged with green. It was understandable: the man had lost not only his wife but his illusions about her.

'Well?' Tom asked curtly. His head was reeling; he had scarcely slept all night, the second without rest, unable to lie in the wide bed he had shared with Laura and which was permeated by her remembered scent. He had gone down to the kitchen and made coffee – not the best recipe for repose – and had sat in his study going over and over in his mind what might have happened on Thursday. If only she'd told him she wanted to leave him! Instead, she had made him so sure of the exact reverse: he had been certain that she was as happy with their life as he was. How could she have been so false? He gave her credit for not wanting to hurt him, postponing a show-down until all her plans were made, but those plans affected him: had he no right to a warning?

He was glad when he could call an end to the night, put on the radio and use the sound of the early farm programme to dilute his misery.

'We're making progress,' Grainger told Tom. 'We're sure that she was hit by a vehicle before being placed on the railway line. Now we have to find the car that struck her.'

'You'll never do that,' said Tom.

'Oh yes, we will,' Grainger assured him. 'We know it was a blue vehicle which was originally painted scarlet. The lab is analysing these paints; they will eventually be able to tell us what makes of vehicle, in which years, were sprayed with that red paint.' The computer would help them to trace possible vehicles whose whereabouts at the given time could then be ascertained. The one they were after had been resprayed; that should have been disclosed on the registration details when the Road Fund licence was renewed, but if it had been stolen, of course that would not have been done.

'You really think she was knocked down and dumped?' Tom asked.

'The medical and scientific evidence points strongly towards that theory,' said Grainger.

'What sort of man would do that?' Tom demanded. 'He must be a monster.'

'There are monsters about, Mr Burdock,' said Grainger. 'And some of them look no different from you and me. I'm just as impatient for answers as you are, believe me, and when we get a bit more from the lab we'll be on our way to getting them.'

'I want to know who that man is,' Tom said. 'Her – her lover.'

'So do I, Mr Burdock,' said Grainger. When they knew that, they would find their murderer.

Tom was thinking that he would kill the man when he knew who he was: a life for a life. It was worth existing until then.

'We're making checks through the estate agents,' Grainger said. 'They've given us various addresses of houses she saw, but most of them have been sold now and the agents don't always know the new addresses of the vendors. We'll find them – the police in the various districts are helping with that now – but again, it takes time. Most police work does, Mr Burdock. Evidence has to be collected and assessed; it's not done by magic.'

'You'll tell me as soon as there's news?'

'Certainly.'

'You've got rid of the press, anyway. I'm grateful for that,' said Tom.

'There's been a shooting over the other side of the county,' said Grainger. 'More's known about that and it's going to occupy them for a while.' Again, it was a triangular set-up: a farmer had shot his wife and her lover, killing the lover and seriously wounding the wife. What would she be left with, if she recovered? Grainger found human passion disturbing and did his best to avoid it in his own life.

'Is that your case too?' Tom asked.

'Luckily not,' Grainger said. 'It's not my area, but it's in the division. It's my chief's worry. We've had a few thefts and break-ins on my patch, but it doesn't need a superintendent in person to look into those.'

'You must be using a lot of men on all this,' Tom said.

'We are.' Grainger was grateful for this sign of appreciation. The case had become a murder inquiry and an incident room had been set up at headquarters. 'All the reports have to be filed and collated,' he explained. 'We're telephoning the traceable people in your wife's address book, for instance, in case any of her friends knows something relevant.'

'Like the name of her lover?'

'Well – that, or about her plans in general,' said Grainger. 'Bear with us, Mr Burdock. It's early days yet.'

Laura had been dead for thirty-six hours, give or take a few either way, Tom reflected. How was she getting on, out there in limbo? Had she just ceased to be?

He did not believe she was having a party in heaven with, for example, her dead parents, and he tried not to think of the waxen face framed by her long hair which he had seen in the mortuary. It had not seemed like Laura at all.

Leonard Masefield had caught a chill on Friday. He had walked a long way that afternoon and it was dark when he returned to the house. Then he discovered that the ancient central heating boiler had found the very cold weather too much for its old bones and had stopped working. He had telephoned the repair service and left a message on the recording machine. No one would come that night.

He made up the fire in the drawing-room and sat huddled over it listening to a recording of Bach's *Christmas Oratorio*. When he went up to bed he could not get warm, despite wearing two sweaters. During the night he went downstairs to fetch an electric fire, stumbled over the cord of his old brown Jaeger dressing-gown and fell down the last steps, breaking his hip.

He lay there until the boiler mechanic arrived the next day and found him.

16

'When will Laura be buried?' asked Peter on Saturday night.

'Oh, Peter, I don't know,' said Marion. 'Not for a bit. There has to be an inquest – that's an inquiry – into what happened,' she explained. 'It can be arranged after that.'

'There's lots of room in the churchyard,' Peter volunteered. 'It's quite nice there, isn't it?' She wouldn't be lonely, with people she knew all around. Of course, he knew she had really gone to heaven to be with Jesus for ever, but she'd be in the churchyard too. That part of things was easier to grasp than the daunting prospect of eternity.

After being sick, Peter's colour had returned. He had had a hot bath and was ready for bed, sitting by the fire with a mug of Bovril and some cream crackers.

'Lovey, try to remember Laura as she was, happy and generous, and so fond of you. Try not to think too much about what's happened,' Marion begged.

'I can't help it,' said Peter.

Marion moved to put her arms round him. He nestled against her, his head resting on her somewhat bony shoulder.

'I'm afraid you'll go away too,' he mumbled.

'Me? Why, Peter? Why should I go away?'

'Mummy did,' said Peter. 'And now Laura. People I like,' he plunged.

'Mummy isn't dead,' said Marion. 'And what happened to Laura was a hideous accident. No one can explain why something like that should happen. There's no comfort to be found, except that we were lucky to have known her at all. Wouldn't it be sad if no one was sorry when someone died? If they had no one who loved them to mourn them?' She gave him a little hug. 'And I'm not planning to die just yet – or to go off to America. Now, let's think of something to cheer us both up. Have you ever read *Treasure Island?*'

He hadn't. Marion had seen an illustrated edition at a village sale and had thought it would be worth having in the house; she kept seeing things that Peter might like one day and there was always some sort of surprise in his room when he arrived.

She took the book from the shelf and began to read it aloud. After two chapters, Peter was agreeable to going to bed and she put the volume on his bedside table, beside the book that Laura had given him.

'Read a bit more if you can't go to sleep,' she advised. 'I'm going to bed soon.'

She kissed him and pulled the duvet up round him. Perhaps it was as well that his new term began on Wednesday; he wouldn't be able to brood so much when he was occupied.

He seemed to be asleep when she went up to bed herself. She left his door ajar so that she would hear if he woke up in the night and called out.

Marion was reading Robert K. Massie's *Life of Peter the Great,* an absorbing book which had increased her existing desire to visit Leningrad. She read on for some time, engrossed by the Tsar's navigational achievements, applying to herself the remedy she had prescribed for Peter. But when she turned out her light, sleep eluded her. Her mind began squirrelling round the events of the last days. In the end she took two of the sleeping pills Dr Bartholomew had insisted on giving her after George's death. They were quick-acting, and she was soon deeply asleep.

When Peter left his room and went downstairs, she did not hear a sound.

He was doing it to protect Aunt Marion. If he didn't go away, something dreadful would happen to her: he just knew it. He must have done something very wicked to bring bad luck to the people he loved. Mummy and Daddy had stopped being in love and Mummy had gone away; now Laura was dead. Something would happen to Aunt Marion too unless he left.

He didn't know where he would go. Daddy was not in danger, because although Peter did love him, of course, it wasn't the same as before Caroline and Sarah were there. So it might be all right to go home, but Dad wouldn't be back from Suffolk until tomorrow night.

He knew that Marion was meeting a friend from America on Tuesday after she had taken him home. Peter was convinced that she would go back to America with her friend or else die unless he made her safe.

It seemed automatic to go to his car while he thought of a plan. How wise he had been to lay in some stores – he had bought a few things in Swindon the day the disaster had happened. Marion had been looking at books at the time; she was never nosey and hadn't asked what was in his carrier bag. He'd stored it away in his wardrobe and he took it with him now – more crisps and sweets, and a tin of lemonade. If necessary, he could stay in the car until it was time for school. Marion wouldn't worry as he'd left her a note. It had been difficult to compose and in the end he'd settled for brevity, writing in green biro on a piece of paper torn from a notebook he'd got in his room. *It's all my fault*, ran the message. He'd wondered what else to say and had finally added, *have got food and drink*, because Marion always took such trouble about meals, saying growing boys needed plenty of food.

He had never been out alone so late – or rather, so early.

His digital watch showed that it was past midnight as he walked through the village carrying his bag of supplies and the book Laura had given him. The night was bitterly cold, but there was no cloud and the full moon cast a light almost as bright as day over the silent houses. Peter had brought his torch, but he did not need it as he walked in the silver-white world of moonlight over the snow. The hedges and trees were rimed with frost and his footsteps crunched as he walked through the copse. His breath wisped before him in visible plumes. He wore his anorak, and his wellingtons with the thermal socks Marion had bought for him, amazed that no one had done so before. She said there was nothing as miserable as cold feet and that she and Daddy had worn special little grey fleecy socks called Arctic Feet in their wellies when they were children. She did lots of nice things for him, almost like Mummy – but Mummy had stopped quite a time before she went away. Peter blinked away tears, thinking of this.

He was glad when he reached the ridge and could scramble down and into his car. Its windows were white with frost but very little snow had penetrated through the brambles. Hugging *Wild Animals I Have Known*, Peter settled down in the driver's seat to wait, if not until term began, at least until morning.

Sharon had very little food in the house. She was taking the children to her parents' house the next day for their Sunday dinner; her mother and father were trying to help her through this difficult time, and one of their methods was to make sure that the little family was properly fed at least once a week. Sharon laid out her own funds very sparingly and she had bought three ounces of mince for Saturday's midday meal. This would feed Emily properly, allow a little to be sieved for the baby, and she would finish what remained with plenty of potatoes. There were ten Brussels sprouts; three for Emily, a small one for the baby and the rest for Sharon.

But Mick had taken them all out for the day and had

spent money on them; she must repay this by giving him a meal.

While he watched television, she put on the mince. Emily had had only crisps at the pub so she could not be deprived of her tiny allotted portion but Mick would have to have what was left. She opened a tin of baked beans to stir into it, for there wasn't enough for a man. There was only custard, made with dried milk, for afters.

Mick appeared in the kitchen while she was preparing this gourmet repast.

'Got any beer?' he asked her.

'Sorry. I never keep any in,' she said. 'You could get some at the pub on the corner.' If he wanted a drink, that was his affair; she couldn't run to that sort of thing.

Mick could not spend a dry evening. He went down to the Rising Sun where he drank two pints before going back to Sharon's place with a couple of large bottles. She'd cooked plenty of chips to go with their meal; they were crisper than Beverley's but otherwise there was an irritating familiarity about the menu. He wouldn't eat the custard; that was only fit for kids unless it was served with a good hunk of apple pie or steamed pudding. Sharon didn't eat a great deal herself, and she drank only a small glassful of beer. When Mick settled down with her on the sofa and drew her towards him, she allowed him to kiss her, but as soon as he slid his hand under her sweater she pulled away.

'No, Mick,' she said.

'Come on, love,' he said. 'No need to be shy.'

'I'm not shy. I don't want to,' said Sharon.

'We'll soon change that,' said Mick.

'No,' Sharon repeated. 'I told you, I don't want to.'

'Oh, come on!' Mick moved his hand and caught both her arms, forcing her back against the sofa. Now her eyes should widen, the pupils darken. He didn't mind a bit of resistance; it would add spice to the conquest. He'd press her and she'd soon give in.

But it didn't happen like that. She made a quick movement with her arms, bringing them up in front of her in some way, and broke free, in the same movement standing up, breathing fast, colour in her cheeks and a look, not of fear but of defiance, on her face.

'Mick, you've given us all a lovely day. Thank you,' she said in a low, steady voice. 'But I'm married. I still hope my husband will come back and when he does, I don't want to have to tell him I've been having affairs.' She moved away and opened the door of the room. 'Thank you for the outing,' she added. 'Goodnight.' She went into the hallway and picked up his leather coat, waiting there until he chose to accept defeat and emerge, which happened quite quickly. Mick found her standing beside the front door, which was ajar, and she opened it wide as he appeared so that they were framed there for any passer-by to see.

For once in his life, Mick was speechless. He snatched his jacket from her and stalked off down the short path to the road where his van was parked. Sharon stayed to watch him go, and she waved, but Mick left without a backward glance.

She cried when she went indoors. Perhaps it was true that men could never be simply friends, and after all, he was lonely too. It would have been nice, in a way, sort of comforting, to have given in, but it wouldn't have been right. Besides, what if she had a baby? She wasn't on the pill.

He'd left an unopened beer bottle behind and she put it away in case he came back, but she didn't think that he would, though perhaps they would meet again in the park.

What a pity it was.

Mick was furious. How had he come to let her get away with turning him out? One minute he'd been pressing her back against the sofa and the next she'd sprung free without any sort of struggle. And after him doing so much for her and her snotty kids, taking them out for the day and spending good money on them. All he'd had was a cup of tea and some runny mince and chips. Well, she could whistle for him to come back. There were plenty more girls who'd jump at the chance of him staying with them. He had only to snap his fingers and they'd come running, Mick assured himself, pushing the van along.

He'd go round to Rene's. It was early yet and she might not have got fixed up. She fancied him all right, she'd proved it often enough.

There was a blue Ford Sierra parked outside Rene's house. It had been there before; the driver was one of her regulars. Well, she could send him away.

Mick drew in behind it, giving its bumper a knock just to show who was top around here. He got out of the van and went up to her door where he pealed the bell. When nothing happened, he pealed it again and rattled the letter-box, making a good deal of noise. A curtain twitched at a nearby window but Mick took no notice. He rang again, and eventually Rene appeared. She was wearing a dark green dress made of some silky stuff and her hair had been freshly rinsed a deep shade of copper. She was heavily made-up and a wave of gardenia scent and her own warm body smell greeted Mick as he made to step over the threshold. My God, she looked wonderful! She knocked spots off that Sharon!

But there was no welcome here.

'How dare you make all this noise?' Rene demanded angrily.

'Come on, Rene. Don't be like that,' said Mick, turning on the smile that was usually so effective.

'Go away, Mick. And don't come back,' said Rene. She lowered her voice. 'Joe's here. His wife's turned him out and he's moving in with me and the kids. We're going to get married. Things have finally worked out for me and I'm not letting you or anyone else wreck my chance. Now, get lost.' She made to close the door and then softened enough to add, 'We've had some good times, Mick, but that's over now. I've got to think of myself and the kids.'

There was the sound of a lavatory flushing in the house behind her. Rene shut the front door in his face.

After that Mick went to the nearest pub where he stayed

until closing time, drinking and playing the fruit machine. Then he went home.

There was nowhere else to go.

On the way back from the park that afternoon, Beverley had gone past the block where her friend Pat lived, and had seen Jim cleaning the car outside in the road.

He told her to go in and see Pat, who would love the excuse for a cup of tea.

Beverley had ended up pouring out the tale of her woes to her friend. Pat had known things were bad; she had seen bruises on Beverley's face and had not believed explanations of collisions with the furniture. Now she heard about the theft of Beverley's money.

'It had to be Mick who took it,' Beverley said. 'I'm leaving him as soon as I've saved up enough.'

'You don't have to leave,' said Pat. 'You should stay – make him go. You hang on to the flat. They can't turn you out. The social security will help with the rent if you can't manage.' Pat's own case was different, she had no children from her first marriage; but she had a friend, Sharon Cole, whose husband had walked out soon after their second child was born. Pat told Beverley about her.

'He wasn't mature enough to cope with the responsibility of a family,' Pat said. 'He went off with some girl he met at a disco while Sharon was in hospital having the baby. She's stayed in her place – thinks he'll come back one day, which is stupid. She's better off without him, but she'll find that out in time.' There was no doubt in Pat's mind that she was better off herself, remarried to Jim who was kind and was also the survivor of a stormy marriage. The sadness was that he saw so little of his two daughters. Pat said she would ask Sharon over so that she and Beverley could meet; Sharon would give Beverley some tips about how to cope as a single parent. Meanwhile, why take any more punishment from Mick? Why not barricade him out of the flat?

'How can I?' asked Beverley.

'Change the locks. Put on bolts. If he tries to get in, call the police. Shout loudly enough and the neighbours will do it,' Pat said. 'I bet they've heard you rowing.'

In the end Beverley had stayed for a couple of hours, during which time Pat had sent Jim off to buy locks and bolts before the shops closed.

They both went home with Beverley and the children, and Jim fitted the lock and a good strong bolt on the door.

When Mick returned to The Buildings late that night his key would not turn the lock, and no one replied when he banged on the door and shouted. At last a light went on inside the flat but the door did not open. He paused in his pounding and heard Beverley's voice. It was not very steady, but the message was clear.

'I'm not putting up with your bullying any longer,' she said. 'I've packed your things. They're on the landing.' Then the light went out.

Mick glanced round and there, sure enough, were a large shabby case and two carrier bags, their tops lashed, neatly stacked in the corner. He began shouting and yelling again, but then Mr Duke called up the stairs.

'If you don't stop that noise now, Mick Harvey, I'm telephoning for the police,' he warned.

Mick believed him. The whole world was against him that night. But Beverley needn't think she'd get away with this. He'd be back, but not when busybodies like old Duke were around. He'd teach Beverley a lesson she wouldn't forget. Who did she think she was, anyway? And who was responsible for all this – for his being turned out of his own home in the middle of winter? Why, those two cows in Didbury, of course, the one who was dead and would cause no more trouble, and that mealy-mouthed other bitch with the peppery hair who'd queened it about giving him tea when he did her a good turn. Mick quite forgot how he had enjoyed that first visit to Lime Tree Cottage as his resentment increased.

No one had ever got away with doing Mick down in the past, and he didn't intend that they should now. All you had to do was to show who was boss; he'd managed that, even in Borstal. No other lad there had been able to frighten Mick Harvey. But he'd hated the restriction of being confined in his tiny cell with its narrow hard bed. The moments when the door clanged shut at night, locking him in until the next day, had been the worst in his life.

In prison it would be the same thing again, but he would no longer be a young offender; it would all be much harder.

But he wasn't going to prison. No one knew what had happened on Thursday. No one would get him for that, nor for what he was going to do now. The only thing the police had on him was a slip with the car, which could happen to anyone, and they'd nabbed him for that because of those two women.

He got into the van and drove off.

From the window above, Beverley saw him go. She went back to bed and slept soundly till she was disturbed again before dawn.

Mick drove through Merston to the Four Roads crossing. An off-duty policeman, driving home with his wife after a night out, noticed the Morris Minor van entering the roundabout but took little heed of it.

It was a beautiful night. The hedges glistened with silver frost and the trees were etched like black lace against the dark sky. Few lights showed as Mick drove on towards Poppleton and took the turning for Didbury. He stopped by the stile over which Laura had climbed just before he struck her down, and got out of the van to relieve himself. Steam rose satisfactorily into the air near the spot where she had fallen. As he climbed back into the van, it began to snow.

Never mind, he'd soon have shelter. That woman could provide it for him. She'd soon smile on the other side of her face if she woke to find him in her bedroom. That would scare her all right. Mick drove past the gates of Clyde House. All was quiet; there was no police presence. He turned into the village street, where there were no lamp-posts to light the road. The houses were in darkness as he

162

glided past them out of gear, coasting towards Lime Tree Cottage.

Pity it wasn't thatched, like some of those others, he thought; still, it was old and full of wooden beams; there were planks across the ceilings and what looked like tree-trunks in the walls. It would burn a treat.

He didn't smoke – it was stupid to fill up your lungs with tar – so he had no matches or lighter, but there'd be those inside for sure, or he could simply pull some of the logs out of the fire in that room where she'd made the toast; they'd soon flare up and it would be put down as an accident when she was found, all crisped up, in the morning. He'd have to make sure the kid wasn't there, though; Mick had no grudge against him and would never harm an innocent child.

Very quietly, having turned off the engine and put on the brake, Mick got out of the van and walked up the path towards the dark bulk of the cottage.

It was bitterly cold in the old Morris. Peter huddled behind the steering-wheel, his arms folded over his chest, the hood of his anorak drawn up over his head.

He was too wound up to go to sleep. He remembered something Aunt Marion had said soon after Mummy had gone away and she had come into his room late at night and found him wide awake, unable to still his thoughts. She'd suggested reciting poems inside his head. She'd been surprised when he said he didn't know many poems. When she was at school, she'd had to learn lots by heart and then, at the end of term, declaim a selected passage in front of the whole school. She had hated that, but other girls had enjoyed it. He tried to remember some of the ones she had read to him then. There was one about an albatross, but he couldn't think how it went; all he could recollect were a few nursery rhymes and some songs. Perhaps a carol would help now. He began to sing *Good King Wenceslas* in a thin treble, but it seemed silly, there in the car alone, unable to see out of the windows because of the frost. A tear trickled down his face. He looked at the time on his watch; it was only one o'clock; there were hours to go before you could call it morning. He composed himself again and began to tell himself a story about a boy who ran away to sea to escape from an evil monster. Gradually he lost sight of the monster and replaced it with images of Geoffrey, now married to Mummy, and soon he was really crying.

This wouldn't do. Peter searched for a handkerchief and found a crumpled tissue in his pocket. He blew his nose and wiped his eyes, then ate some crisps, but he felt no more cheerful afterwards. He was so cold. He told himself that he was an Arctic explorer. The car was his bivouac and outside was his team of Huskies, tethered to an ice-floe and with seal meat for food. The blizzard was blowing, but the brave explorer's spirits were high as he set an example to the men he was leading.

The brave explorer's teeth, however, had begun to chatter as he shivered in his shelter. He had better get up and move about to restore his circulation.

Peter got out of the car. It had started to snow, and huge flakes were drifting silently down through the trees. He moved to where there was a clear space near the car and began jumping up and down, moving his arms and legs as they did at school in PE. Then he looked at his watch again. It was twenty minutes past one.

Perhaps it would be best if he went back to the cottage and got into his nice warm bed for an hour or two, until morning. Aunt Marion never got up before half-past seven in the winter. He could set the alarm on his watch, put it under his pillow, and slip out again at six. By then buses and things would be running, thought Peter, unaware of the limitations of Sunday timetables. He would walk to Poppleton. The bus came through there and he'd take it to the motorway, or the nearest point it went to in that direction.

He realized then that he'd forgotten his money. He'd need that; to pay for the bus, though he'd hitch a ride to

London. He could spend the day in a museum, until Dad arrived back.

This justified his return. The intrepid explorer's spirits genuinely rose as he started off through the copse, a small figure soon covered in snow as he came out into the lane and walked on through the silently falling flakes.

Wild Animals I have Known lay abandoned in the car.

Mick walked all round the cottage surveying the windows. He had tried the front door, which was made of solid oak with an iron latch. It was firmly locked. There must be some easier point of entry. People were very careless; before now, he had climbed into a house through a half-light that had been left open.

All the ground floor windows were securely fastened. He could break a pane and put his hand in to turn the catch, but there might be another way. Passing the back door, he tried the handle. To his amazement, it opened.

Stupid bitch, Mick thought, slipping into the house. Heated by the Aga, the kitchen was warm. Mick was grateful for that. He closed the back door and pulled up a blind to let the pale light from outside illuminate the room while he listened to make sure that no one was stirring. All was quiet, so he turned on the light and went into the hall, then across to the sitting-room. The fire had burned down but the ashes were warm. There was a pile of newspapers and magazines on a stool; they'd soon catch and when the place was blazing she'd be properly scared, but he needed more than that; before the final panic from which there would be no escape but which he wouldn't be able to see, he needed to witness her naked terror.

Naked. He could make her strip. She wouldn't like that, a prissy bitch like her. And he wouldn't give her the satisfaction of doing it to her; he'd just mock her.

Mick went back into the kitchen to find a knife. The first drawer he opened held neatly folded tea-towels; the second was full of various kinds of kitchen paper and polythene bags. In the third he found what he wanted, a knife with a strong blade and a serrated edge. He looked about for some stockings or tights. Disguise didn't matter as he was going to make it impossible for her to call the police ever again, but features distorted by a stocking mask were frightening in themselves. Marion had not, however, left any tights in the kitchen. He saw a torch on the shelf by the back door. How very convenient; he could use that instead of turning on any more lights.

Pointing it towards the ground before him, Mick began climbing the narrow twisting staircase, ducking under the beam that crossed it at one point, testing every tread before trusting it with his weight in case it betrayed his presence by creaking. It was exciting. He had never broken into a house at night before; all his thieving had been of the opportunist kind, done during the day. On the landing, he paused. The kid's room was here, to the right. There were several other doors; the place was quite large though all on different levels and really old-fashioned.

The door of the boy's room was not closed. Mick pushed it wider and shone the torch round. The beam picked up the bed with the duvet neatly drawn up. So the kid wasn't here; that was good. He'd have been a problem; Mick wouldn't have known what to do with him. He'd have trussed him up, probably, and taken him out to the shed where he would have had to take his chance. The fire might spread that far before anyone came; who could tell?

Mick would take the woman's car. Her red Fiesta would be better than his old van. If he put that in the garage, and fired it, who'd know the difference? He'd have to get right away after this; there was nothing here for him now so he'd make a new start. He would have her car to sell, and he'd take anything else she'd got that he could turn into money. He could get into the big time in London. Good drivers who could lift cars were always needed, and when he'd got a few grand put away, he'd go to South America. He'd send for Cliff then, bring the kid up there. Ronald Biggs had done something like that, hadn't he?

Mick wasn't sure of the details but he knew you couldn't be brought back from there.

Now for the woman.

Marion was deeply asleep. She did not hear Mick enter her room, nor was she roused when he opened her dressing-table drawer and found the box in which she kept her few pieces of jewellery. Laura's hat was still in his pocket; he drew it out to use as a bag, dropping them into it and folding it round them before stuffing it back. Her handbag was on a chair and he opened that, taking out her notecase and cheque book. She'd have a banker's card, too; Mick looked in the notecase and there it was. He'd have funds for a long time. He was elated, already planning the high living he would soon be able to enjoy.

There was a telephone on the bedside table. Mick tweaked the wires away from the wall and the slight sound disturbed Marion. She stirred as Mick turned the torch towards her. When she opened her eyes, all she could see was a white dazzle of light which made her blink; then she felt a sharp nick on her cheek, an instant of pain, and the warm trickle of blood.

'There, that's to show you what you'll get if you try any clever stuff,' Mick warned. 'I've got a knife, and it's sharp, and it will be your throat next. Get up.'

Marion's first thought was of terror for Peter, her next for herself. She was going to be raped here, in her own bed, and she would have to submit without a struggle because of the boy. But she was being given the chance to stand up on her own two feet. What could she do? How could she warn Peter? If she called out, he'd come running and the intruder would go for him. In spite of her shock, she felt muzzy from the effects of the sleeping pills she had taken, and she shook her head to clear it as she slid her legs over the side of the bed and stood up. Thank goodness she had kept on her warm bedjacket and her shoulders were covered. She was perfectly decent, standing there in her pale blue Marks and Spencer's nightdress with the lace trimmings, taking deep breaths to try to steady herself.

'What do you want?' she asked. 'My handbag's there on the chair.'

If he turned towards it, she might be able to hit him with something. *Peter the Great*, which lay on her table, was quite hefty. Would it knock him out or just make him angry?

But he was talking.

'I've found it,' he said. 'And your jewels.'

What a grand name for her bits and bobs. Marion felt a brief pang for her grandmother's garnet brooch.

The man had shouted the words. He'd wake Peter.

'Please keep your voice down,' she said. 'There's a baby in the house. You'll wake it.'

She suddenly felt a stinging blow across the face where he had already cut her as Mick struck her. The pain was intense and her eyes watered.

'Don't try tricks like that on me,' Mick said. 'I know there's no kid in this house.'

What did he mean? Had he watched the house, as thieves did, and learned that she lived alone? If Peter had woken up, would he have the sense to stay quiet?

Mick grabbed her arm and twisted it behind her.

'Now get going,' he said. 'Downstairs, and fast.'

He frogmarched her out of the room. On the landing sh_ twisted her head and saw Peter's door wide open, with the room in darkness. He must be hiding. If that were so, he would give the alarm – use the telephone when she and the man were downstairs. She clung to the thought that Peter was keeping his head as she stumbled downstairs.

The alternative – that the intruder had already found Peter – was not to be contemplated for one second, not now, when she needed to keep her wits.

Only when they were in the kitchen, where the light was already on, did she recognize her captor.

17

As Marion absorbed this fresh shock, she realized what an opportunity he had had to look round; she supposed that he'd seen she had a few things worth stealing, but then so had most people. He had woken her by shining his torch in her eyes. Why do that, when he could have come and gone without discovery? He must have known she would recognize him if she saw him. He could have everything she possessed as long as Peter was safe. She must try not to aggravate him. Marion suppressed a shiver; no matter what happened, she was not going to show fear.

Her thinking was sluggish, her head still heavy. Concentrating hard, she asked Mick again what he wanted.

'You'll see,' said Mick.

He didn't know why he had brought her downstairs. He had intended to roast her to death in her bed, but not until he had made her thoroughly afraid. Then the desire to exert power over her, make her jump to his bidding, had been irresistible. She was sly, making out that the kid was in the house when he wasn't. He gave her arm an extra wrench as a punishment for this offence, and another for pretending there was a baby; then he let her go.

Marion rubbed her aching arm, but when she saw Mick gloating because he had hurt her, she stopped.

'I'm cold,' she said. 'There's a coat on the back of the door. May I put it on, please?' It hurt her to make the request, but if he allowed it, it would mean a small victory. She would also be better equipped to tackle whatever lay ahead.

'Get it, then,' said Mick, gesturing with the knife. 'But no tricks.'

Marion kept an old anorak hanging on the door. She crossed to take it down and considered throwing it over

Mick's head. Could she do it? Could she overpower him, if she did? He was taller than she was, and very much stronger. She turned slowly.

He was glaring at her, the knife held out in a threatening gesture, his eyes glittering, sweat shining on his face, the lines of the soft moustache lending menace to features she had paid little attention to at their other meetings. Deciding to wait for another chance to outwit him, she put on the coat and fastened it across her chest. That was better; now she had acquired some protection; the padded sleeves would to some extent shield her from the knife if he used it, and if she were to shiver again, it would not be because she was cold. She curled her toes up on the cork-tiled floor. If she tried to kick him, bare feet would not do much damage. She must stay alert, watch for an opportunity if he relaxed his guard. Meanwhile, where was Peter? All the time she was straining her ears to catch a sound in the house, but she could hear only her own rapid breathing. She tried to control it, to draw in deep, even breaths and allow her pulse rate to slow.

'Take that look off your face,' said Mick, for to him the settling of her features as she strove for calm appeared like a sneer.

Marion did not understand what she had done to provoke him as Mick launched into what was, for him, a long speech.

'I know your sort. Think you're bleeding Lady Muck, don't you? "Would you like a cup of tea? It must be cold up that ladder. Thank you, my good man."

Marion had never addressed anyone as 'my good man' in her life, nor heard anyone else do so. The line from *Twelfth Night* about thanking heaven fasting for a good man's love shot into her mind with startling irrelevance and she smiled, but that was wrong too. Mick slapped her again, this time for laughing at him.

'Try laughing that one off,' he said, in the voice that made Beverley cry for mercy.

Marion was not smiling now. She caught the inside of her cheek between her teeth to counteract the sharp pain and help her to hold back the ready tears which had sprung by reflex into her eyes. What was in his mind? Why had he brought her downstairs? This was no ordinary burglary. Did he mean to rape her? To be violated by this delinquent boy, for so she thought of him, would be so obscene that she would lose every ounce of her self-respect. He would have to kill her first, she resolved, and she looked at him coolly, weighing him up. He had on a leather jacket, which hung open revealing the beginning of a beer belly above the tight waistband of his jeans as he leaned back against the wall, still pointing the knife at her. He could not be very old – twenty-two, perhaps. If the cards of his life had fallen another way, he might have gone into the Army, harnessing his physical energy into legitimate pursuits. She would try to think of him as a young soldier run amok, who whould eventually respond to authority.

'Would you like some cocoa?' she suggested. Cocoa was a comfort, a settler. If he let her make some, she might be able to think of a way to defeat him as she moved round the kitchen.

'All right, but shut up. No talking,' he said.

Marion crossed to the fridge and took out a bottle of milk. She fetched a pan from the cupboard and set it on the stove, making her movements measured and precise. As she went to the larder to fetch the tin of drinking chocolate, she felt in one of her anorak pockets to see if there was anything in it that might be useful. There were only a tenpence piece and a crumpled tissue. Patting her other side, she knew there was no potential weapon there, just a toffee.

She needed a spoon, however.

'This is sweetened already,' she said, displaying the tin. 'Do you like extra sugar?'

'Yes, two,' said Mick.

How slow she was, setting out the mugs and the sugar bowl. He saw the two teaspoons laid on the table but he had not seen Marion take a small stubby knife from the drawer and drop it into her pocket. As she did so, she took out the tissue to dab her cheek.

The knife gave her a surge of confidence until she noticed what was sticking out of Mick's jacket pocket as he turned to sit at the table. He had made her sit down first and had wedged her chair against the wall so that she could not suddenly spring to her feet.

It was Laura's hat, or its twin. Marion could see a piece of the plaid facing under the brim. She thought back quickly. He had not worn a hat when he was cleaning the windows, nor when he delivered her chair, and she had particularly noticed his curls when she met him in Merston with his small boy. She had decided then – correctly – that his hair was permed. Perhaps he'd got a hat because of the cold weather: but cheap rain hats were not lined with tartan. Could he have found Laura's somewhere? But how?

'There's some cake,' she said. 'Would you like a piece?'

'No,' said Mick.

'Why are you here?' she asked, trying to speak very calmly and evenly.

'To teach you a lesson, like that other bitch,' said Mick, tired of the tea-party atmosphere that was developing. 'Thinking all you've got to do is go to the police and they'll believe you against me. Setting a trap against me when I was only a couple of days late with my insurance.'

'What do you mean?' asked Marion, but as she spoke she felt a great wave of horror sweep physically over her from her scalp to her toes.

'Don't pretend you don't know. Careless driving, indeed! I'd as much right on the road as you had,' said Mick.

Even then Marion was reluctant to understand.

'Making me lose my job,' Mick went on.

Still Marion stared at him.

He was getting to her now.

'Reported me, didn't you?' he said. 'It was only a bit of fun but of course you had to go to the nick and they sent a copper round when I was in bed with my wife. Quite frightened little Cliffie, it did, having the law in like that in the middle of the night. Wanted my licence, didn't he? And my papers.'

Cold sweat washed over Marion as at last she accepted

what these words meant. This was the man who had buzzed her and Laura on their way back from *Giselle*. They had not known his identity but he had learned theirs. He had said he was going to teach her a lesson 'like that other bitch'. He had killed Laura and he meant to kill her. It was shock, not terrror, which now darkened Marion's eyes as she watched him drain the last of his chocolate from the mug she had bought in Liskeard. She would throw it away, smash it in pieces; no one else should ever again drink from that contaminated article. She put her hands under the table, ready to tip it up against him, hoping it would wind him for long enough to let her seize something heavy and hit him over the head.

But at that moment the back door opened and Peter came in. He was half-crying with cold, his jacket and hair covered in snow, but he tried to smile.

'Peter!' Marion made to get up but Mick pushed the table tight against her and she sat back, turning her face so that Peter should not see the cut on her cheek.

'I went for a walk in the moonlight and it started to snow,' Peter said, his voice rather unsteady. 'Hullo,' he said to Mick.

He'd gone for help and failed to find it, Marion thought, otherwise why had he come back? No one in any of the houses would have allowed him to return alone. Perhaps he had gone to the telephone box by the crossroads, but surely, if he had dialled 999, the police would have told him to wait where he was until they arrived? But there was no time now to wonder what had gone wrong; the tears were evidence enough of failure.

'Come in and get warm,' she said. 'I'll make you some chocolate. We were just having some.'

Would he take the cue, behave in a friendly way? And would Mick play along?

He had been just as startled by Peter's appearance as she was, and he let her get up to put on more milk.

To Peter, approaching the cottage from outside, the scene through the window had looked normal except for the hour at which it was taking place. He had seen Mick's

173

van parked in the lane and at first had thought it was something to do with the police. Perhaps Marion had woken and missed him and called them in. But police vans were usually white. Sometimes, though, they used others, for disguise, hiding in them when they were watching suspects. He looked fondly at this one, an old Morris Minor, kin to his own. A beam of light from the kitchen window slanted across the path as he trod softly in the snow. Through the window – unscreened because Mick had earlier drawn the blind – he observed his aunt and that man who had delivered the chair. Peter recognized him at once, sitting chatting at the table over hot drinks. It was a strange hour for a social call, but perhaps the man's van had broken down and he had come in to use the telephone or something like that. Peter knew you should not let anyone into your house whom you didn't know, especially at night, but this man wasn't a stranger.

He was too cold and miserable to wait outside until the visitor had gone, and besides, Marion wouldn't be angry in front of a third party.

Mick said nothing as Marion made the drink. She was about to tell Peter to take off his coat when she changed her mind. He had better stay dressed for outdoors because they might both need to run for their lives. The snow on his clothes was beginning to melt as he took his mug. Marion had gauged the temperature exactly so that it was just right to drink at once.

Mick had not spoken since Peter appeared. He had been trying to decide what to do with the boy.

There were two sturdy oak doors in the kitchen wall facing the stove. One led to the larder, a small room full of shelves laden with stores of which Mick had caught a glimpse when Marion fetched the chocolate. That would do at a pinch, but it had only a latch to close it. The other door was fitted with a strong bolt.

'What's behind that?' Mick asked Peter.

'It goes to the cellar,' said Peter.

'What's in there?'

'Not a lot. Some drink and things,' Peter said.

'Has it got another door?'

'No.'

'A window?'

'No.'

These were strange questions. As he answered them, Peter was suddenly aware of how motionless Marion was, standing over by the sink. The man was still, too, a hand behind his back. And why was Marion wearing her old anorak and not her dressing-gown? And how had she cut her face? There was blood all down her cheek.

'Show me,' said Mick.

Peter opened the cellar door. Steps dropped away sharply from the aperture – the reason it was kept bolted, in case it was carelessly opened and someone fell down them. There was blackness beyond.

'There's a light,' Peter said helpfully, and he reached out to turn it on.

The next moment he had been pushed through the door and was pitched down the stairs, taken so much by surprise that he had no time to attempt to save himself.

Above in the kitchen, Marion leaped at Mick as he thrust Peter through the cellar door. She drew out her small knife and struck out at Mick, but he stamped on her bare feet so hard that she fell back. Mick seized her wrist and forced her fingers apart so that she had to drop the knife.

'If you try anything else, the kid gets it,' Mick told her.

She believed him. She watched while he bolted the cellar door and she allowed him to tie her wrists together behind her back with a torn-up tea-towel. Then he ordered her to walk out to his van.

'I need shoes,' she said.

He was going to take her away, out of the place, leaving Peter who would then be safe. Someone would find him in the morning. There was air in the cellar, and light. It would be very frightening for him, but not fatal unless he had been badly hurt falling down the stairs. She could do nothing to help him now, and she did not think she could do much for herself if she were to be barefoot in the snow.

Neither did Mick. He kept her that way.

18

Mick bundled Marion into the van where he tied her legs together with more shredded tea-towel. She tensed her muscles, hoping that when she relaxed them the bonds would also slacken and allow her some movement. Then Mick shut the van doors, got into the driving seat and drove off.

She was not gagged, but what use would it be to scream? No other house was near enough for her to be heard, and if she made Mick angry he might go back and do something to Peter. She drew her body up into a ball to protect herself against the bumping she was sustaining as Mick drove fast through the village. It was still snowing, though not very hard, when they left the cottage. Mick had turned in the gateway, so she knew the direction they were following, but after some time she became confused about where they might be. Her worry was centred on Peter. Who would find him in the morning? The house would look normal from outside. Would anyone notice if her curtains were undrawn? No one would find it strange if she did not answer the telephone they would think she was out.

She must try to escape. That was the quickest way to help both Peter and herself, but it wouldn't be easy. This was a violent man who considered himself above the law. He had virtually admitted to killing Laura. Had she lain in the back of this van, just as Marion did now, at his mercy? Had she tried in vain to find a way to escape?

If they had not reported the buzzing incident, Laura might still be alive. Marion replaced this thought with anger at the police – or the court – she did not know which was to blame for taking so long to bring him to justice for the other offences of which he was accused. He should have been off the road by now.

But he wouldn't have gone to prison. He could still have sought vengeance.

Like Scarlett O'Hara, Marion decided not to think about that now. What were Mick's plans at the moment? Would he hit her – wound her in some way, as Laura had been injured before she was cast on to the railway line, and then do the same thing to her?

If he did, Peter would know who was guilty. Mick Harvey would be brought to account for his actions.

Marion began to work at the bonds which tied her, drawing her feet up, trying to pick at the knots with her cold fingers. The tea-towel Mick had used was very old; she might be able to tear the fabric apart.

Now that he was behind the wheel of his van Mick was thinking more calmly. His plan had gone all wrong when the kid appeared, but he'd make another. He didn't like talk; you could be trapped by folk who were clever at talking and it was easy to get confused and forget what you'd meant to do. But with an engine purring in front of you and four wheels driving you forwards, putting distance between you and them – the people who were out to get you and do you a bad turn – you had power. You were in charge.

He drove on through Poppleton and turned towards the motorway. London was where he was going, and on the way he'd get rid of the interfering cow in the back of the van.

He should have set fire to her house, as he'd planned. He'd meant to crisp her up thoroughly, but the kid had turned up. He'd intended to take her Fiesta but she'd made things go wrong. He should have done that – left the kid in the cellar and fired the van with her in it. He'd have been well away by now if he had.

Mick had reached this unsatisfactory point in his thoughts when the van's engine began to misfire as it laboured up a hill. On the far side of the long rise the road divided. To the left lay the loop to the motorway; to the right a lane passed through fields.

Marion heard Mick curse as the van juddered and

jerked. He was already in bottom gear; then, as it began to move more evenly, she sensed they were going downhill. Suddenly the van stopped and she heard the ratchet sound as the handbrake was fiercely applied.

Mick had run out of petrol again.

Marion had made no progress with untying her bonds. She lifted her head and saw Mick's dark bulk in the front of the van as he opened the door and got out. A gust of icy air blew in and the van moved again as Mick, from outside, leaned across the driver's seat, turned the steering-wheel to the right and released the hand-brake. He came round behind the van and pushed it to start it off down the hill. On it hurtled, gathering speed.

He saw it run through a hedge at the bottom and then, as it turned over, its lights went out.

He had no matches. He could not set it on fire.

Mick hesitated at the brow of the hill. It was a long way to walk to make sure she was dead, and he'd have to walk back up the hill to go to the motorway. After a crash like that, at such speed, she had to be dead, or hurt badly enough to die before anyone found her; anyway, she'd freeze to death by morning. With the kid locked up there was no one to give the alarm, and the wrecked van on a lonely road like this might not be seen for some time.

Mick left her.

PC Coates was in bed in his one-roomed flat with the girl-friend he planned to marry. He had tested her over the past year and she had never complained when he had had to stand her up because of extra duty, or was late for any date. She was cheerful and unflappable, and she enjoyed her food. He felt happy whenever he was with her and knew she would give him lovely children.

But tonight, instead of drifting into a dreamless sleep tucked close to her warm body, Coates chased an elusive thought. It had been there, a niggle, when he went home, the awareness of some very significant fact about which he should act without delay, but he could not think what it was. Coates mentally ran over his last actions before going off duty and hurrying back to the flat where Sue had already arrived, having let herself in with her key and started to prepare their meal. She was a nurse, and she lived in a hostel in Fordbridge.

Coates saw himself back at the station, making his report, reading the orders. The big case in the division at the moment was the mysterious death last Thursday of that woman who had been found on the railway line over at Hickling. The investigation was being conducted by officers from that area, but all stations were circulated with relevant information. She was one of the women who had made a complaint about Mick Harvey's reckless driving.

Coates sat up in bed as he realized what had been nagging away at his mind. He'd pushed it aside because he had wanted to get back to Sue. When Coates had spoken to him that morning, Mick Harvey had known that Mrs Burdock was one of the women who had reported him back in October and led to his being summonsed. How had he known her identity? The women had dropped their charges and Mick could not have learned her name from any police officer.

There would be no more sleep for Coates until he had obeyed the inner voice which instructed him to find the answer. He got out of bed carefully, not wanting to wake Sue, and dressed quickly. As he pulled on his uniform jacket – this was police business – she stirred and reached for him in the bed. Then she opened her eyes. Coates dropped on his knees beside her and stroked her long straight brown hair, which looked so neat tucked up under her cap in the ward but now, spread out on the pillow and smelling of lemon shampoo, tempted him to linger.

'I've got to go out, Sue,' he said. 'It's to do with that woman who was found on the railway line over Hickling way. I've just thought of a scoundrel who might be mixed up in it somehow, though it seems a long shot. I should have remembered it sooner and chased him up before coming home.'

'Oh dear,' Sue sighed. 'All right. Don't be long.'

'I don't want to go at all,' Coates replied. 'But it must be done.'

'I know,' said Sue.

At the door he paused.

'Will you marry me, Sue?' he asked her.

'After my finals, yes,' said Sue. 'I thought you'd never get around to asking.'

He heard her soft laugh as he closed the door.

In his own car, for another officer was using the patrol car he drove on duty, Coates went straight round to The Buildings. When he reached the street there was no sign of Mick's van. Coates got out of his Renault and went up to the Harveys' flat. Outside their door he saw a large shabby suitcase, and two carrier bags bound round with twine. He knocked and waited, then knocked again, harder, and called through the letter-box that it was the police outside. He heard no sound from within. Did the cases belong to the wife? Had she walked out at last and left her things here for collection?

He knocked again.

'Police. Open up,' he said, more firmly than he had spoken before.

Beverley had heard the first knock. She'd lain still in bed. That wasn't Mick; he would make much more noise; he'd fairly shout. Then she heard Coates's voice. Maybe Mr Duke had done as he'd threatened and rung the station, but they'd taken their time about coming. At last, when Coates called again, she turned on her light, put on her shabby pink dressing-gown and went to the door, opening it cautiously, leaving it on the chain which Jim had fitted. She peered out and saw Coates's serious face under its thatch of blond hair.

'Mick's not here,' she said.

'No. Well, can I come in for a minute, love?' Coates requested. 'It would be better to talk in private.'

Beverley unhooked the chain and let him in. She led the way to the sitting-room and bent down to light the gas fire.

'What's he done now?' she asked, and wondered if it was

very wicked of her to hope he had smashed himself up and was dead.

'I don't know that he's done anything else yet,' said Coates. 'But I want to ask him some questions. Do you know where he is?'

'No, and I don't want to,' said Beverley. 'I'm not letting him back in.'

'Does he know that?'

'Yes. I told him tonight, when he came home.'

'What time was that?'

'Oh, late. After midnight,' said Beverley. 'He couldn't get in because I'd had the locks changed. He made a dreadful noise. I thought Mr Duke from downstairs might have called you. He said he would if Mick didn't shut up.'

'That's not why I'm here,' said Coates. 'Never mind, love. It doesn't matter now. You go back to bed. Sorry I woke you.'

'I wish you'd get him and lock him up,' said Beverley bitterly. 'He'll find some way to get back at me if you don't.'

Coates hesitated.

'He's been cleaning windows lately, hasn't he?' he asked.

'Yes.'

'Where? Round the town?'

'Yes, and in the country parts. He had posters done,' said Beverley. 'Look, I'll show you.'

She went to the drawer where she had put the last leaflets and took one out which she gave Coates. Then her glance fell on the business ledger and small cash book. She took them out, too.

'Here,' she said. 'There's some addresses in this of where he went. I knew he ought to keep records because of tax but he didn't bother after the first week or two.'

Perhaps that was why the policeman was here. Mick hadn't filled up the right forms. But it was a strange time to call about something like that; more likely he hadn't been able to keep his hands off any stuff that was lying about where he was working.

Coates looked at the leaflet.

'This your phone number?' he asked.

Beverley shook her head.

'We've not got the phone,' she said. 'It's some friend of Mick's who takes messages for him.'

'I see.'

Coates turned over the pages of the ledger. The word *Didbury* sprang at him from the page and he saw the names Quilter and Burdock. He snapped the book shut.

'I'll take these, Mrs Harvey,' he said. 'You'll get a receipt in the morning. And while I'm about it, I'll take Mick's things, too. That's his case outside, isn't it?'

She nodded.

'What if he comes back for them?' she asked.

'You can tell him where he can find them,' Coates replied. 'You'll get a receipt for them, too.'

'I'm not bothered,' said Beverley. Then she shivered. 'He'll not leave Cliff,' she added. 'He'll come back for him.'

'I doubt it,' said Coates. 'Don't you fret, now. Take care of yourself and the kids.'

After he left, Beverley sat staring at the fire which hissed in a comforting manner. What was that all about? The bobby had looked closely at Mick's ledger and had gone all still for a second. There had been more on the telly that night about the railway woman, as the media were calling the poor soul who'd been run over by a train and killed. Beverley drew the newspaper out from under the settee cushion where she had put it only that morning. She stared at the dead woman's face.

Mick couldn't have done that, could he?

He might, if she'd somehow crossed him.

Beverley didn't want to believe it, not even of Mick, but it wasn't impossible. When she returned to bed at last, she felt very cold, chilled through with fright.

Down in his car, Coates looked at the ledger again. There was Mrs Burdock's name and address, mis-spelt and inscribed in ill-formed script. He looked at the poster on which Mick advertised his services, and at the telephone number printed below. Then he drove straight to the station, where, when the duty sergeant heard what he had to say, connection was very soon made with the officers investigating Laura Burdock's death and a call was put out for Mick's van. And for Mick.

It did not take long to trace the address whose telephone number was given on Mick's hand-out, and within a very short time two uniformed officers were ringing Rene's bell. They asked her if Mick was in her house, and when she said he was not, they wanted to know when she had last seen him. She told them the truth.

Coates was some time making his report, and after communicating with Detective Superintendent Grainger's headquarters it was arranged that he should deliver to them the items he had taken from the Harveys' flat. Grainger himself was there when Coates arrived. He listened to Coates's description of Mick's van: an old Morris Minor, the same type as those once used by the Post Office and long since superseded. It was painted dark blue. Blue paint over red, Grainger thought. He paid particular attention to Coates's assessment of Mick Harvey; Coates described the bruises he had seen on Beverley Harvey's face and mentioned her fear of her husband.

'You did well,' Grainger said at last.

'Sir,' ventured Coates at this.

'Yes?'

'If there's anything in this, there's the other lady. Mrs Quilter, her name is. Harvey didn't reply to the summons. The two ladies hadn't gone ahead with their complaint but he didn't seem to know that. He bore a grudge, sir.'

'You think Mrs Quilter may be at risk?' Grainger looked at Coates's pink, earnest face. 'If he's our man, you could be right,' he said. 'We'd better send someone out there.'

19

Peter had fallen the full length of the cellar steps. During the descent he experienced the suspension of belief common in moments of peril when the person involved feels as if they are observing their danger from outside, as though in a dream. He was bruised and shaken, but not seriously injured, and his immediate reaction was fright mingled with baffled rage. Was it some sort of joke? He sat at the foot of the stairs trying not to cry and expecting the door to open and his aunt to come pattering down after him.

Nothing happened.

At last Peter picked himself up and groped his way in the dark to the top of stairs where he pounded on the door with his fists.

'Let me out! Let me out!' he yelled. His aunt could not possibly approve of such a rotten trick. Why didn't she open the door? He made his fists sore with the force he used.

Finally he paused, partly from exhaustion and partly to listen to what was happening in the kitchen. He could not distinguish a sound. He banged again and shouted, then stopped to listen once more. The silence beyond the door was total. Perhaps that man and his aunt had moved to another room? The strangeness of Aunt Marion wearing an anorak, not her dressing-gown over her nightdress, combined with the cut on her face, now registered and with it the recognition that the man in the kitchen, although known to them both, was up to no good. Aunt Marion would never have let him be shut in the cellar if she could have prevented it; she would have thought it a poor sort of joke. Perhaps she'd been locked up too and the man was robbing the house?

He'd got to get out. That was the first thing to do.

Snivelling a bit, his nose running as much as his eyes, Peter felt for the cellar light switch on the wall at the top of the stairs, and at last he found it. He cheered up fast when he was no longer in the dark, and he went down the pitted, old stone steps again to look for something to use to break down the door.

Marion kept a few bottles of wine in the cellar, and spare flower vases and other things she used rarely. There was no handy iron bar or hammer lying about; no poker; not even a golf club. In a corner there was a large tin trunk with Uncle George's name and regiment written on it in chipped white paint, and some suitcases, an upright chair with a leg missing, a dressmaker's dummy, a folding screen with the hessian cover torn and partly detached, and a wooden clothes-horse. Peter opened the trunk. Inside was a large, heavyweight polythene bag containing some khaki garments: Uncle George's uniform. Peter lifted it out and found another bag which held his navy-blue mess kit. In a third bag was his full dress uniform. In other, smaller bags were the various caps that went with these outfits. Further down, wrapped in newspaper inside yet more polythene, was a long rigid object.

Peter lifted it out and undid the wire tie which secured the end. He pulled the wrapped bundle out of the polythene and unrolled the newspaper. Inside, in its chased scabbard, was Uncle George's sword. Marion had been unable to decide what to do with these relics and had postponed action.

Peter took the sword out of its scabbard. It was quite heavy. The blade shone in the weak light that came from the single bulb suspended from the ceiling. He tested it with his thumb. It was very sharp. Carrying the sword, still unsheathed, in both hands, Peter went back up the stairs and looked at the door, which opened towards him. He knew that the bolt on the kitchen side was a strong one.

Forcing it and the latch would not be easy. It might be better to tackle the hinges. They also looked strong, and the sword was so long that it would be difficult to force its tip under the metal. If only he'd got a penknife to use on the screws, which were old and pitted. Peter held the sword by the hilt and poked at the top hinge with the tip of the blade, digging at the wood of the door frame; gingerly, he slid one hand along the blade to steady it. Luckily for him, woodworm had once attacked the surround and, though no longer active, had left the old oak soft and allowed the screws to move. The top hinge came away without very much effort, though the door was still held in position by the bolt and the lower hinge. But now Peter was able to work the sword into the gap and behind the second hinge, and he could put his weight on the hilt as he pulled. The blade of a lesser weapon might have snapped under the strain, but this one did not; the lower hinge tore away from the woodwork and Peter almost fell back down the stairs as it gave, held by just one remaining screw. Holding his breath, Peter cautiously propped the sword against the wall and gripped the hinge. The screw was too rusted to be turned by hand but he was able to pull it away from its worn housing. The bolt, however, held the door rigidly across the aperture, and he was still a prisoner. This was nearly too much for him and tears started up again. He tried pulling the door towards him but he was not strong enough to break the bolt and there was little room to manoeuvre on the narrow top step. Almost in despair, he kicked at the door where it held on his right. The action was inspired by frustrated rage, but then he realized that, as shown on television, this was what the police did when they broke into a house to make an arrest. Perched on the top step, he could not aim at the right level, but in the end, after a great deal of kicking, with intervals for tears and despondency, the strength of the actual bolt forced the screws out of the socket end where it was secured, and the latch bent sufficiently to let Peter open the door wide enough to get out.

He stood in the kitchen at last. The light was on – Mick had not switched it off when he took Marion out – and the house was silent, but Peter went all over it, seeking his aunt in every room and in every cupboard, even the oak chest in the hall. She was not to be found, and when he saw the telephone wires pulled out of the wall in her bedroom, any last doubts he had about Mick were swept away.

Mick never liked walking at the best of times. He liked walking through snow still less as he trudged back to the fork where the road divided, and took the left turning which would lead him to the motorway. His cheap ankle boots, bought for style, not for strength, were not waterproof and soon his feet were damp as well as cold. He pulled Laura's hat out of his pocket to put on his head, forgetting he had packed Marion's trinkets inside it, and then had to scrabble about in the snow collecting them up. He put them in his pocket and plodded on towards the motorway, wearing Laura's hat with its distinctive tartan lining showing under the brim and with his coat collar turned up.

He must have transport. Without that, Mick was unable to function. Sooner or later he would surely come to a house where there would be a vehicle garaged or parked outside, but as he walked on there was no sign of human habitation. Mick tried to remember the area. When you were in a car, you soon hit the motorway and he had never troubled to notice landmarks. It seemed to Mick that he had been walking for several hours when at last he came to an extended roundabout above the motorway link and saw, beside it, the lights of an all-night filling station.

The snow had almost ceased falling as he reached it. He could see the bright forecourt, the small shop and pay area, the self-service pumps. On this bitter night few motorists were out and the attendant, who had not had a customer for more than an hour, was dozing over his paper. Normally there were two people on duty together, but one of tonight's pair, on his way to work, had been involved in a collision in the icy conditions and had not turned up, so the man was alone. He did not hear Mick open the door, and his eyes were still closed when Mick plunged the knife he had taken from Marion's kitchen into his back. It slid in so easily: Mick had been told during his Borstal spell that providing you didn't hit a rib it was like slicing butter. He had also been told that a person could walk about although fatally wounded, even run for a hundred yards before a final collapse, but this did not happen now; the man – he was bald and fat, the father of four – slid to the ground with a gurgle. Mick kicked him out of the way under the counter and was sitting in his place when ten minutes later a car stopped to fill up.

He had taken all the money out of the till, and had withdrawn the knife from his victim, the blade wiped on a rag he found handy. Mick knew how to turn on the pumps; he had watched it being done only the other day. He was ready to act when the customer, having filled his car, came in with a ten-pound note. He was a big man in his forties, and Mick hesitated. With the counter between them, he could miss the target.

The man laid the note down on the counter.

'What a night,' he said. 'I don't envy you this job in such weather. Still, you're snug enough in here.' The shop was warmed by a portable gas heater. 'I'll just go round the back,' he added, and swung out to go to the advertised toilet.

Mick didn't wait. He was in the man's car – a Volvo 343 – in seconds. The car had no lock on its filler cap and the man had not had one fitted; his keys were in the dash.

He deserved to be done.

The Volvo's owner heard the car start up and move off; there was no other sound in the night. He came running on to the forecourt shaking his fists and took a full minute to calm down enough to realize that it was the pump attendant who was the thief. Mick had not thought of disconnecting the telephone in the pay-booth and the man was able to report his loss at once. He did not go round the counter while he waited for the police, but they did, and they found the real attendant.

The Volvo driver had taken scant heed of the man he had assumed to be in charge. He had been wearing a fawn hat of some kind, he remembered, and a black leather jacket, but he had barely looked up as he took the banknote.

He'd worn gloves, the man recollected; he hadn't thought much of that at the time, for the night was cold, but it was unusual, perhaps, when handling money, and the small shop was well heated. Of course he would co-operate over a photofit picture if the police thought that would help but he really had no idea where to begin a description. All that had been in his mind was his need for a leak and the desire to get home as soon as he could.

PC Coates knew that a police car would soon be in Didbury making sure Mrs Quilter was safe, but he decided to go home from Grainger's headquarters by way of the village, even so. The nearest patrol car might be delayed; on nights like this motorists frequently got into difficulties and had to be helped, and country roads could soon get blocked in the icy conditions.

He did not know which was Lime Tree Cottage, and when he reached the village he drove slowly along the main street looking for names on gates and doors. Not every house was labelled. He thought about ringing someone's doorbell to ask where Mrs Quilter lived, but it was past three o'clock in the morning and it would be better if he could find the place for himself. The village was quiet, the snow no longer falling, not masking two sets of tyre tracks in the road. It looked as though only two cars had passed that way during the night. Coates drove on slowly and saw a shaft of light ahead: despite the hour, someone was up.

As he drew to a halt outside a long, low timbered cottage, Coates saw that both sets of tracks stopped here. He parked on the left side of the road so that the rear of his car with its red light was presented to his colleagues if they approached from the same direction as he had done and walked across to the gate, which was open. Shining his torch, he read the name neatly painted in black on the gate-post: *Lime Tree Cottage*. He saw that a vehicle had turned in the gateway and gone back through the village, and halved his estimate of the night's traffic flow. Several sets of footmarks could be distinguished in the snow, some of them blurred by the subsequent fall; one set, however, stood out clearly: the ridged trail of a child's or a small person's boots walking away from the cottage. Coates followed them round to their source by the back door, taking care to keep his own large feet well away from the rest of the marks.

Peter had shut the kitchen door behind him. Before trying it, Coates looked through the window. He saw an empty room with three mugs on the table. All looked tranquil. From where he stood, the cellar door was concealed. Coates did not expect the back door to be unlocked but he tried it, instinctively holding the knob lightly with his own gloved hand. The door opened, and once inside, Coates immediately saw the damaged cellar door, the shot bolt.

He stood at the top of the cellar steps and shouted.

'Anyone there?' he called. The light was on below, and when there was no answer, Coates went down the stairs.

Peter had taken the sword with him, reasoning that if he met Mick he would need a weapon. Coates found the empty scabbard, worked out what it was and thought it could be Mick Harvey who was thus armed. He was officially off-duty and had no radio with him. He made sure there was no one in the house, searching every room quickly. He saw Peter's note, but it made no sense to Coates who did not know of the boy's existence. He left it where it was. The disturbed bed in the main bedroom and the telephone wire ripped from the wall added to the evidence of serious trouble.

Coates went outside and examined the footmarks so revealingly left in the snow. The blurred tracks ended among the confused tyre marks, which indicated that whoever had made them had gone off in the vehicle which had turned in the gateway. The single, sharper set went on up the road in the same direction and whoever made them had not been gone long. Perhaps Mrs Quilter was a small woman.

Coates got into his car and went on down the road to

turn, not wanting to add his own tracks to those in the cottage entrance. Headlights full on, he drove back, following the footprints but avoiding the existing tyre marks.

The footprints went straight through the village and turned down the Poppleton road. A short way further on they passed between some large entrance gates. Coates followed them up a curving drive which led to a big square house and he saw an extraordinary sight: a small figure had turned to face him, a long sword held upright in both hands, its blade glinting in the headlights. Coates drove on, very slowly. The sword wavered in the holder's grasp but its bearer stood firm, legs slightly apart. Coates dipped his lights, turned off the engine and got out of his car. Peter retreated two steps; then he saw Coates's uniform. He dropped the sword in the snow and his two arms fell to his sides as Coates, at last certain that this was a child, approached.

'Whatever's been happening, son?' he asked, putting out his hands to grasp the boy's shoulders. He could feel Peter trembling.

'He's got Aunt Marion. That man's got Aunt Marion,' Peter said. 'The van man. He locked me in and took her away.' To his utter chagrin, he burst into tears as he spoke.

Amazingly, though, the policeman seemed to understand without a great deal of explanation. He even understood that this was Tom's house, where Peter had gone for help because the telephone wasn't working at home. He knew about Laura, too, although he wasn't one of the policemen Peter had met before. He rang Tom's bell and banged on the door until at last Tom came and let them in, then said he must use the telephone at once. Tom took Peter into the study, where it seemed he'd been when they arrived; he was still dressed. The electric fire was on and there were bottles on the table. Tom made him swallow some brandy before he would listen to what Peter had to say; it made him cough and splutter but it sent a warm fire right through his middle and down to his toes. Tom also produced a not-

very-clean handkerchief so that Peter could blow his nose.
By the time Coates joined them he had stopped crying.
Now the policeman wanted to hear a full account of his
adventures. Peter glossed over his reasons for being out
late and simply said he'd been to his den in the copse,
which satisfied Coates. Boys did these things.

'We'll soon find your auntie, lad, never fear,' he said.
'You stay here with Mr Burdock now. Keep each other
company, eh? I'm going off, but I'll be back, and Mr
Grainger's on his way. You know him, don't you, Mr
Burdock?' he asked Tom, who nodded. Peter had called
Mick the van man and had said that he recognized him
because he had delivered a chair to his aunt at half-term.
He had not known the man's name. He had also described
the van, an old Morris Minor. 'I expect you saw the tyre-
tracks in the snow, didn't you, Peter?' Coates said. 'I'm
going off after them. I'll maybe catch up with them before
long.'

'You can take the sword if you like,' said Peter. 'It
belonged to Uncle George.'

Coates did not think a sword would be a great help in
arresting Mick Harvey, which he meant to do very shortly.
Mick was unlikely to be armed, and if he were, a sword
would be no great protection against a sawn-off shotgun
or other firearm. However, it still lay in the snow outside
and must be retrieved.

'Thanks,' he said. 'I'll take it.'

Burdock had been swaying about when he opened the
door, but he had sobered up rapidly as he tried to follow
Peter's very strange story. No wonder he'd got drunk, poor
sod, thought Coates, who knew only that Burdock's wife
had been savagely killed but nothing of the puzzle she had
left behind her. He'd have to take a grip on himself now
and do something about the kid, give him something to
eat and get him warm, for a start. If he couldn't think of
that by himself, the super would when he arrived.

But Grainger was somewhat delayed. There had been
an emergency call from a motorway filling-station on his

patch, where a car had been stolen. When police arrived at the scene, a man had been found stabbed.

It was proving to be quite a night.

20

Mick, in the blue Volvo, raced round the roundabout and roared off towards London leaving the filling-station a blur of light far behind as he whooped for joy, pressing his foot down hard on the accelerator. Gritting lorries had passed that way earlier but the road surface was treacherous; however, there was very little traffic about as he sped on through the spectral white countryside. After his old van, it was a treat to be driving a lively car and it rode well; the heater played warm air comfortingly around him. The radio was tuned to some concert or other, a foreign station. Mick twiddled the knobs and found one that was relaying pop music. He shot past a trundling lorry, eating up the road, putting miles between him and the scene he had left. It seemed as if he was almost alone in the world.

A police traffic car picked him up because he was going so fast. Blue light flashing, it set off in pursuit, unable to get up close enough for the driver to read the number. But a call had gone out for the stolen Volvo when the police had reached the filling station and seen that the thief was a killer. The pursuing car's driver and his partner soon knew whom they were chasing.

When Mick saw the police car come up behind him, he drove even faster, the tyres slurring in the slush but the Volvo holding the road as he pushed it to its limits. There was more traffic about now as the motorway turned into dual carriageway through a built-up area. Mick swerved in and out of vehicles in front of him, passing wherever there was space, missing a pick-up truck by a whisker as he overtook on the wrong side.

Traffic lights lay ahead. Mick shot across the first set at red and at the next turned off into a street which in daytime was so busy that it was impossible to traverse at any speed. The police car was held up by two law-abiding citizens who had stopped at the lights and then, as it pulled out to pass them, by a car legitimately crossing ahead. By the time it had turned to follow Mick he had made another turn himself and was haring down the side streets among a sleeping conurbation of houses and apartment blocks.

He emerged at another major crossing and took the motorway again, this time going west. The police car had not reappeared in his mirror when he left the Volvo across the carriageway with its doors open and its lights full on. He seized the keys as he ran off; they might be useful.

Mick was high on excitement as he raced down a street past some shops. His feet left tracks in the snow so he ran in the gutter. They'd be after him soon, he hadn't got long to give them the slip. It was a great shame to give up such a good car with its tank half-full.

Mick hurried on, turning left and then right past lighted shops and dark ones, and past tenement houses. By the time the police had penetrated the area in any strength he had slipped round the back of a public house, long closed and the landlord asleep with his takings under the mattress. Mick used his knife on the padlock securing the door of the ladies' toilet which was in the yard at the rear, and which the landlord kept locked after hours against vandals.

Mick shut himself into a cubicle. No one came to disturb him, and though it was exceedingly cold and uncomfortable, he knew he would be safe there till morning.

He must have dozed off. Mick was suddenly aware of the quiet sounds of Sunday: the first cars, a distant church bell. He was cold and cramped; his feet had dried off in the Volvo but had been soaked again during his run through the streets, and his jeans were sodden, but he had escaped. In fact, the police searching for him had thought he must live in the district and had gone to ground. It was some time before his identity was known.

Mick, the night's euphoria now dispersed, was as nearly

miserable as he ever allowed himself to be without doing something about it, usually at someone else's expense. Well, he had money now, and with that he could buy some comfort. He left his uncomfortable, dank, sour-smelling shelter and headed off in what he thought was the direction for central London. He wore Laura's hat, pulled well down, and he still had on his gloves. He would not have left a print anywhere, he thought with complacence, forgetting that he had taken one off when helping himself from the till. Now he'd just vanish. They would never catch him. He felt no remorse for his attack on an innocent stranger, just as he felt none for what he had done to Laura and Marion. They had all got in his way.

Mick had been walking for some time when he saw a thin man on a bicycle come out of a side road and pedal slowly ahead of him. The man wavered on the slippery road surface, where frozen slush overlaid by new snow lay in ridges. He wore a long black raincoat and had cycle clips round the ends of his dark trousers. Mick followed him, wanting the cycle.

The man was a Roman Catholic priest on his way to take Mass at a nearby church. Mick watched him wheel the bicycle round to the back of the church and he saw the man's flock arrive, mostly on foot though a few had cars. Fancy turning out for that rigmarole in this weather, Mick thought, as he understood what was happening.

He decided not to take another car just yet, and controlled his impulse to seize the bike straight away, waiting until no more people seemed to be entering the church, which he watched from a bus shelter opposite. Then he went where the priest had gone. The cycle was not to be seen, but there was a side door leading into the vestry. Mick listened and then cautiously opened it: there was the bike, not even padlocked, just asking for someone to take it.

He wheeled it away and pedalled on up the road till he came to an underground station, where he caught the first train into London that came along. He was safe; he had got right away and no one would find him now. The kid might put the finger on him for that Mrs Quilter when she was found, but no one would link him with anything else.

The cycle which Mick had left at the underground station entrance was retrieved by a passing boy who went for a joy-ride on it and then dumped it; its next finder sold it for twelve pounds – it was too old and rusty to be worth any more – and its true owner never saw it again.

Marion had been unable to protect herself as the van gathered speed, hurtled down the hill and careered through a hedge into a field, just missing a tree. It made a lot of noise as it crashed through the short, twiggy hawthorn and bumped over the frozen, snow-covered ground before rolling over and ending on its side.

Marion had drawn her knees up to her chest but she could cling to nothing for support and as the van turned over, she went with it, prepared for agony, prepared even for death.

She hit her head and was showered with broken glass from the shattered windscreen and windows, but most of that fell on the two seats in front which to some extent shielded her. A petrol can hit her; she banged her sides and her elbows. When the van stopped moving she lay still, sure that she must be injured but feeling no serious pain. She tried moving her limbs; confined though they were, she could do it; it seemed that nothing was broken.

There was silence around her. The van's engine had stopped before the mad rush down the hill and there were no instant flames. Marion waited for Mick to appear. She understood what he had done: the van had broken down and he had pushed it to start its momentum. Now he'd come to make sure that this incomplete action would have done the job intended; someone who had put a still-living woman on a railway line wouldn't be satisfied unless he had made sure of her, too. He wouldn't be long, and he'd use that knife.

She set about trying to free herself before he arrived. Her arms were still tied behind her back; they and her shoulders ached but she forgot that as she groped about for any sharp object which might help her. She was lying on the van's side and could feel the plastic pail near her feet. Her hands met the rubber-flanged scraper which Mick had used on the windows. The rubber blade was held in a metal grip. Marion worked away with her fingers which were clumsy because they were so cold; she tried to detach the rubber and expose the blade, hoping to use it to cut the linen binding her wrists together. She did not succeed, but she managed to edge the scraper under the knot and to work the fabric against the handle. It took her a long time to wear it apart and her wrists and arms ached almost unbearably by the time she won through, but when Mick had not arrived after the first anxious minutes she gained heart; perhaps he wasn't returning after all.

She rubbed her arms to restore circulation to her weary muscles and then tackled the bands round her legs. She was tied at the knees and the ankles, and blood had soaked into both sets of bonds; her body had been protected by the anorak but her bare legs had been peppered with flying glass. She ignored that as she worked away to free herself. The knots had pulled tight; she had to use the scraper again, but now she knew that it could be done.

The next thing was to get out of the van. It had rocked alarmingly when she moved to sit up, and she dared not climb over into the front to escape through the uppermost door; she would never be able to climb out of there without help, and to go through the windscreen would mean being cut still more. She edged cautiously towards the double doors at the rear and drew her legs up to kick at them. Her feet were bare, so she tried to use her heels. The worn doors gave at once and she fell out into the snow, where she lay for a few seconds drawing in lungfuls of icy night air before struggling to her feet. She was chilled through and very stiff, and she had no idea where she was as she looked across the white landscape palely showing against the dark sky. There was not a light in sight. They seemed to have been driving for hours, but that could have been her imagination because of the horror of the situation. Now a new fear came into her mind. What if Mick Harvey, thinking she was disposed of, had gone back to Didbury to deal with Peter? It would take him some time to walk there, so he might not have arrived yet, but if he did, he would take her car; he knew it was there in the garage, and he could soon find her keys. He might even take Peter with him to use as a hostage.

It was no use staying here, getting colder with every minute; she must seek help.

Would her feet drop off with frostbite if she walked barefoot through the snow? She thought about tearing up her bedjacket to provide some wrapping, but decided the wool would soon get so wet that she would be no better off, and at least it, combined with her anorak, was keeping the worst cold from her body. Then she remembered the sacking that had been in the van and which must have helped to protect her during the crash. She found two thick, scratchy sacks and put one leg in each, like enormous socks. Thus garbed, she set off across the field, holding the sacks up and following the trail left by the van, blundering through the hedge and turning uphill the way they had come.

It was a weird progress, the land greyish white and still, not totally dark because of the snow. In time she must surely meet a landmark she could identify, if not a house, she told herself, drawing the old anorak round her, clutching the sacks. She had felt blood trickling down her legs and knew they were cut; in a detached way she wondered what had been in the sacks, what infection might enter her wounds. Her progress was slow as she slid her feet over the ground.

She had walked more than a mile when she saw the lights of a car on the road ahead. At first she thought it was Mick returning to complete his mission; if it was, he would see her at once; there was nowhere to hide. But when the car stopped, she found it was driven by a police officer who knew who she was and why she was there, and who told her that Peter was safe.

So he had somehow raised the alarm, Marion thought,

as for the first time in her life she almost fainted. The policeman saw what was happening and helped her as she leaned forward in his car, sitting beside him in the front with the heater full on blasting warm air over her cold legs and feet. He took off his jacket and wrapped it round her.

'Mick Harvey killed Laura Burdock,' said Marion.

'I know,' Coates replied. 'Don't worry. We'll get him.'

He took her to hospital and as soon as she was safely receiving medical care, he reported what she had told him during their journey.

Because of his report, a name could be put to the man who had made the attack at the filling-station only two miles from where Marion had been found. There could not be two such villains about in such a small area on such a night. The various sets of prints on the till had yet to be separated into those of the attendant and his colleagues, and others who might belong to the assailant.

The police ran a check on Mick Harvey. His record was uncovered, and his fingerprints tallied with some on the till.

A warrant was out for the arrest of Mick Harvey on a charge of robbery with violence. The stabbed man was in intensive care, in a very critical state. Journalists, summoned to a briefing by Detective Superintendent Grainger, picked up the inference: if the victim died, the charge would be murder.

At this stage, Grainger disclosed nothing about Mick Harvey's involvement with Laura Burdock's death. He had as good as admitted his guilt to Marion Quilter, but hard evidence was needed to prove what had happened. It would soon be found: his van lay on its side in a snow-covered field; it would be removed to be examined, and its paint could be matched with the chips found on the dead woman's clothing. Other traces of her might remain in the van; even a dot as small as a dust-mote could be of significance.

While Grainger was setting up the investigation into

the motorway incident, Detective Inspector Masters and
Detective Sergeant Norris had gone out to Didbury, where
a patrol officer was on guard at Lime Tree Cottage
awaiting their coming. On the way they called at Clyde
House, where they found Peter wrapped in a rug in front
of the electric fire in Tom's study. He seemed rather dazed
but said he was perfectly well and that Mick had not hurt
him. He had bumped himself a bit when he fell down the
cellar steps and his legs were bruised, but he had been
dressed in his padded jacket and thick corduroy trousers
which had protected him from grazes and cuts.

The main concern of both Peter and Tom was for
Marion, and while Masters was there, Coates telephoned
from the hospital to say she had been found and was safe;
she had some cuts which needed attention and she would
be kept there for what was left of the night.

'What were you doing out of doors, Peter?' Masters
asked.

'I've got a den. I went out there,' said Peter, and
Masters, like Coates, accepted the explanation. 'I'm sorry,'
Peter added.

Masters thought it was lucky indeed that Peter had set
forth on his nocturnal escapade; who knew what might
have happened if he had not surprised Harvey by returning
when he did?

'Can you keep Peter for the rest of the night, Mr
Burdock?' Masters asked. 'Or is there a neighbour – ?'

'Oh, please let me stay,' said Peter.

'Of course you can,' Tom assured him.

'I can ask for a woman police officer to come out,'
Masters offered.

'Whatever for?' asked Tom. 'I think Peter and I can look
after each other all right. Can't we?' he added to Peter,
who nodded.

Masters and Norris left them going upstairs together to
find a bedroom for Peter among the several available, and
something to wear, for as Tom pointed out to the boy, he
had not brought his pyjamas. Masters heard Peter laugh;

such a positive sound could not have been heard in that house since Thursday.

Tom took Peter to the yellow spare room, which was nearest the bedroom he had shared with Laura.

'I don't have to have a bath, do I?' Peter asked. 'I've had one already tonight.'

'Not unless you're still cold,' Tom said. 'If you are, it would warm you up.'

'I'm quite warm, thank you,' said Peter politely. Then he giggled. 'I think I'm a bit drunk. That brandy's made me go woozy.'

'Never mind,' said Tom, and added, 'are you too young for it?'

'I don't think so,' said Peter. 'Aunt Marion gave me some, too.'

'If you were older, I'd give you some more, to make you sleep,' said Tom.

He led Peter into the main bedroom.

'You hadn't been to bed,' Peter said.

'No.' Tom had not been able to face a repeat of the previous night's misery, when there had seemed to be no future. He had hidden his face in the silky softness of Laura's nightdress and had told himself that she was lost to him anyway, just as his mother, through whatever cause, had forfeited the love of his father. The pattern was set, and he could take the same way out.

Now he put morbid thoughts away and marched forward to open a drawer. He pulled out a blue sweater of Laura's. 'Here, how about this?' he suggested. 'It's smaller than a pair of my pyjamas would be. You could wear that as a top, and what about these for bottoms?' He had opened another drawer and seen a pair of cotton shorts Laura wore in the garden. 'You're thinner than Laura,' he frowned.

Peter was pleased at the thought of wearing these garments in bed.

'They're fine,' he said. They would bring Laura nearer, make him think that she wasn't really dead, after all.

By now he was reeling with fatigue and the effects of the

brandy. He pulled off his clothes and put on his new sleeping attire, almost asleep before he crawled into bed.

Tom was not used to children and he had known minimal parental cherishing himself as a boy. He stood over Peter, hesitant. Then a dim memory came to him and he bent to tuck in the blankets.

'Sleep well, old man,' he said, and patted the small bump of shoulder under the quilt.

'Night,' Peter mumbled.

Tom left the door open and the landing light on. He went into his own room and undressed, and he took Laura's nightdress from under the pillow and put it into a drawer. Then he climbed into bed, turned his back to its centre, and closed his eyes.

21

Mick had left the train at Earl's Court. He walked about till he found a café that was open. He felt better after a hot meal and several cups of sweet tea.

He'd got enough money to last for some time, and he had the Quilter woman's bank card. During his long wait in the toilet, he had counted the loot from the filling station. There were over three hundred pounds in cash. Unfortunately a lot of people had paid for their petrol by cheque or account card, which had deprived him of some gain from his night's exercise.

Sauntering along, looking in the windows of closed shops, Mick told himself that with money you could do anything. He could drop his old identity, say goodbye to the dull past and begin a new life with a new name. He stared at packets of pasta in a small grocery shop and they seemed to sway in front of his eyes. The large meal was combining with shortage of sleep to make him drowsy. He must get his head down somewhere.

Mick had been to London often enough, but he had never stayed overnight, though he had left amusement arcades and bars in the small hours before going home to Merston. That was when he still lived at home, before he was married and before his mother had left the district. He'd even brought Beverley up once, but she'd spoiled the evening as usual; she'd felt sick. It was when Cliffie was coming. Well, now he must find a bed. There'd be plenty of hotels around here, Mick thought, and with visions of luxury accommodation in his mind, he started to look for one. The receptionist at the first place he tried took one look at him, in his jeans and leather coat and Laura's hat, and with his unshaven face and no luggage, and said there were no vacancies, but eventually he found a place where for twenty-five pounds a night he could have a room. As he had no case with him, he had to pay in advance.

Mick was soon in bed, between rough drip-dry sheets, unwashed and naked. While radio news bulletins informed the nation that he was wanted by the police, he slept dreamlessly, having signed himself in as Joe Smith.

At Clyde House on that Sunday morning, Peter woke first. Usually he was alert in an instant and ready to spring out of bed, but today his instinct was to pull the bedclothes tight round his ears and sink once again into the safety of oblivion. But sleep wasn't safe: he had had a frightening dream. It was something about being chased through a copse by a monster who was going to throw him into a pit. The dream faded as he looked round the unfamiliar room, where the flowered curtains were drawn but were pale enough to reflect the light from outside. Everything was still and silent. Peter sat up, wondering what time it was.

Laura's perfectly appointed spare bedroom had a clock on the bedside table; it was a quartz one and so had continued to function despite the events of the past days; it was now ten-fifteen.

Goodness! What a time to wake up!

Peter got out of bed and went along to the bathroom.

When he emerged, Cleo was outside on the landing; she wagged her tail and made snuffling sounds indicative of pleasure at seeing him, and he patted her big heavy head.

'Good old girl. Come on, then,' he said, as she followed him into his bedroom where he began to dress as fast as he could, folding up Laura's sweater and shorts and placing them neatly on the bed. As he did this, he wondered about Mick. Had he been caught yet, or was he wandering about the district, unable to get away because he had smashed up his van? That was an uncomfortable thought, and fast behind it came another: Peter had left the book which Laura had given him in the Morris Minor.

He must rescue it. It would get damp in the car, as his comics had, and anyway, it was special and precious. The fact that he had forgotten it made him feel bad; it was a sort of betrayal of Laura.

Tom had probably been up for hours, Peter thought, but when he looked round the half-open door and peered into the main bedroom, the curtains were still drawn and he could just distinguish a large hump in the big bed. Faint snores could be heard.

Grown-ups often slept late at weekends. Mummy and Geoffrey did, and waiting for them to wake up, Peter had spent hours watching television in their apartment. There were masses of stations to choose from in America, and it was company of a sort.

He tiptoed away. He felt rather hungry, so he went into the kitchen and helped himself to bran flakes. They tasted quite like Weetabix really, he thought, stirring them round in a sea of milk. This was his second breakfast at Clyde House and he sighed with a weary sadness at its cause. His appetite suddenly vanished, and he poured the unwanted milky cereal down the sink. His boots and anorak were still in Tom's study, where he had taken them off last night, or rather early today. He put them on, and as Cleo saw these preparations she started to fuss round him.

'Well, Cleo, do you want to come for a walk?' Peter

asked her. 'I suppose you should go for a run, at least. All right, then. We'll probably be back before Tom wakes up.'

He found her lead; although she was obedient and usually kept to heel if so instructed, Laura always took it in case they met other dogs. Then they set off together towards the copse.

The sound of the front door closing woke Tom. Peter had gone out that way, giving it a good bang from outside and testing it to make sure it was fast, in case Mick Harvey was still around. Then he set off through the snow. More than an inch had fallen during the night, enough to transform the countryside into a Christmas card scene. Snow was fun in the country, thought Peter as he scuffed it up round his boots. He might make a snowman later. He strode on through the bright winter day; the sky was blue and the sun shone, and the snow was powdery as he stamped his way forward. Now the brave explorer of the previous night made headway, his husky dogs turned into one lumbering Labrador. Peter ran and skipped and tried to slide.

When he reached the car, he ushered Cleo into the back where she stretched out on the rear seat. The book was quite safe. He had read a lot of it now; he liked the story about the Springfield Fox. Perhaps there were foxes here in this wood. He was looking at the picture of Vix when he heard a sound outside the car and a shadow fell across the window beside him. For an instant Peter was terrified; he could see nothing through the thick frost that covered the glass and he thought it was Mick Harvey. The driver's door was opened, and just as he thought he would die with fear, he heard Tom's voice.

Trembling, Peter scrambled out of the car, the book clasped to his chest. Cleo followed, wagging her tail. Tom did not realize how badly he had frightened Peter; he had had a severe fright himself when he found the boy gone, but he had easily tracked him through the snow.

'Peter, you shouldn't have gone out without telling me,' he scolded.

'You were asleep,' Peter accused.

Tom's relief that the child was safe had turned into anger.

'You should have woken me up,' he said. 'Or waited.'

'I'm sorry,' said Peter in a sulky voice. People usually stopped going on at you if you said you were sorry, even if you didn't mean it.

'Come along, then. We must get back,' said Tom, though really, what was the hurry? There was no one at home wondering where they were.

He climbed up the ridge and waited there for Peter to follow.

Peter turned to look at the car. He closed the door. Now Tom knew it was there, he might have it removed; in any case, it would never be the same. He blinked fiercely to stop himself crying as he blundered along beside Tom, who had calmed down and knew he had been unfair.

'I'm sorry I was cross,' he said. 'But if it hadn't been for the snow, I wouldn't have known where you were and I would have been very worried.'

'I went to fetch my book,' Peter said. 'I forgot it last night.'

'You went to that old car last night?'

'Yes.'

'Why?' Had he made a habit of such nocturnal trips?

'It was my den,' Peter said. 'No one else knows about it, not even Nick Carey.'

'But why did you go there during the night?' Tom pressed.

'I was waiting for morning,' Peter said.

'What for?' Tom persisted. Had he set himself some sort of endurance test?

'I'm not saying,' Peter answered, and resolutely folded his lips together in a scowl.

The two marched on in silence. Tom understood about the den; in his case, a tree in his grandmother's garden had been a retreat from the world.

206

'I won't tell anyone about the car, Peter,' he said as they reached the house.

'It doesn't matter,' said Peter ungraciously. Tears were very close. 'I don't care now.'

Tom ignored this surly reply.

'We'll go round the back,' he said. 'Laura doesn't – didn't like boots in the hall.'

He led the way round through the yard to the back door, which he had left unlocked. Peter followed in silence and took off his boots before entering.

'We'd better have breakfast,' said Tom, removing his jacket and hanging it in the rear lobby.

'I've had mine,' said Peter, also hanging up his anorak. 'I was going to bring you yours in bed, if you weren't up,' he volunteered.

Tom interpreted this as a change of humour.

'That was a kind thought,' he said. 'Perhaps you could manage some more?' He was longing for a cup of strong coffee, and went into the kitchen to make it. A mug and a cereal bowl, both clean, rested on the drainer. What a tidy child, clearing up after himself before setting forth on his expedition. It didn't seem natural. 'What about coffee?' Tom asked. 'Would you like some? Or tea?'

'I could do with some hot chocolate, please,' said Peter.

'That was your and Laura's speciality, wasn't it?' Tom said. 'All right.'

'I can make it myself,' said Peter.

'Fine. You do that,' said Tom.

He had already put the kettle on. He made a strong cup of instant coffee for himself while Peter concocted his brew. Tom thought of lacing his own with brandy, as he had done the previous day, but he banished the temptation. He put some bread in the toaster and when it sprang up, gave Peter a slice.

'Here, keep me company,' he said.

Peter had taken his drink to the table. He spread butter and honey on the warm toast and nibbled a corner. Tom, meanwhile, had put more bread in the machine. The rapid walk on such a beautiful morning had made him hungry.

It was the first time his grief had lifted even slightly and it was some minutes before he saw that Peter was only playing with his toast. His head was bent and he seemed to be inspecting the texture of some crumbs. He was silently crying.

Poor little blighter! He'd had a terrifying experience the previous night and here was he, Tom, taking it out on him when all he'd done was run off on some harmless errand.

'I'm sorry, Peter. I didn't mean to be angry,' he said. 'It's over now. Please don't cry.'

Peter turned a face of misery towards him.

'It isn't that,' he wailed. 'It's all my fault.'

'What's your fault?'

'Everything.' Peter made a large gesture, waving his toast.

'What do you mean?'

'Laura being killed, and Aunt Marion nearly was. That's why I had to go, last night – in case it happened to her, but I was too late.' Peter's words were choked with sobs as he laid his head on his arms on the table and sobbed with the abandonment of a devastated adult. Tom heard the word 'Mummy' muttered among some other indistinguishable sounds.

'Peter, you must explain,' Tom urged, shocked and alarmed. How on earth did one comfort anyone in such a state of profound misery?

It took Peter some time to comply with his request, and Tom had difficulty in understanding even when he did.

'But that's not how it was!' Tom exclaimed when at last he had disentangled Peter's meaning. 'And anyway, your mother isn't dead. You'll often see her.'

But how could he console Peter over his mother's disenchantment with her life? How explain her wish for a fresh start in America? How account for what had happened to Laura, when as yet no one knew exactly what had started the chain of events that had ended in death?

'Grown-ups do awful things,' he said. 'Being grown-up, even middle-aged, doesn't mean someone's always right or won't make a mistake. But there isn't a jinx on you that causes you to bring bad luck. That's what you mean really, isn't it?'

Peter nodded, his face bleak.

'This man who locked you in the cellar – he's evil, Peter. He's a real villain. Mad, perhaps. Laura got in his way, that's all – like a road accident, where you have no chance of avoiding some car that drives straight at you.' That was exactly what the police thought had happened to Laura. 'It had nothing whatever to do with you,' Tom said firmly.

He was still trying to make Peter believe this when Marion telephoned from the hospital to say she was being released. Would Tom and Peter come and collect her?

22

She was waiting for them in the day room attached to her ward, wearing clothes fetched for her from Lime Tree Cottage by a police officer. She was pale but was not on crutches, and at her request had been brought some slacks so that the bandages on her injured legs did not show, but there was the tight line of a cut on her left cheek. She was, however, very definitely not dead.

She looked at Peter with as much anxiety as he was inspecting her, for her last sight of him had been as he was dispatched down the cellar stairs.

He put his arms right round her waist and hugged her.

'Are you really all right, Peter?' she asked. 'How long were you down in the cellar?' Detective Inspector Masters, to whom she had given a statement earlier that morning, had not been able to answer the question precisely.

'Not long,' Peter said. 'I escaped.'

'I know. I want to hear all about it,' said Marion. 'Let's get out of here, Tom.' She was very glad to see him; his sheer bulk was reassuring.

Peter was eager to relate how he had got out of the cellar.

'The door's a bit bust,' he said, at the end of his story.

'Never mind,' she replied. 'You did well.' She had already heard PC Coates's incomplete account of what he had done, and of how he had turned in the snow, holding the sword, ready to face an enemy. 'You were very brave.'

'I wasn't really,' said Peter. 'I cried a bit.'

'I'm not surprised,' said Marion.

He had shown qualities that could turn him into a leader of men. That was what George would have thought. Marion felt mild surprise that her mind should have turned towards her husband at this moment; he would have been a support now, whereas it seemed likely that she must resume the role of propping up Tom which had been hers since Thursday.

There were other duties, too: David must be told of his son's adventures before he learned of them through the press or in some other way. She still did not know why Peter had gone out during the night unless it was to get help, and if that was the reason, why his mission had failed. But explanations could wait.

'You'll come back to Clyde House, won't you?' Tom said. He felt they must all stay together while this nightmare went on.

'I'd like to go home first,' Marion said. 'Just to see what's happening there. I think the place is full of policemen.'

'All right.'

Tom drove straight through the village, most of whose residents were spending their Sunday morning unaware of the night's drama on their doorsteps, though the stabbing at the motorway filling station had been mentioned on the radio.

The police were just finishing at Lime Tree Cottage when Tom's BMW drew up outside. Detective Inspector Masters and Detective Sergeant Norris were there, and two other CID officers whom Peter recognized from among those who had been at Clyde House. While Marion was looking at the damaged cellar doorway, he ran quickly up to his room, but the note he had left for her had gone.

Masters had followed him.

'Is this what you're looking for, Peter?' he asked, taking a piece of paper from his pocket.

Peter seized it.

'Yes,' he said.

'Your auntie won't have seen it,' said Masters. 'What did you think was your fault, son?'

Because he had already tried to tell Tom, Peter found it easier to explain to Masters, who nodded thoughtfully.

'It's as if I'm a sort of unlucky mascot,' he ended.

'I think you're a lucky one,' said the detective. 'I'd be glad to have you around if I was in trouble. Something worse might have happened to your auntie if you hadn't turned up when you did.' He looked down at Peter. 'I ran away once,' he said. 'I'd accidentally broken my mother's best teapot – it was an heirloom she'd had from her grandmother. I'd been trying to help by washing up and I dropped it. I got into much more trouble for running off than I would have for breaking the teapot.'

'How far did you get?' asked Peter with interest.

'About a mile,' said Masters. 'I ran into my dad on his way back from work.'

'What work did he do?'

'He was a copper, too,' said the officer.

'Hm.' Peter took it in.

'Believe me, Peter, if someone gets struck by lightning, it's not because someone else happened to tell a lie that day or forgot to wash his neck, or anything like that. It's a random accident.'

'A random accident?' Peter repeated the phrase.

'Yes. Seems your auntie and Mrs Burdock met Mick Harvey one night when they were coming back from Fordbridge. He was driving dangerously and they reported him. Of course, they didn't know who he was but they took his number. When the local station followed it up – PC Coates did, the bobby who picked your auntie up last night – he found Mick Harvey wasn't insured and had no

MOT certificate. Those are serious offences and charges were brought. Mick had it in for your auntie and Mrs Burdock on that account. It was nothing to do with you.' Coates, in fact, had been the catalyst.

'Was it him who did that to Laura, then?' Peter asked.

'We think so. We aren't sure yet,' said Masters. But they were. Mick had as good as confessed to Marion Quilter. 'You saved your auntie,' he added.

'Did I?' Peter didn't see how. Luck had, or God, keeping her safe when the van crashed.

'Yes,' Masters said. 'Now, shall we go and see what she's doing? I should just flush that note down the toilet on the way, if I were you, and forget it.'

During the afternoon, David arrived. Marion had given him a played-down account of the night's events but had praised Peter's courage. David had decided to make sure for himself that Peter was unharmed, and was taking him back to London; Didbury seemed to be far from peaceful just now.

She had told him to come to Clyde House. She was snoozing on the sofa while Peter watched a film on television, and Tom was trying without much success to read the paper, when he arrived.

Peter now had to tell his father how he had found the sword and prised open the cellar door. He was in high spirits.

'But what were you doing out at night?' David asked. Marion had given him no satisfactory reply to this question on the telephone.

'Oh, just having a walk,' Peter said airily. 'I know it was wrong. I'm sorry, Daddy. I won't do it again.' He glanced at Tom, who could give him away, but Tom said nothing.

David, once he was sure that Peter was unharmed, was concerned as to what the boy's mother would say about the affair if she heard about it. He did not think she was likely to spirit Peter off to New York at once and seek a reversal of the custody order, but he must give her no grounds for questioning his care of their son. Spirited boys were, however, adventurous; a worse fate might have befallen Peter if he had decided to go roaming about London at night. Not for the first time, the notion of sending him to boarding school crossed David's mind; there was a good preparatory school only twelve miles from Didbury.

This was all a terrible business. You read about such things but you didn't expect them to happen to people you knew, much less your son and your sister. Most of David's legal work was conveyancing, and he was not as well versed in aspects of human frailty as some of his colleagues.

Marion said she would make some tea, and David followed her out to the kitchen so that they could exchange some words in private.

'What about Caroline?' Marion asked. 'Is she staying on at her parents' place?' Who would look after Peter till term began on Wednesday if that was the case?

'Her father's taking her back now. She's going to see that everything's ready when we get there this evening,' said David. 'She wants to make Peter feel really welcome. It is home, after all.'

'Yes.' Marion said. 'I feel so guilty, David. I ought to have heard him leave the house. Ordinarily, I would have, I'm certain. But I'd taken a pill after all the upset over Laura. Peter's very sad about that, you know. He was very fond of her.' She sighed. She felt dead inside. 'Goodness knows why he went out like that. Some dare, perhaps.'

'He seems to have kept his head remarkably well,' said David.

'He did. Of course, he didn't realize Mick Harvey was up to no good, as he'd seen him before when he – Mick – delivered that new chair from Patchett's. If I hadn't insisted we go to the police when he buzzed us on the road, none of this would have happened,' she said.

'Why so?' David had not heard the full story.

Marion told him as much as she knew.

'You did the right thing,' he said. 'If people are afraid to testify against scoundrels, anarchy will prevail.'

Marion laughed.

'That remark's worthy of George,' she said. 'Anyway, we weren't going on with the charge. Tom didn't want Laura involved. But the police found out that Mick Harvey was guilty of other offences and they charged him with those.'

'If you'd gone ahead, the police might have told you who he was,' David said.

'So that we'd have been on guard, you mean?'

'Well, you wouldn't have let him clean your windows, would you?' he pointed out.

'Don't tell Tom that,' said Marion. 'I don't know how Harvey found out who we were. Recognized Laura, perhaps, or her car. I'd have known his if I'd seen it – a clapped-out old Maxi – and I'd got the number, but he was driving a van when he came again.'

'You didn't get a look at him?'

'No. I only caught a glimpse of a face and some hair as we passed. He might have been any young man,' she said.

'Poor old Tom,' said David. 'Will he ever get over it?'

'I doubt it,' Marion answered. Tom had more to get over than Laura's death, but she was too weary to explain all that. 'Does one ever get over a tragedy?' she added. 'One adjusts and accepts. Isn't that all? He'll do that, I expect, in time.'

'You should get away from all this morbidity,' David said. 'You were coming up to town on Tuesday with Peter – got some date, haven't you? Don't stay here holding Tom's hand or he'll never be able to let you go. Come up and spend a few nights with us. Get to know Caroline better. She's nervous of you, you know.'

'Nervous of me? Goodness, why?' Marion was amazed.

'Well, you're older, and you're so clever – or she thinks you are,' David said, grinning. 'I told her it's all bluff, you just have the gift of tongues, but you could be her mother, you know, old girl, age-wise.'

Marion knew it only too well.

'We can't have her feeling like that,' she said. 'Yes, I'll come, but only to tea this time. Thanks.'

'We're fine, you know. Caroline and me, I mean,' said

David, looking sheepish. 'It's heaven, actually,' he confessed.

'Good,' said Marion. 'Then that's all right. Come on. You carry the tray.'

While she and David were in the kitchen, Tom picked up *Wild Animals I have Known*.

'Don't forget this again,' he said to Peter.

He did not know that Laura had given it to Peter. She had said that one of the parcels for the boy was a book, but it never occurred to him that this old volume with the faded green binding was the particular one.

He glanced at some of the illustrations and smiled. Then he handed it back to Peter.

At The Buildings that Sunday morning, Mrs Duke made sure that Beverley learned what Mick had been doing.

'I thought you might not have heard,' Mrs Duke said, well pleased with the effect of her visit.

Mick was wanted by the police in connection with a motorway stabbing during the night: imagine it! Beverley turned white at the thought and sat down abruptly.

'I didn't know,' she said.

Mrs Duke had always known Mick was a bad one, but he had proved to be worse even than she had imagined.

'He must have gone straight off and done it after he left here,' Mrs Duke surmised, also sitting down, prepared for a good chat. The radio bulletin had given no precise time for the incident, but no doubt tomorrow's newspapers would have every detail; there was nothing about it in the *News of the World* which Mr Duke had already collected.

'You're well rid of that one, my lass,' Mrs Duke told her. She had no very high opinion of Beverley, but the girl didn't deserve this load of trouble.

Beverley had not a moment's doubt but that Mick was guilty of what was alleged. The copper who'd come round in the night, though, was on about the woman in Didbury. Her head reeled.

'You must look to the future,' Mrs Duke was advising.

She stayed quite a time, making tea for them both and clearing up some of the muddle in Beverley's kitchen. When a journalist rang the door bell, she told him briefly, 'No comment' and closed the door in his face. Later, she spoke to another reporter and said she had always thought Mick Harvey a bad lot. He hadn't been a considerate neighbour at all, she said, and it was the kiddies she felt sorry for, if the reporter got her meaning.

Beverley cowered inside the flat with the children while other reporters came to the door after Mrs Duke had gone. She left the bell unanswered and at last they moved down the road to await events in the Cricketers, where they learned a lot about Mick and his heavy drinking.

The police would soon catch him, wouldn't they? They'd put him in gaol and Beverley would be safe.

Now she really was on her own.

She was still feeling stunned when PC Coates arrived with her mother. He had found it quite difficult to persuade Mrs Wayne that she must go to her daughter's aid.

'What sort of a mother are you?' Coates had demanded at last. 'Didn't you know he knocked your daughter about? Haven't you seen her bruises? You shouldn't have let her marry him in the beginning. She can only have been a kid herself.'

'Got herself into trouble, didn't she?' said Mrs Wayne.

'Didn't you?' Coates riposted with a random shot.

It went home. Mrs Wayne went first red in the face, then white. She accompanied Coates to The Buildings and offered to have Beverley and the children to stay.

'Just till all this dies down,' she said.

'It won't. Not ever,' Beverley answered. 'It can't be forgotten. I'll stay here. The welfare will help us.'

Coates regarded her approvingly. Then he looked at her mother, in her jersey-knit two-piece and mock fur coat.

'Your daughter could do with some cash,' he said bluntly. 'I'm sure you can help her out, Mrs Wayne.'

He had the satisfaction of watching while Mrs Wayne opened her notecase and took out a ten-pound note; under his unrelenting gaze she added another. He left her to find her own way home. Mr Wayne could pay for a taxi if she was too grand to go on the bus.

Later that morning Pat and her husband came round. They took Beverley and the children home with them to share their Sunday dinner – roast pork and steamed pudding – and then they all went off to the park so that the children could play in the snow. While they were trying to build a snowman from fine powdered snow which did not want to bind together, a young woman pushing a baby in its pram and with a small girl beside her, approached. Pat recognized her friend Sharon at the same time that Sharon was staring at Cliff.

'This is Beverley,' Pat introduced.

Cliff and Emily had run towards one another, then halted in the manner of small children too young for much conversation.

Sharon took it in: this was Mick's wife.

She knew nothing about what he had done until she saw the television news that night. It showed a mug shot of Mick at the age of sixteen and a photofit which was remarkably accurate. It seemed that no one had a recent photograph of the wanted man; Coates had asked Beverley if she possessed one but there was not even a wedding picture.

Sharon could not believe it. She had to wait until the next day to read a fuller account of Mick's infamy, when it was revealed that before the stabbing he had abducted a woman from Didbury. She still thought there must be some mistake.

23

The inquest on Laura, opened on Monday morning, was adjourned. Grainger was not yet ready to present the facts that would ensure a verdict of unlawful killing. Unless Mick Harvey, when he was arrested, admitted to killing her, the case against him would depend on the scientists' evidence.

The weather was appropriately sombre, the sky heavy and grey, and snow fell intermittently during the morning. A few reporters were in court. Grainger, at a briefing the previous evening, had disclosed that Mick Harvey, wanted for the motorway stabbing, would also be charged, when caught, with other offences including abducting a woman whom the police did not name. She had escaped with minor injuries. So far, no indication had been given that there was any connection between these cases and Laura Burdock's death.

Mick's van had been removed from the field and transported to the laboratory. Detectives had examined the snow-covered ground at the site of the crash, picking up fragments of glass and searching for clues that would tie the van in with evidence already collected. Paint scrapings from the van were being compared with what had been found on Laura's clothing. Marion had seen a waterproof hat resembling Laura's sticking out of Mick Harvey's jacket pocket; if that had been found in the van, it would have been strong evidence of guilt, but it was not there. There was no sign of the missing button, though detectives searched for it in the snow. It might have dropped down somewhere inside the van and would yet be found.

Marion and Tom went to the inquest together. Afterwards, Grainger told them that he had a list of people whose houses Laura had visited. Most of the sellers had now been seen by police in the various areas, and all had said she had been alone. One vendor had moved to Guernsey and would be interviewed by the Guernsey police. No contact had been possible with the owner of the last house she was known to have had an appointment to view. She had been there in October and had said she might visit it again but the agent did not know if she had done so. Now the owner was in hospital, gravely ill.

Tom was not interested in the vendors of houses; he was no longer sure that he wanted to know the name of her lover. It seemed that this unknown man had not been involved with her death after all, and for their own part the police no longer needed to trace him.

'You'd think he'd have come forward, though, wouldn't you?' Tom said to Marion, when they had parted from Grainger. 'He must know what's happened. It's been in the papers. Anyway, if he didn't know he'd have rung her to make an assignation, and one of us would have answered.'

'Tom, there's no proof that she was having an affair. You're just guessing,' Marion said. She thought that if he was right, it was not surprising the lover had stayed in the shadows. He would want to avoid exposure and subsequent scandal. Whatever the truth, Laura had certainly been guilty of deception. 'She may just have enjoyed looking at houses,' she suggested.

'Whatever for?' Tom asked. 'If it was historic houses she wanted to see, it would be different, but it wasn't like that.'

'Well, I think you should try to put it out of your mind,' Marion said, knowing that this was useless advice.

'I hope the police pick up Mick Harvey soon,' Tom said.

'I expect they will,' Marion answered.

'No one's safe while he's around,' said Tom. The man could be skulking about in the district, ready to stab some other innocent person who got in his way. Had he stabbed Laura before dumping her on the line? The police hadn't mentioned stab wounds.

Grainger had said that a portable radio found in the crashed van had turned out to be stolen from a house in Flintsham on the day Laura died; fifty pounds had been taken then, too. What else had he done? Marion remembered that he had a wife and two small children; she had seen the little boy. What would happen to them? What about the filling-station attendant's family? The repercussions of this sad affair would endure for years. She and Laura, setting out innocently for the ballet, had embarked on a collision course with a destroyer.

Tom went back to the office after the inquest. It seemed the best way to spend the rest of the day. Marion asked him to come round for a meal in the evening. She had a rest herself, spending two hours in bed with a hot-water bottle and Radio Three. She slept for a while, but still felt numb and exhausted when Tom arrived in the evening. She cooked the half shoulder of lamb that had been intended for yesterday's lunch. Tom had achieved a certain amount at the office, he said, and his staff had been very helpful.

'Come to dinner tomorrow,' he said before leaving.

She agreed. Getting it ready would give him an aim, and she would be glad not to be alone. She locked up securely when he had gone and tested the telephone; the police had arranged for it to be repaired at once.

Mick wouldn't come back: of course not. He'd be miles away from the district by now. Unless he had learned that she was still alive and he came to finish off what he had begun.

The idea was stupid. Someone else would be his victim, if the police didn't find him first.

Mick, with regret, had shaved off his moustache. To be on the safe side, he had his hair cut short, and he'd moved his hotel. He had bought some new clothes on Monday, a sheepskin coat and a pair of tweed trousers. All this considerably changed his appearance. He made his purchases in different shops and he paid cash. That Quilter woman had signed her cheque card with her full name and no one would take him for a Marion, so the card was worthless, a further mark against her.

She'd survived, too; he knew that from the paper. He'd quite enjoyed reading about what he had done but he was very annoyed at the woman's escape.

He had spent most of Sunday asleep but by Monday evening he was ready to start his new life.

A watch had been brought into Merston police station on Monday afternoon. A jeweller in the town had bought it and when he heard that inquiries were being made about one that was missing, he knew that his uneasy feeling about the deal had been sound.

Detective Inspector Masters took it over to Didbury for Tom to identify before he left for the office on Tuesday.

It was Laura's, or its twin.

The jeweller had not taken the name of the young woman who brought it in, but he would know her again. It seemed possible from her description that she was Mick Harvey's wife; she had said that it was a gift from her husband. Prints on it were smudged but the original jeweller's mark would be on the inside so that its provenance could be proved.

Meanwhile, a statement had been taken from Beverley Harvey about Mick's movements on Saturday night; it confirmed what PC Coates had already reported.

The paint scrapings found on Laura's clothing had been analysed and the scarlet under the blue was of a type used on Morris Minor vans supplied to the Post Office some years ago. The fragments could now be matched with paint from the van itself. A hair similar to Laura's had been found in the van, and others that matched Marion's. When Mick was arrested, the hair caught in Laura's belt could be compared with one from his head.

It was unreal, thought Tom: a watch, hairs, a missing button which might yet be found, paint scrapings: these were the things that could send a man to prison, but there was no way to restore a lost life. Nor a dream.

Two lives had been forfeit: the pump attendant had died.

Marion travelled up to London on Tuesday to meet Hugh and go on to Putney for tea. Next time, she would stay for a night or two, but this evening she must return for dinner with Tom.

Hugh's letter had revealed that during his time in America his wife had had a tremendous affair with a much younger man, a student on the campus. The tottering marriage had become, as a result, still more unsteady, and

Hugh had decided to end it. He planned to return to England, where he was in line for a chair.

Marion had mixed feelings about their meeting. She was partly excited, partly afraid, and as she entered the restaurant where they had so often met before, apprehension prevailed. After her recent experiences, she felt too drained to cope with more emotion, but of course Hugh did not know what had been happening to her.

There he was, waiting to greet her, standing up as he saw her arrive, a tall, thin, slightly stooping man with steel-rimmed spectacles. His hair was greyer and had receded further from his forehead and his face was more lined, but it creased into the familiar smile of delight as he greeted her. His lips were warm, dry and soft: familiar, yet strange. He was a man she knew intimately and also a stranger.

During lunch, Marion kept the talk turned to him and how things had gone in the States. Although he had enjoyed the experience, he had missed England. She asked about his children and was told of their satisfactory lives. She and Hugh had not communicated during their time apart; Marion had insisted that it should be a complete break. Now she realized that although she was going to see him so soon, she had never once wished for his presence during the dreadful last days with all their sorrow and fear, but her thoughts had twice turned to George.

Gently, she told him to count her out of his future plans. He wanted to know if there was someone else.

She hesitated.

'I see that there is,' Hugh said bleakly.

He had noticed that she had cut her face; a neat line, healing now, marked her cheek. She had seen him glance at it and had said she had caught it on a bramble when she was having a bonfire in the garden.

Marion thought about Peter.

'It's not what you think,' she said, but she did not explain.

They parted rather sadly, without arranging another meeting.

Marion hurried off to Putney, where Peter, pink-faced

and happy, showed Marion a wild mustang which Caroline had drawn for him to paint. She had copied it loosely from an illustration in *Wild Animals I have Known;* she had also done Redruff, the owl, and a very intelligent-looking fox. Peter intended to adorn his room with a frieze of wild creatures.

'She draws jolly well,' Peter said, and Marion saw the two exchange pleased grins.

She had not known that her sister-in-law possessed this talent; in fact, she really knew very little at all about Caroline.

'It's a restful old book,' said Caroline. 'Who was Leonard Masefield?'

'I don't know,' answered Marion. 'Why?'

'It belonged to him,' said Caroline. 'Hadn't you noticed his name in the front?'

Marion saw the neat, faded inscription. Then she remembered what Peter had said. An old friend had given Laura the book. She hadn't paid attention to that at the time.

'I hadn't seen this,' she said slowly as she realized the significance of the initials.

She continued to wonder about them during the rest of her visit as she set herself out to be pleasant and not alarming. She dandled her niece on her knee during tea and hoped she would have more rapport with Sarah in time. When she left to catch her train home in time for dinner with Tom she felt completely exhausted.

I'll go away, she resolved. When all this is over I'll go right away, quite by myself, to Greece or Australia or somewhere, and forget all this horror.

Meanwhile, should she tell Tom the name?

She bought an evening paper, hoping to learn that Mick had been caught, but news of him consisted of just a few lines which said that the search was continuing and that he was believed to be somewhere in London.

A man could hide for weeks, even for ever, without being found, unless he committed fresh crimes and left new clues.

24

Mick hadn't enjoyed Monday night. He had gone looking
for some excitement around Soho and had been ripped off
in a strip club. Imagine charging all that for a drink and
a tit show! He'd refused to pay at first, but then the atmosphere had turned bad and he'd left; he certainly didn't
want to be faced with the law.

After that, he'd gone to a disco where he'd picked up a
girl and bought her some drinks, but then he lost interest;
she was only a kid who ought to have been at home with
her mother. There was no one around for him to impress
and no one paid him any attention. If only they knew!

He'd spent most of Tuesday in his room enjoying its
luxury. He had his own well-appointed bathroom, a kettle
and packets of coffee and tea, and a bottle of whisky he'd
bought the day before.

The maid came wanting to clean it, so he went out. He
itched to have his foot on an accelerator pedal, his hands
on the wheel, and he wanted the vehicle's metal body
around him; Mick felt unsafe without that carapace. He
had a pie and some beer in a pub, then spent the afternoon
on his bed watching television.

He went out again in the evening and ate steak and
chips in a steak house, then tried several pubs where he
drank beer and played the fruit machines, just as he did
in Merston, but here he was elbowed out of the way by
regular customers, just as he elbowed others at home.

He was back in his hotel room in time for the ten o'clock
news and near the end of the bulletin there was a shot of
Beverley and the children hurrying into The Buildings.
Mrs Wayne was there too, being interviewed; she said she
had never liked Mick and was heart-broken on behalf of
her daughter.

The old bitch!

Watching her, Mick seethed. But for her, he and Beverley wouldn't have got married.

Then he remembered Cliff – little Cliffie. Mick, lying on the bed fully dressed, drinking whisky neat from the bottle, felt tears spring to his eyes at the thought of the fine little son whose company he was being denied – and for ever, if he succeeded in getting away, as he would.

Cliff thought the world of his dad; everyone said so. Cliff would be missing him.

A boy should be with his dad.

As always, an idea had no sooner entered Mick's head than he acted upon it. He got up and bundled his possessions into the holdall. In any case he'd planned to move on soon, before the hotel gave him a bill which he didn't intend to pay.

Mick took the lift down to the first floor and just in case there was someone nosy at the desk, he left by the fire exit on that landing. Now the let-down feeling he had been suffering from departed as he moved into action, running down the last flight of stairs and merging into the shadows. Some cars were parked behind the hotel. Mick decided against lifting one of them in case it was missed at once. He'd go a bit further, pick up something decent, maybe with its key already in it; then he'd get Cliffie. They'd travel north together. In London you needed contacts; up north, it would be different.

The night was bitterly cold. Mick snuggled into his coat. He had left his leather jacket in a litter bin after he bought the new sheepskin, but he'd kept the hat. He put it on. The pavements were icy and, in places where the snow had not been properly cleared away, were treacherous to his smooth leather soles. He slipped several times, and when he saw a bus approaching, he decided to take it and find a car further west.

Mick left the bus at Shepherd's Bush and walked on till he came to a filling station. The knife was in his pocket and he clasped his hand round it, but the same trick wouldn't work here; the place was too busy.

He took his hat off and put it in his pocket while he watched a man fill his Rover 3500 – a car Mick fancied driving – and when the driver returned from paying, Mick asked for a lift. The man hesitated, but only for an instant; Mick looked very respectable in his new sheepskin coat, the neck of a scarlet polo visible, his hair neatly trimmed. He told a plausible tale about his own car being put off the road by some idiot skidding into it, and he'd got to get home to Swindon.

The man faced a long, solitary drive through the bitter night and welcomed the chance of company.

'Jump in,' he said. 'It's a cold night to be out.'

'It is,' Mick agreed.

All the way to Swindon he sat lapped in the car's comfort and warmth, planning to kill the driver. He longed to be at the wheel himself, but if he attacked the man while they were travelling at speed, they would crash and Mick himself might get hurt.

They never slowed down, so Mick spared the man, who made a detour and dropped him in the outskirts of Swindon where Mick said he lived.

He soon picked up a Vauxhall which yielded to a key in the collection he had gathered over the years and always kept with him. Just over an hour later he was parked outside The Buildings.

There were no policemen on guard and the cold weather had driven the press away. The street was deserted.

Beverley would never get over it, not if he took little Cliff. The police wouldn't touch him if he'd got the kid; Cliffie would be his passport to safety. They'd head for Scotland, maybe cross over to Northern Ireland.

The ladder was still propped up at the side of The Buildings, where Mick had left it before he took Cliff to the park. He sat there looking at it, devising his plan.

He'd have to go in through the children's window. The living-room overlooked the front of the block, and the sight of a ladder against it would attract attention if anyone were to pass by.

If he'd planned this sooner, he could have brought scotch tape to secure the glass while he broke it. He'd have to hope Mandy would sleep through any noise; it didn't matter about Cliff – he'd be thrilled to see his dad.

Mick took off his coat, which was too bulky for ladder-climbing; he bundled it into the back of the car, then set the ladder in position, making sure there was no one in sight as he began the ascent.

With his gloved hand he smashed the window close to the catch and reached in to undo it. He was over the sill in seconds, the curtains parting as he thrust through them. Enough light filtered in from the street lamp outside to let him see his way, and he scooped Cliff out of his cot.

The child woke. His sleepy stare showed him, in the half-dark, a total stranger, for he did not recognize Mick with his trimmed hair and without a moustache. His face crumpled up in fright and he opened his mouth to bawl.

Mick clamped it shut with his hand.

'It's all right, Cliff. Don't you know your dad? I've come to take you away. You and me's going to have rare old times together.'

Cliff was far too terrified to take in any of this. His small heart pounded as he wriggled and twisted his head about, trying to break free and to yell.

Never mind. He'd soon give over, once they were out of here and in the car. Mick wedged Cliff's limbs against him with one arm; the other hand was still firmly gagging the child. He'd never get back down the ladder like this; he would have to leave by the door.

'It's Dad,' he kept saying, in a harsh whisper. 'Stop, Cliffie. It's your dad.' He edged to the door and pushed the handle down with his elbow. As he stepped out to the landing, the main bedroom door opened. Beverley had heard an unfamiliar sound and sensed movement; she wondered if Cliff had climbed out of his cot. He'd nearly done it once before.

It was Cliff she expected to see on the landing. Instead,

the bulk of a man showed up against the pale oblong of the children's window, and he held something which made mewing sounds in his arms. He was stealing her child!

'Put him down!' Beverley screamed, and sprang at him, fists starting to pummel him.

Mick dumped Cliff on the floor with some force. As the child started to yell he caught her by the shoulders and pushed her back into the bedroom, finally giving her a powerful shove which sent her staggering across the room in the darkness. She gave one shrill cry as she lost her balance, and there was a loud crack as her head met the corner of the dressing-table; then she was silent.

But Cliff was bellowing now. He'd wake the Dukes and the old fool would come thumping the door down, complaining as usual. It had all gone wrong again.

Mick had to get out, and fast.

He left his son wailing there in the hallway, and went back the way he had come, down the ladder.

It just wasn't fair. By now he and Cliff should have been on the road together, speeding north, and here he was on his own with the whole world against him. If it hadn't been for those two bloody women he'd still be at Patchett's and well on his way to driving a lorry all over Europe.

That patronizing bitch with the red hair was still alive to put the finger on him. He should have made sure she was dead, but instead he'd gone soft, because of the kid.

He would deal with her now.

Didbury seemed as quiet tonight as it had been on Saturday. Fresh falls of snow had obliterated the single attempt by a gritting lorry to keep the road clear; outposts like this, off main routes, were the last to receive attention in such weather. Severe frost had turned the slush into ridges over which the new snow lay and Mick's stolen Vauxhall crunched its way through the village towards Lime Tree Cottage.

A light burned over the porch and the empty garage was open. She had gone out, leaving an invitation to thieves.

Mick was again obsessed with the notion of vengeance. He could wait until she returned, but when would that be? It was already four o'clock in the morning. He could fire the cottage now; she wouldn't like that but physically she would escape him again and he wanted to frighten her to the depths of her soul. He'd like to see her beg him for mercy. She'd shown no fear on Saturday except when he'd threatened the boy.

She'd not have gone far in this weather.

Mick turned the car and went slowly back through the dark village. He turned down the Poppleton road and paused at the entrance to Clyde House. Plenty of furrows going to and from Poppleton showed in the snow, some covered by the fresh fall. A single, recent set of tyre tracks led to – or from – the village. Mick got out of his car to inspect them. They dented the dry, icy surface and were made by a fairly small wheel. The woman's Fiesta might leave marks like these.

Mick drove slowly up the drive to Clyde House. The place was in darkness, but there, parked outside, was a red Fiesta.

The dirty bitch! She'd not even waited for her pal to be buried before having it away with the husband. And her so toffee-nosed, too! It just went to show.

This man had a BMW. Mick remembered the neighbour mentioning it when he pumped her about the Burdocks. He'd take a look at that before deciding what to do next.

Mick turned off the Vauxhall's lights and made his way round to the yard. The garage doors were locked. He could soon break them open, but it might make a noise. The keys and those to the car would be in the house. The man would have a credit card, too, and money. He'd have a passport Mick could use. If he took his time and searched carefully, he might get a good haul here, and find a way to get at the woman, too, though that wouldn't be easy with the two of them in bed together.

The house had sash windows. They were easy to force unless fitted with security locks, and these were not. Mick still had his knife, and he was soon inside.

The knife was in his hand when he heard a rustling sound in the dark passage and then a low growl. That damned dog! He'd forgotten about her. As she sniffed at his legs he bent down and struck out with the knife, and he killed her at once.

It shook him a bit. On the whole he liked dogs and it was a shame this one had got in his way. He felt for the light switch and when he had found it he opened the back door and dragged the dog's body outside.

Then he had a look round.

There were bottles of drink in the dining-room, set out on a sideboard. That reminded Mick that it was hours since he'd had one. He poured Scotch into a heavy cut-glass tumbler and drank it down neat. Ah, that was better. Mick followed it with another. Now for the keys and whatever else he could find.

And he needed a knife to replace the one he had left in the dog's body. He went into the kitchen to look for one, searching through the drawers.

He had a knife in each hand, weighing their merits, when Tom came into the room.

Mick's remaining mental balance left him. He plunged straight at Tom, who immediately picked up a chair to fend him off. One of the legs caught Mick's wrist and the pain fed his rage but he kept hold of the knives, moving about, making dabs towards Tom who was able to use the chair as a shield.

Tom, at this point, thought he had surprised an ordinary – though obviously violent – burglar. He had never met Mick Harvey, and this man bore little resemblance to the mug shot and photofit pictures he had seen.

'Drop those knives,' Tom commanded.

Mick answered him with an expletive, still moving round like an unsteady boxer. He had edged away from the sink and now had his back to the stove.

'There's a chair over there. Go and sit down,' Tom ordered.

'Get stuffed,' answered Mick. 'That's what you were doing to her upstairs, isn't it? They're all tarts. What's it like doing it in your wife's bed with a cow like that scraggy old carrot-top?'

What did this foul-mouth mean?

A burglar would know whose house this was; indeed, he could have picked it because it had been in the news. But how did he know who owned the car outside? For the man's insulting words must relate to Marion. Had he been watching them through some gap in the curtains, waiting until it was quiet before breaking in?

'Who are you?' Tom demanded.

'Don't you know?' Mick taunted him.

Tom stared at him above the barrier of the chair which divided them: he saw the mean mouth, the short brown hair, the slightly spotty skin, and he suddenly understood.

He really went for Mick then, ramming the chair into his stomach, pinning the younger man against the Aga cooker. Tom was big, and though overweight, he was fit and strong.

When Marion, who had been woken by sounds from below, came into the kitchen, Mick was rammed against the stove and the lid of the hot-plate behind him was raised. He had dropped the knives and was screaming to be released as Tom hit him on the jaw.

'That's for my wife,' he cried, and cuffed him again – awkwardly, for he was not naturally violent. 'And that one's for Peter. And here's one for Mrs Quilter. And now I'll roast you.'

He threw aside the chair and pushed Mick by the shoulders so that his upper body and ultimately his head drew nearer to the exposed hot surface of the stove.

'Tom, it's all right. The police are coming,' Marion cried.

'I'm going to pay this fiend out if it's the last thing I do,' Tom gritted. His face was red and contorted with anger.

Marion had seen the knives on the floor. She picked them up quickly and shut them inside the nearest drawer. As she did this, Mick's arm met the hot plate and he let out a yell. There was the smell of singeing wool as the sleeve of his sweater frizzled.

'Tom, stop!' Marion said. 'You've got him – he can't get away. The police will be here in a minute.'

The scene before her was dreadful: two violent men locked in combat, the one pallid with terror, the other's face crimson with hate.

Her words got through. Tom twisted Mick's arm up behind him but he let him move away from the stove. Mick was snivelling and he muttered curses, saying he would have Tom up for assault.

'Shut up, you creep,' said Tom, and hit Mick across the face again.

Well, that was better than frying him before her eyes, Marion thought. It was effective, too. Mick's obscenities ceased but his snivels continued as over his head Tom looked at Marion to see if her words about the police were true or a bluff.

Understanding, she nodded.

'I heard what was going on and phoned,' she said. 'Here they are.' Sure enough, a siren wail could be heard outside. 'I'll let them in,' she added.

While she was gone, Tom stood over Mick who cowered away from him nursing his arm where he had sustained what later turned out to be a second-degree burn about as large as a fifty-pence coin. Tom lifted his arm to hit him again, then dropped it as his anger ebbed. It wasn't worthwhile; the man was a mean, sniffling, vicious coward and beyond contempt.

Only then did Tom wonder where Cleo had been all this time. A police constable who had been directed to approach the house from the rear found her lying stretched out in the snow, with the knife that had killed not only her but the pump attendant still fast in her side.

Later, a forensic pathologist showed that its blade exactly fitted the wounds on the human corpse.

25

'If he'd had a gun, he'd have shot me,' said Tom. 'As it was, he couldn't get in range with those knives. Why two?'

'One for each of us, maybe,' said Marion. 'He seemed to know I was here.' Tom had given her an edited version of Mick's remarks.

'If you hadn't come in then, I'd probably have killed him by slow degrees,' said Tom, shocked, now that it had abated, by the force of his own rage.

'I wonder if it would have counted as legitimate self-defence,' said Marion lightly.

The fact that Tom had raised the Aga lid had shown what was in his mind. Thank goodness she had woken when she did. She had recognized Mick's voice as she came to investigate what was going on downstairs. She had dialled 999, thinking that would be quicker than trying to get hold of Grainger direct, but he and Masters had arrived very soon after the car that had answered the call.

Tom and Marion had both drunk rather a lot during the evening. Marion had told Tom about Hugh and had revealed Caroline's discovery of the name in the book Laura had given Peter. They had looked for Masefields in the local telephone directory but none were listed. Then Tom had shown Marion something he had noticed when preparing the salmon his secretary had bought for their dinner. He had not known how to cook it and so he had consulted Laura's special recipe file. Some figures, which could have been a telephone number, were written on the cover. On impulse, Tom had dialled them; there had been a ringing sound but no answer. He told Marion about this and they had gone on to discuss Laura's funeral. By midnight, they had both become very melancholy and Marion had needed very little urging not to return alone to her cottage but to spend the night in the spare room. When he came downstairs and saw the light on in the dining room, Tom had expected to find her looking for another drink, but the room was empty. He had gone on down the passage towards the kitchen and discovered the intruder.

Masters had cautioned Mick and then charged him with the murder of the filling-station attendant. The other charges could follow. There was going to be a formidable list, enough to send him down for a very long time.

Mick had complained a great deal about his sore arm and Masters inspected the burnt sleeve of the red lambswool sweater.

'Left the stove open, hadn't you, Mr Burdock, before retiring?' Masters had said. 'It's easily forgotten when you're making tea and have something else on your mind.' He gazed at Tom stolidly as he spoke, a wise, experienced man who would never make higher rank but who had seen it all.

Mick had blustered that Tom had tried to kill him, but no one paid any attention. The police took him away at last. They did not allow him to put on his sheepskin coat which was still in the car. Laura's hat was stuffed into its pocket and they took it away sealed into a large polythene bag. They would spend the rest of the night interrogating him, and while his resistance was low they might get him to admit everything, though he would deny it all again as soon as a lawyer took over his defence.

The police would tell the stolen Vauxhall's owner that the car had been found, but he would not be able to claim it yet; it must be gone over thoroughly by the forensic scientists. There was a cheap holdall bag in its boot; later, Marion's jewellery was found inside it.

'Why did he come back?' Tom asked Masters.

'Felt homesick, maybe,' said Masters percipiently.

'He was fond of his son,' said Marion. 'I'm sure that was genuine. Maybe he was on his way to see him.'

'Maybe he'd been there already,' said Masters and spoke

to Detective Sergeant Norris who immediately went out of the room.

Ten minutes later two officers from Merston police station arrived at The Buildings and found Beverley lying in the bedroom while Cliff, who had discovered her unconscious form on the floor, had cried himself to a standstill and then fallen asleep beside her.

'You were splendid, Tom,' Marion told him. 'I mean, I didn't really think you needed to roast him alive, but you gave him a taste of his own medicine. You scared him rotten.'

Even though it was fuelled by fury, she would never have expected Tom to be capable of such passion; had he ever shown Laura the same depth of feeling, channelled tenderly into the rites of love?

'It's easy to kill,' Tom said. 'I know that now.'

He held out his arms, and Marion, who was in need of comfort herself, allowed him to hold her close to his large, dressing-gowned body. How simple it would be, how natural, what a healing experience for them both if she remained there and let follow what would. And how they might both regret it later. It would jeopardize the friendship both of them needed much more than the brief relief of their isolation. She drew back after several seconds.

'It's almost morning,' she said. 'Not really worth going back to bed just for an hour. You go and shave and I'll fix us some breakfast.'

They both spent a long time with the police that morning. Masters and Norris returned soon after eight with the statements Tom and Marion had made earlier, neatly typed. They went over them and signed them.

Masters told them that Mick Harvey had admitted running over Laura; he'd said she stepped into the road in front of him and that he had no chance to avoid her. He had thought she was dead when he dumped her.

'Do you believe that?' Tom asked.

Masters didn't, and neither did the superintendent.

'How's Mick's wife?' Marion asked.

'Not too good,' Masters said. 'She's got a fractured skull. But she'll be all right. We haven't been able to talk to her yet, but we're sure he entered the flat through a window. He's clammed up on that – hasn't said why. He knocked her about – Coates knew that. I daresay she won't be sorry to see him locked up.'

'What about the children?'

'The boy was very scared. The baby was asleep – she may have slept through whatever happened. They're both with foster parents now,' Masters said. 'Mrs Harvey's mother didn't want to know.'

'Oh dear!'

'Well, they come like that sometimes,' said Masters. 'The kids are probably better off where they are.'

After he and Norris had gone, Marion said to Tom, 'If I hadn't insisted on reporting that young man for buzzing us on the road, he wouldn't have become a murderer.'

'You can't know that,' Tom answered. 'He might have killed both of you that night. He might have killed his wife any time, from what we've just heard. The chance part was that he ran into Laura again.'

And I'm alive and she isn't, thought Marion bitterly. She shivered.

'You're cold,' Tom said.

When she had appeared in the kitchen that morning dressed in Laura's nightgown and robe, she had looked quite young, colour high, eyes bright as she made him calm down. Now she looked every day of her true age, the lines round her eyes sharply etched, faint vertical threads radiating from her pale, soft-looking mouth, her neck no longer smooth. Perhaps she would change her mind about that man Hugh, he reflected; it was rough for her, being alone. He was glad he had not yet offered her a job; he thought he would wind the business down, sell the goodwill and the house and start something else, go into manufacturing himself.

Mrs Rigby had already arrived and could be heard upstairs wielding the vacuum cleaner. Marion had left her bed unmade; best quash rumour right at the source, a rumour she would have minded more for Laura's sake than her own. Mrs Rigby had wept over Cleo. The police had taken the body away; it was evidence because of the knife, Marion told Tom, who had been upset at not being allowed to bury the dog in the garden.

'Have you paid Mrs Rigby?' she asked him.

Tom hadn't.

'I'll go and ask what we owe her,' he said.

Marion's ruse to get him out of the kitchen had worked. She hurriedly took down Laura's recipe file and made a note of the mysterious telephone number from which there had been no reply last night.

She tried the number again that afternoon. After ten rings, when she was on the point of giving up, a woman's voice answered.

Was this Mrs Masefield? Did Leonard Masefield live at this address? Marion plunged; she asked to speak to Mr Masefield.

The voice told her that he was seriously ill in hospital after a fall at the weekend.

So he couldn't have heard about Laura.

'Oh dear,' she said, 'I'm sorry.'

'This is his daughter,' the voice went on. 'Can I help you?'

His daughter, not his wife: if Marion mentioned Laura by name, would she be setting a cat among pigeons? She decided to take the risk; no further hurt could touch Laura now, and if Leonard Masefield had been her lover, he must fend for himself during whatever ensued.

'He doesn't know me,' Marion said. 'I wanted to give him a message from Laura Burdock.'

'Oh, that's the woman who came to see the house, isn't it? He told me about her. She didn't turn up on Friday.'

So Leonard Masefield had a house to sell! He must be

the vendor the police had not been able to contact; they'd mentioned no names.

The voice now sounded warmer.

'My father was very disappointed,' said the woman. 'He knew she didn't want to buy the house but he liked her and had asked her to come again. He'd put a book out for her daughter – an early edition of *The Secret Garden*. I believe he'd already given her one for her son. Peter, isn't it?'

'Her son?' said Marion faintly.

'Yes. So he said,' the voice stated.

Marion took a grip on herself.

'What hospital is your father in?' she asked. 'I – we'll send some flowers,' she managed. What fable had Laura been spinning?

The voice told her where Leonard Masefield was; he had been moved from the general hospital into a private one. Then the daughter asked where she should send *The Secret Garden*.

'I'm clearing the house up, you see,' she said. 'My father will never come back.'

Marion suggested the book should be sent to her. She would see that it reached Peter's sister.

Sarah would love the story one day, she reflected, and thought how easy it was to evolve a deceit.

Marion had to make sure. She was at the hospital just over an hour later, and posed as a very old friend. She was allowed in to see Mr Masefield, though warned that he was very frail and might not be up to much conversation.

She hoped the daughter would not be there. If she were, Marion would have to match Laura's powers of invention to account for her presence.

But she was the only visitor.

And Leonard Masefield was a very old man. She read his age on his chart. He was asleep.

Marion had brought some spring flowers. A nurse gave her a vase so that she could occupy herself by arranging them while she waited for him to wake up. There was a cradle over his legs to protect them from the weight of the bedding; his face was grey, the cheeks hollow, his eyelids transparent, like wax. A trickle of spittle emerged from his mouth and the nurse wiped it away with a tissue. She shook him gently.

'Mr Masefield, wake up,' she said. 'You've got a visitor.'

'Don't worry – I'm in no hurry,' Marion said. 'I'll be quite happy to sit here for a bit while he rests.' She wanted no witness to their conversation.

When the nurse had gone, she crossed to the bed and took the thin old hand with the big brown blotches and knotted veins on the back in hers, holding it firmly.

'Mr Masefield, please wake up,' she said. 'I've come from Laura.'

She said it several times, praying that no one, and particularly the daughter, would come into the room, and at last the translucent lids lifted.

'I'm a friend of Laura's, Mr Masefield,' Marion told him as he gazed at her with bewildered, unfocused eyes. 'She couldn't come on Friday because she had an accident.'

'Oh!' Suddenly the faded blue eyes looked alert.

'She wasn't able to let you know,' Marion continued.

'Oh dear,' he said. 'Is she in pain?'

'No,' answered Marion steadily. 'Not now.'

The old man closed his eyes while Marion waited for his response. If he asked her, she would tell him the truth but she would not lead him to find it. He seemed to be dozing again; then he opened his eyes once more.

'It was good of her to come and see me,' he said. 'I persuaded her. She said her husband wouldn't want to buy the house. Tom, that's his name, isn't it?'

'Yes.'

'She seemed lonely,' Mr Masefield said. 'With the children away at school and Tom having to go abroad so much. Did Peter like the book?'

'Oh yes,' said Marion, ready now. 'He loved it. It was kind of you to give it to him.'

'Jane must have hers,' said the old man. 'I've asked my daughter to see to it.' His voice trailed away, then he said, with sudden firmness, 'Tell Tom not to leave her alone too much, and give her my kindest regards.'

His eyes closed again. An *old* friend, Peter had said.

On the way home, she called in at Clyde House and told Tom where she had been.

'Leonard Masefield is eighty-four years old,' she said. 'He was selling his house. He persuaded Laura to return because he liked her and he was lonely. She took pity on him and went. She mentioned Peter and he gave her the book. She spoke most warmly of her husband. Mr Masefield knew your name, Tom. Now does any of that fit in with your idea that she had a lover? I think she simply liked looking at houses.'

'Why didn't she tell me, then?'

'Because she didn't want you to think she was unhappy,' said Marion.

'But she must have been,' Tom said.

'No. Bored, perhaps. Not unhappy,' said Marion.

There was no need for him ever to learn about the fictional children.

'Thank you,' he said, accepting what she had told him.

Two days after Laura's funeral, Marion saw the notice of Leonard Masefield's death in the paper. Now that last secret had been taken safely to the grave.

She went to finish her packing. The book for Sarah was already in her case; she was going to London.